The Last Perfect Summer of Richard Dawlish

Dottie Manderson mysteries book 4

Caron Allan

In memory of

Joyce Ellen Anscombe.

One last summer would have been perfect.

THE LAST PERFECT SUMMER OF RICHARD DAWLISH

DOTTIE MANDERSON
MYSTERIES BOOK 4

.

Chapter One

Hamfield, just outside Nottingham, June 1919.

The war was over. That was the main thing. That was all that mattered. Not the lives lost. Nor the devastation. Not the hostile, resentful power struggle throughout Europe. Not even the victory. In the end, all that mattered was that the long years of anguish and despair had come to an end.

Up and down the country, people celebrated the fact that life could now go back to normal. Whatever that was. Women left their war-jobs in the factories in their tens of thousands, and went home to cook, clean and have babies. Men, scarred inside and out, lay aside their rifles and bayonets and took up their hammers and saws once more. They hammered their swords into ploughshares, figuratively if not literally, and tried to forget what they had seen.

Across the nation, there were street parties, tea parties, balls, lunches, drinks evenings, galas and dances to celebrate the return of the heroes, and the prospect of returning to everyday life as it had been years earlier.

No one mentioned the dead.

The Member for Hamfield and West Nottingham, the Honourable Norman Maynard, with his charming wife Augustine, hosted one such event at their elegant home in the leafy suburb of Hamfield.

It was a glorious evening. The weather for the first week of an English June was perfect: warm and sunny, with a cloudless blue sky. There was the merest hint of a breeze ruffling its fingers through the early roses, bringing their fragrance lightly into the house.

The ballroom, a recent and somewhat garish addition when viewed from the outside, inside flowed neatly on from the other reception rooms. By the simple expedient of moving the furniture and flinging wide the folding doors that separated the rooms, the whole of the downstairs was transformed into a vast space where guests could mingle, and roam drink in hand, from the dancefloor to the buffet and back again.

In one corner of the ballroom, on a small raised platform, the little orchestra played a series of popular dance tunes, and couples, young and old, circled the floor just as they had done five years earlier. All around them, people gathered in little groups, laughing and talking. Cocktails of all kinds were knocked back in massive quantities.

And obviously, no one mentioned the dead.

The war, Richard Dawlish reflected as he sipped his champagne cocktail with great reluctance, might never have happened.

No one mentioned the dead, but he could still see them, their clutching, decaying flesh protruding from muddy dips and hollows, and at night the rats would come out of their hiding places and nibble the naked vulnerable limbs. Richard didn't even need to close his eyes. The images were always before him. He carried them with him wherever he went, whatever he did, in his head, in his dreams, his mind, his eyes. He began to think they would never leave him. Even when he was an old man, he would still see those corpses, like so many strange species growing in a wasteland of mire.

Turning, he looked out through the open doors at the long lawn surrounded by blossoming borders. Was this what those millions had died for? A perfect flat green lawn? He took another drink. He couldn't think of anything else to do, so like all the others, he just took another drink.

Behind him in the ballroom, someone tapped a spoon against a glass to get everyone's attention. The chattering stopped, the laughter faded, and everyone turned to face the Honourable Norman Maynard positioned at the front of the stage. He embarked upon a rambling, largely predictable second-hand speech, culminating in, 'So let us raise our glasses in a toast as we welcome back our heroes, and thank them for their part in keeping England's green and pleasant land free of tyranny and destruction.'

There were loud shouts of 'Hear, hear', and 'Just so', and everyone repeated some jumbled form of the toast and drank. Maynard then said, 'And another toast to celebrate the fine achievements of some very special young men in the field of combat, and who are here with us this evening. Please join me on the stage: Captain Algy Compton!' There was a loud and raucous cheer. Maynard continued, 'Next, I'm very proud to be able to honour my son, Group Captain Michael Maynard.' There was a further, louder chorus of cheers and catcalls, then someone at the back shouted, 'Thinks he can bloody fly, so he does!' There was general laughter, though some of the ladies tutted at the language. Norman Maynard, smiling proudly, responded with, 'Aye, well, from what I hear, he *can* fly!'

'Showed the bloody Boche a thing or two, let me tell you!' came another voice from the back. Again, everyone laughed, and Maynard said, his good humour slipping slightly, 'Indeed. But let's keep it polite, gentlemen, remember the ladies.' He looked down at his bit of paper. 'Er, next on the list, is some young scallywag by the name of Second Lieutenant Gervase Parfitt. A second lieutenant at only twenty years of age! That's a sterling achievement, Gerry, my dear boy!' A lanky youth nodded, and received with blushes the back-slaps and cheers of those around him as he made his way forward.

The audience, less bored now and enjoying the fun, turned back to Maynard, whose glass was being topped up by a servant. 'And we mustn't forget Gervase's little brother Reggie, better known as Sergeant Reginald Parfitt,' Maynard paused to drink his toast, then went on, 'Then there's yet another of these overachieving Parfitt brothers, this time it's none other than Artie, a Lieutenant in His Majesty's navy, which as we all know, is just some strange, salt-water name for a Captain! Lieutenant Arthur Parfitt, ladies and gentlemen. Then last, but by no means least, my nephew Algy's comrade-in-arms, Lieutenant Richard Dawlish. Richard, my dear fellow, do step up with the others for the photograph. Let's have some applause for this excellent display of British—er, and Colonial, of course—manhood.'

Richard had smiled dutifully and raised his glass for each toast. He had wondered if he would be mentioned and was a little surprised that he was. As a ripple of polite applause went around the room, he made his way forward, embarrassed but smiling. Maynard shook his hand, then the six young men stood together whilst the photographer arrived to capture the moment for posterity. The photographer had some difficulty getting the right light reading and focus, no doubt due to the dozens of dazzling artificial lights in the ballroom coupled with the bright sunlight coming in from outside.

'Your black face is mucking up his lens, Dickie,' Reggie laughed. He swayed, clearly fairly tipsy. The others joined in with the joking and laughter. Richard smiled politely and said nothing.

'Everybody stand perfectly still, please,' called the photographer.

'Don't call him Dickie, he doesn't like it,' Gervase said.

'Oops I forgot! So sorry, Rich-*ard*,' Reggie said, slapping Richard's shoulder. Reggie pronounced the name with the emphasis on the second syllable, in an attempt at mimicking Richard's strong Jamaican accent. Again everyone laughed. Richard looked at his feet.

'Hold still gentlemen, and—smile!'

It seemed to take the photographer forever to get everything how he wanted it and take the wretched photo, but at last they were free to go back to the dancing and drinking.

Richard felt a hand on his arm, and looked round to see Miranda Maynard, smilingly standing on tiptoes to plant a kiss on his cheek. She kept her arm through his, a show of solidarity it seemed. She, the darling of the ball, and he the outsider with the black skin, united against the rest of them.

Richard couldn't help but notice one or two ladies shaking their heads in disapproval. These ladies muttered to their gentlemen escorts and together they all turned away. Richard was neither surprised nor offended. The British almost universally despised him for his skin colour. And not only them. Even the enemy soldiers he'd come across had been surprised to observe a Jamaican among the British armed forces that had overwhelmed them. Especially a Jamaican who gave orders. In their eyes, his honoured achievements and Courage Under Fire would never rise above his complexion.

Miranda gazed into his eyes. 'Take no notice, darling. They don't know you as I do. They can't help being fearfully ignorant.'

She kissed his cheek again. Richard felt she was in danger of incurring her parents' wrath. He was about to tell her he wasn't upset by the cold shoulders around him or the comments, but she carried on speaking.

'Algy, Michael and the rest of them are planning a little drinks party in the pavilion. They've snaffled a couple of crates, Mike said, and I'm going down to join them now. Algy is bringing Dreary Deirdre, but in spite of that it should be laugh. You could come too, it'll be good to let our hair down away from this stuffy lot. And you can keep that awful limpet Reggie away from me. What about it?'

It sounded like a good idea to Richard.

'And you never know,' Miranda said softly for his ear alone, 'you and I might finally get some time alone, if you know what I mean.' She gave him a wicked smile. Yes, he thought, he knew exactly what she meant.

'I don't know. They didn't invite me, they might prefer it if I didn't come along. I was thinking of getting back to my lodgings.'

She slanted an eyebrow at him. 'Good idea, I could come with you.'

That wasn't what he had in mind. He hastily added, 'On the other hand, why not, we deserve to relax a little.' Miranda wrapped herself around his arm and giggled.

A few minutes later they reached the 'pavilion', as the Maynards called it, but which to Richard appeared to be a spacious if somewhat dilapidated summerhouse. Two wide, long steps led up to the door, and the group of young men and girls were sprawled all over the steps, smoking cigarettes and drinking beer.

'Hello Dickie-Dick-Dick!' Arthur Parfitt called and cackled at his own hilariousness. Like his brother Reggie, he was quite obviously very drunk.

'Don't call him that, you know he doesn't like it, *Artie*.' Miranda snapped, folding her long skirt neatly about her and taking a seat on the bottom step. She took a drag of her friend's cigarette, and watching him through the blue swirling smoke, like the starlets she'd seen in her favourite films, she added, 'It's not like you to be so queerly bitchy.'

'That's because he's a bitchy little queer!' Gervase, drunk, said. Everyone, including Richard laughed at that.

Artie clapped his hand to his heart as if mortally wounded and subsided theatrically onto the step. 'Oh Miranda, Gervase *mon frère*! I'm cut to the core by your marvellous jibes! Though actually, darling, I prefer to be called Artie. It's better than Arthur any day of the week. Anyway, Dickie knows it's just a bit of fun, don't you Dickie-Dick-Dick?'

Richard ignored him, and took a seat on the other side of Miranda. He accepted a bottle from one of the other girls. She must be Margaret, Richard thought. Her errand completed, she turned back to Gervase, who put a possessive arm about her shoulders. Beyond her, Algy and his girlfriend Deirdre were kissing with complete abandon, ignoring the others nearby. Richard hoped things wouldn't get too out of hand. The fourth girl was Miranda's little sister Penny, a sweet kid who looked almost as uncomfortably out of place as Richard felt. She was too young to be drinking beer and talking about the kind of things the rest of them were likely to talk about. He'd give it half an hour, walk Penny back to the party, say goodnight to the Maynards, then make his escape.

He sat in the shade of the large and very beautiful copper beech. It was no blue mahoe, and the leaves were far smaller but they were still more or less heart-shaped, like those of the trees from his homeland. He repressed the aching flashes of memory: playing outside his grandfather's hillside home, of the little village where his family had been schooled for the last three generations. Lois looking into his eyes, the sound of her laughter. Not long now. He'd be home in six weeks, and still be able to enjoy the long Caribbean summer.

There was an aged swing hanging from the lowest branch of the beech, and at intervals one or other of the girls went to sit on it, and the men took it in turns to push them, although really it was a contest to see who could get the girl to fall off, perhaps flashing her underwear at the same time.

Miranda was chatting with the other girls, and Richard drank another beer Algy handed him, then found he had another in his hand, and he drank that too without even really thinking about it. After half an hour or so, Miranda stubbed out her third cigarette, took his hand, removed and set down his fourth bottle of beer, and pulling him to his feet, drew him off into the copse of rhododendrons and azaleas, amid catcalls and jeers.

They were gone for twenty minutes. When they returned to the group, both of them were sullen and silent. Miranda went to sit with Deirdre, Algy, Margaret and Artie. Richard sat for a moment beside Penny before asking if she wanted to go back to the main party. She jumped up, relieved, and they set off back to the house.

'How any lady can go home in just one shoe and not notice is beyond me,' Norman Maynard's butler remarked. It was early the next morning, and he, the footman and two maids, were surveying the scene of the party with dismay. They had brought boxes into the ballroom to clear away the debris, which consisted of discarded food, drink, crockery, glasses, napkins, items of clothing, cigar and cigarette butts, the lady's shoe in question, a cigarette case, two pipes and a host of other oddments. The house was a mess, and on inspection it was discovered that the lawn outside was hardly less strewn with rubbish.

George Blake, the footman, was despatched to the pavilion to clear up after the 'secret' drinks party enjoyed by some of the young people. He was pleased to go, as it meant he could enjoy a sneaky cigarette and dawdle for a few minutes in the sunshine. He paused to light his cigarette as soon as he rounded the shrubbery which hid him from the house. He stood for a moment, holding the smoke in the back of his throat before raising his face, eyes closed to the sun, then slowly releasing the held breath. It was a perfect morning.

But as he neared the pavilion, something odd on the ground caught his eye. As he came up to it, he saw it was the narrow piece of wood that formed the seat of the swing. He picked it up. Coming slowly closer to the pavilion, the hair on the back of his neck prickling with caution, he beheld the body of Richard Dawlish, hanging by a rope from the stout lower branch of the copper beech tree just beyond the building. The man's tie was hanging loosely down, his hands swinging freely by his sides, the feet together and turning as if by their own volition as the body swayed with the breeze, first to the left, then to the right, then a little left again, his boots still smartly polished. George Blake vomited onto the bottom step of the pavilion, then throwing aside his cigarette and wiping his mouth on his sleeve, he ran back to the house, saying over and over to himself, 'Oh my God, oh my dear God.'

Later, under the watchful eye of the local police, Richard's body was cut down and carried into the house, where it was laid upon a table in a back room. Several of the young men were up and about by this time, and stood about the room, eyeing the proceedings and sharing cigarettes. The Honourable Norman Maynard was consulting quietly with his friend, Edwin Parfitt, the chief inspector sent out from Nottingham. For once, no one felt much like making jokes about Richard's name.

Gervase, pale and shocked and looking far too young, said, 'Never thought he'd be the sort to hang himself. Bit of a quiet one, a loner perhaps, but suicidal? What do you think, Algy, was he the mental sort?'

'I wouldn't have said so.' Algy's hand shook as he lit a cigarette. Reggie and Artie were already smoking. Reggie's hands shook as badly as Algy's and he said, 'No one knows what someone will do when they're a bit queer in the head. Penny said he was saying all sorts to her last night. She was glad to get away from him and back to the party. Drink makes some people more depressed rather than cheering them up. And old Dickie had had an awful lot to drink.'

As the door opened to admit the doctor, Miranda was also there, shocked, her hand to her mouth as she took in the scene. She pushed past the doctor and rushed to Richard's side, sobbing hysterically, forgetting that she wore only her nightgown and that her negligee was not tied about her. Gervase Parfitt and her brother Michael between them tried to drag her away.

'Come away, old girl, nothing we can do for the poor fellow now,' Mike said.

'You don't understand!' she cried, turning to face the lot of them. 'None of you understand. I loved him! We were going to be married!'

Then she fell down in a dead faint upon the floor.

Chapter Two

June 1934, York.

The power of a random word or phrase to come out of nowhere and to destroy everything, Dottie thought, as she edged forward in the throng of people leaving the platform. Behind her, she heard the train puffing out of the station, carrying William with it, and the ashes of her dreams.

'Change at York for all stations to Scarborough.' That had been the guard.

'George's sister Diana is staying there for a while. She's been ill.' Dottie herself had said, and how she wished she'd said nothing, just said nothing at all, then everything would still be all right.

'I'm not sure we could still consider pregnancy an illness in this day and age,' William had then replied. And in those few words, he had revealed, quite unwittingly, his prior, privileged knowledge.

Everything seemed to recede around her now as she ran through it all again, what had happened between them just a few minutes ago. How close she had been to complete happiness, promised to William forever, kissing him, holding his hand, feeling his arm strong and protective about her, then that one little phrase had come out of nowhere and had set off an avalanche that had brought her world crashing down.

Diana wasn't married, that was the problem, and she had been having an affair with a married man, one that resulted in his death. Now Dottie had discovered, completely by chance, that Diana was pregnant. She had been sent away to have her child in secret then give it away to strangers to bring it up. Like Dottie's recently deceased friend and mentor Mrs Carmichael, Diana would never see her baby again. But she would always wonder, Dottie felt certain, and always hope. And William—he had known. All this time. And he had said nothing. Even the recent events in Scotland had not loosened his policeman's tongue. Dottie saw with clarity now all the years ahead of them, her and William, if she married him, and all the secrets he would keep from her, all the silence, the unspoken thoughts and quiet knowledge. Part of him that would never be hers.

'This ticket's for London, Miss,' the ticket collector told her. Dottie focussed on him with difficulty. He smiled at her kindly, seeing a tired, upset-looking young woman standing in front of him, jostled by the crowd, looking fit to drop. Quarrelled with her sweetheart, no doubt.

She said in a faded kind of voice, 'Yes, but I'm staying here for a few days, or possibly a week.'

'It'll still be valid in a week's time, Miss, or if you decide not to travel back for a while, you could apply for a refund on the unused portion.'

'Thank you, I'll think about it.' She took the ticket and followed everyone else out into the street. She stood there, dazed, a bit frightened to think too closely about what she had just done. No, she knew what she had done. Her head had told her to hold back, not to speak out, not to act rashly, but she hadn't been able to stop herself, passion and shock causing her to blurt out her hasty words. And so it had happened. The end.

'The world's shortest engagement,' she told herself with an unsteady laugh which very nearly gave way to a sob. She bit her lip and hefted up her suitcase. Now what? She forced herself to be practical. She needed somewhere to stay. She had said she would go to the Station Hotel in Scarborough, but she really didn't feel as though she wanted to go anywhere right now. She would stay in York overnight and travel on to Scarborough in the morning. She was exhausted, even though it was only mid-afternoon, but the last week had been busy and emotional, and she had left Scotland early that morning. In the station yard there was the ubiquitous Victorian-era hotel, a lovely old building, and she made for that, hoping they would have a room.

'Then tomorrow,' she told herself as she went, 'I can get the train to Scarborough and get a room at the Station Hotel and wait for W—for Inspector Hardy, I mean—to telephone with Diana's address. And I must telephone to my parents, they'll need to know where I am.' It was a relief to deal with practical matters. She went in the front door of the hotel and up to the desk.

'Yes, Miss?'

'I'd like a room, please. Just for tonight.'

'Of course, Miss.' And the clerk took her through the rigmarole of checking-in, then summoned another young man to carry her suitcase up wide shallow stairs, thickly carpeted, to a room overlooking the side entrance and a brick wall.

The youngster hovered, disposed to talk, but Dottie cut him off with an imperious, 'Thank you, that's all for now.' He left, with a look of unsatisfied curiosity, something he wouldn't have dared had she been with her parents or a husband, or if she had just been a little older than her twenty years. The door closed behind him and she was at last alone with her thoughts.

She sat on the bed. It was high off the ground, and even she, tall for a woman, couldn't reach the floor. Her legs dangled like a child's; she leaned back on her elbows and looked around the room.

How had it happened? She couldn't seem to stop that question arising time and time again. She fell back on the bedclothes, giving in completely to the misery that had engulfed her as soon as she'd stepped off the train.

'Oh William!' Dottie clutched the pillow to her face and wept.

Finally, exhausted by the emotion, she slept. When she awoke, she felt better. More resigned. She would compose herself and get on with her life, she decided. Nothing was so bad that one couldn't recover from it with time and by keeping busy. She washed her face, brushed her hair, repaired her make-up and changed her dress. Then she went down to dinner, pausing at the desk to arrange a telephone call to her parents.

Dining alone was no fun, and she ate quickly and with little regard for what was put in front of her. Her head was full of ideas as she mentally sketched the conversation she was about to have with her parents. She returned to the reception area, still not sure how much she would say or leave out.

The telephone for the use of guests was concealed in a little booth at the rear of the lobby. Dottie went in and pulled shut the jerky sliding door. These things never closed properly, she thought. She made herself comfortable on the little padded butler's stool and waited for the call to come through. It was a relief, though hardly a surprise, to hear her father's voice, not her mother's. In a few short words she told him she's decided on an impulse to overnight in York before setting off for Scarborough in the morning to visit George's sister Diana, leaving out the fact that she had yet to obtain an address for Diana.

If her father thought any of this seemed peculiar, all he said was, 'You sound a little odd, dear. Is everything all right?'

'Yes, Father, I'm perfectly all right.'

'Do you have enough money?'

Bless him, she thought. Aloud she said, 'Er, well, no not really. I have enough ready cash, if I could leave the bill at this hotel and the one in Scarborough to you?'

'Of course, my dear, I'll sort those out for you,' he promised. She just had time to thank him and assure him once again that she was all right, and to ask after her mother and her sister Flora, who was expecting her first child. Then the operator ended the call. She left the telephone booth and followed the direction of the discreet sign that indicated 'sitting room for hotel's clients' and found herself in a dowdy, slightly dusty room, full of sofas and easy chairs, each one looking as if it was at least a hundred years old. An elderly lady sat at a tiny desk in the corner, writing letters. She turned to stare at Dottie through her lorgnettes then looked away.

Not wanting to stay in that dreary place, Dottie went back to her room. On the stairs she passed a fair-haired man. And just for a moment... But the chap went right on past her with only the slightest smile and nod, and she saw it was not William Hardy at all but a complete stranger.

She sat by the window looking out at the busy streets. It was rather early, too early for bed, but she couldn't think of a thing to do other than brood. She wondered what time William would be likely to call. It was then that she remembered. She had told him she would be in Scarborough. And here she was still in York. And—she looked at her watch—he probably wouldn't be home yet, in any case. The train should have arrived in London about an hour ago, and then he would have to go straight to his office and find the address to give to Dottie. Or perhaps he wouldn't. Perhaps he would—out of spite or anger, or simply because he was tired—perhaps he would wait until the morning and the resumption of his duties before looking out that information? Which meant that Dottie would not be likely to see Diana tomorrow. For a moment she had the panicking thought, what if he didn't ring at all? What if he was so angry with her, so resentful, that he simply ignored her request for the information, or rejected it on the grounds of police confidentiality, or some such thing, and he never called her. What would she do then? For a bleak moment her thoughts ran aground on this awful possibility, but then she mentally swept it away with a brisk, silent, 'Nonsense!' There was no point in considering such a devastating consequence until it happened—if it happened.

Her father would by now have spoken to her mother about what Dottie had said. Then her mother would doubtless convey the information to Flora and thus to George. So if Dottie didn't hear from William by tomorrow evening, she could telephone Flora and ask her to ask George to ask his parents for the address of the old nanny with whom Diana was staying in Scarborough. Until then Dottie would just have make her way to Scarborough and while away the time there as best she could until she had the information she needed. It felt good to have come up with a plan.

But she had not told William—Inspector Hardy—that she was still in York. She didn't want to speak to him, but there was another way. She ran back down to the reception desk and asked for another telephone call to be put through to her parents' home. Her father would certainly have a large telephone bill to pay when he settled her account here. She was relieved that Janet answered the phone. The maid Janet was walking out with Sergeant Frank Maple, Hardy's most regular assistant. Cutting through Janet's chatter and enquiries, Dottie said, simply, 'I need you to tell Your Frank to let Inspector Hardy know that I am at the Metropolitan Hotel in York. I had told him I'd be in Scarborough, but I'm staying here tonight and won't be going on to Scarborough until tomorrow. In case he asks.'

If Janet was surprised by either Dottie's tone or the way she called William 'Inspector Hardy', she said nothing, assuring Dottie only that she would get it done straight away, then adding, 'Are you all right, Miss? You sound a bit queer?'

Dottie told her she was just tired, and in need of a good night's sleep. She thanked Janet, said goodnight and hung up the receiver. She went back to her room, gathered her things, and went along the corridor to the bathroom for a deliciously hot bath, then felt it was a reasonable hour to turn in.

She slept fitfully, tossing and turning, and waking from horrid but already-forgotten dreams. She knew she had called out William's name at some point, as the sound of her own voice woke her, sweating and trembling, from the dream, and it took over an hour to go back to sleep. Somewhere around dawn, she had a passing thought: I'd almost forgotten I'm Mrs Carmichael's heiress. The girls at the warehouse must be wondering what's going to happen to them. I must go back next week and start sorting everything out.

Finally, she fell deeply asleep and woke at nine o'clock feeling reasonably refreshed.

It was a good thing she stayed in the hotel after breakfast, for William's phone call came at eleven-fifteen. The clerk directed Dottie to the same booth at the back of the reception hall that she had used the previous evening. As she stepped inside and pulled the door closed, her heart was pounding. Her hand shook as she took up the receiver.

'Hello?' At least her voice sounded more or less normal. After a short delay, there was William's dear voice coming down the wire to her.

'Dottie? It's William,' said William, from his desk in London. In York, Dottie rolled her eyes. Well, of course it was, Dottie thought, who else would it be? He continued in what she thought of as his policeman's voice, officious and to the point. 'Are you all right? Look here, darling, this is madness, you can't simply...'

But Dottie wasn't having any of that. As coolly as she could, she said, 'Inspector Hardy, how kind of you to call. I hope you have that address for me?'

At the other end of the line, she heard a sharp intake of breath, followed by a very bad word indeed. When he spoke, it was as if through gritted teeth. 'So that's how you want to play it? I see. Well in that case, Miss Manderson, here's your information. Bessie Brown, 71 Seaview Terrace, and much good may it do you!' With a loud bang, he slammed down his receiver and left Dottie with the echo of it going round and round in her head. Fighting back tears, she told herself she deserved that.

She ran up to her room, repeating the address under her breath, afraid she would forget it before she wrote it down.

Slamming the phone down did not relieve William Hardy's temper at all. He was aware only of a deep sense of grief. Something vital— Dottie's heart—had been irretrievably lost.

He had been at his desk at eight o'clock to catch up on the events of the past week. He had an appointment with his superior officer at 4pm. Until then, time hung on him like a pall. He decided he would take an early lunch. A very early lunch. The clock in his office at the police station showed 11.20. He made his way to Mr Bray's office, and spent far longer with the solicitor than he'd anticipated.

Mr Bray, a middle-aged bachelor who took a great interest in the lives of others, especially with regard to their romantic involvements, had been looking forward to seeing Inspector Hardy. He had hoped to see the lovely Miss Manderson too, but it quickly became clear, as the young policeman began to explain what had happened in Scotland, that there had been a falling out. Mr Bray felt a huge wave of disappointment but tried to give William his full attention.

William ended his rather long account with, 'So you see, there's still quite a lot to do if my half-brother is to be exonerated and the real killer brought to justice.'

'And that is...?' Mr Bray pressed, though he felt sure he already knew the answer.

'Well, there's no clear evidence either way, which is part of the problem. It is either Mrs Louise Denholme, the dead man's wife, or her mother, the novelist Miss Millicent Masters.

Both women are of small stature, which fits perfectly with the position of the wound on the body, and both women had the opportunity of committing the crime. And both women wanted the man dead. I'm absolutely certain in my own mind that Mrs Denholme is conducting a romantic involvement with the local procurator fiscal, and that he used his position to ensure evidence was either lost or ignored. Again, I'm convinced it was he who fixed on my half-brother to take the blame, but theories are not proof. However, I have a meeting with my superiors this afternoon to discuss what may be done.'

Mr Bray's eyes lit up with interest as he listened to all this. William went on,

'I shall lay everything I know and have discovered before my superiors, and I have every hope that at the very least, we might be able to force an inquiry into the conduct of the procurator fiscal and the possibility of him abusing his position. This could lead to a re-evaluation of recent criminal cases. But otherwise, it's out of my hands...'

'Hmm, yes of course. Mr Hardy—excuse me, I mean, of course, the other Mr Hardy—will need to keep out of sight for a time. I suspect these matters could take quite a while to be resolved, if in fact, it is possible to resolve them at all. Well, do please keep me informed. That seems to be all for the moment. Now if you will just sign here.' He indicated a place at the bottom of a form he now set in front of William. William duly signed the papers without taking the time to read them. 'And here—thank you—it gives me great pleasure to hand over to you the remainder of the monies which were your fee for going to Scotland and tracking down your own brother. I apologise, incidentally, for the deception, but I'm sure you would agree that, had I been explicit about your task, you would have declined to undertake it.' He cast a look at William, who gave him a brief nod in reply, his expression inscrutable. 'This envelope contains the £250 we agreed. And this other envelope contains some papers and a set of keys. These are also for you, and left to you by Mrs Carmichael as one of her bequests. Her only proviso being, that if your half-brother should ever need shelter, you would provide it.'

'Well I'm in lodgings at the moment, so there's no room. But in any case, I couldn't do that while he is a wanted man; as a police officer I'm prohibited from any involvement with criminals. Even if they are waiting to be proved innocent.'

'Quite so, well if he should turn up to beg a bed for the night, do send him to me, won't you?'

But William wasn't listening. He was looking at the small bunch of keys that had fallen out of the envelope. 'What...?'

'Ah. Those are the keys to Mrs Carmichael's residence, which she has left entirely to you. The papers you so trustingly signed without reading just now relate to that property. The envelope also contains the deeds, of course. You may take possession immediately, or whenever convenient to yourself. So you see, you shall have room for a guest if someone should turn up on your doorstep late one night. I'm so sorry to hurry you, but I'm afraid I have another client waiting.'

Mr Bray got to his feet. He didn't add, I had thought it would be the perfect first home for you and the delightful Miss Manderson. He suppressed a sigh of disappointment and extended his hand. 'Goodbye, Inspector Hardy. Thank you for your assistance. I hope we won't have to wait long for a happy conclusion to the events in Scotland.'

Chapter Three

It took Dottie almost no time to pack, and soon she was at the railway station and waiting for the train to Scarborough. How she wished—not for the first time—that she could drive. It would be so convenient to bundle everything into a car and leave immediately, instead of all this hanging around and waiting for the train. As soon as she got back to London, she must insist on George teaching her.

She bought a newspaper from a young boy on the platform, the train journey was a little over an hour, and she had no book to read, and no wish to be drawn into conversation with any of the elderly ladies waiting on the platform.

The train left on time, and she opened her newspaper, reading it carefully from front to middle, then skipping over the sport and financial news without interest. The small section on page four under the heading of Lower Bar, Scotland caught her eye. She read:

'Police investigating the death of local laird, Howard Denholme, late of Lower Bar, urgently want to speak to a young man named locally as William Hardy. Mr Hardy has not been seen in the area for two or three days, and is believed to be accompanied, either willingly or unwillingly by Mrs Anna McHugh the wife of a local publican. If anyone knows of the whereabouts of either party, or has any other information to offer, they should contact the authorities immediately. When asked about the presence of a detective from Scotland Yard, the procurator fiscal said the officer had been operating in an advisory capacity only, and had since returned to London.'

With a sigh, Dottie folded the newspaper and set it aside. She hoped William... She groaned, annoyed with herself for keep slipping over his name. Inspector Hardy. She hoped Inspector Hardy would be able to solve that case very quickly, so that his half-brother could be exonerated and would be able to settle down with his lover, Anna McHugh. Because whilst the local police, aided by the procurator fiscal, no doubt anxious to cover his own part in the crime, wasted their time searching for the other William Hardy, the real perpetrators were going unpunished. Dottie hated to think that Will Hardy, local rogue and wife-snaffling scoundrel, might be arrested and charged with a crime he didn't commit. Especially such a serious crime as murder.

She sat lost in her own thoughts for a while. The motion of the train lulled her mind, and soon her thoughts returned to London and all that was waiting for her return: her parents, her home, her sister and brother-in-law, and soon, their first child would be born and she would be an aunt, and she would take care to be the fun sort of aunt who took pleasure in spending time with their niece. Or nephew. She wouldn't be the kind of aunt who didn't understand anything about life and all the latest things, or was only interested in ensuring the child did their school work.

And, increasingly persistent, increasingly forcing itself into her consciousness, was the newly-inherited fashion warehouse, Carmichael and Jennings, Exclusive Modes, and all those women who depended on it for their living. If only it wasn't hers, she suddenly thought. If only Mrs Carmichael was still alive, and would go on living for years and years, and would have time to teach Dottie everything she knew, so that when Mrs C did finally pass away, she, Dottie could step up and run the business properly, and everyone who worked there would prosper. It was her greatest fear that she would, through lack of experience, run the thing into the ground within months or even weeks, and all the mannequins and dressmakers would be unemployed. If it was a tremendous honour to receive Mrs C's bequest, it was also terrifyingly onerous for her, a young woman—a mere girl really—of just twenty years old. She couldn't afford too long a delay here: she had to be back in town to take up the reins and ensure the transfer of the business went as smoothly as possible. Too many people depended on her for their livelihood. But her only experience was as a mannequin. What if she had no head for the business side of fashion? What if she was a failure?

And yet this, this impulsive quest to find George's sister, seemed so pressing, so important. In one way, she could quite see it was really none of her business, but at the same time, she knew Diana, and counted her as a friend— kind of—and she couldn't bear to think of her shoved off somewhere out of the way, feeling the disgrace of her illegitimate pregnancy, the anxiety of childbirth ahead of her. Surely all first-time mothers felt that fear? And then to be followed almost immediately by the wrenching misery of separation from her child. To go through all that alone—well, not quite alone, but with just her old nanny for company and support...

No. Thinking it through again, Dottie felt sure she was doing the right thing. She felt a kind of sisterly solidarity with Diana. After all, there but for the grace of God... Dottie had been tempted more than once to throw convention to the wind and spend the night with William. Who knew what might have happened if she had? If he had asked her to stay, begged her, kissed her just once more. What might have happened had she found herself in Diana's predicament? Men could afford to have affairs, and everyone thought it was acceptable, even laudable. There was no shame, no guilt, no disgust for a man's behaviour. Jokes were made, elbows nudged knowingly, eyebrows raised. Other men envied them; women found them virile and desirable.

But what of the women these men left trailing in their wake? What was their lot? Even in this modern era, Dottie thought, women were expected to remain spotless until marriage, beyond reproach. It was decidedly Victorian, but decidedly real. A woman who had affairs, unless of course she was a successful actress, or a Bohemian, was despised by all. God forbid she should have a child too; her reputation, even nowadays, would never recover from the shame of her guilt.

The sun shone in at the window. There was no sign of the sea, the coast was still a little way off, but a refreshing breeze came into the carriage where a gentleman a few seats away had let down the glass. The breeze ruffled Dottie's hair and soothed her skin. She dozed, her hands neatly folded in her lap, her hat and overnight bag on the seat beside her.

When she woke a short while later to find herself almost in Scarborough, she felt relaxed and calm. She would find Diana, relieve her own mind that Diana was all right, and hopefully assure her of any help should she need it. At this point Dottie faltered somewhat—what could she actually do? Anyway... she left that on one side... then she would return to London and bury herself in her new role at the warehouse: it was the beginning of June, and she would have to start thinking about the Spring range for the following year. William Hardy would be forgotten. After all, just how often did one cross paths with the police? Once in a blue moon? Yes, he would soon be forgotten, and eventually perhaps, her heart would mend.

The Station Hotel was full. Then it was borne in on Dottie that she had come to the seaside, so why not go down to the promenade and look for a nice hotel there. Here too, many hotels were rather full, but there was an attractive one called The Grand Hotel. It had a charming-looking glass sunroom at the front that faced the prom. Beside the front door, gleaming in the sunshine and well-polished, hung a discreet sign stating, Vacancies. It all looked beautifully clean and comfortable, and very expensive. Dottie went inside to enquire.

They had a number of rooms available, the clerk told her, and she opted for a room with a sea view. A price was agreed, and the clerk slowly wrote her details on a form. Dottie wondered how it was possible to write so slowly and not accumulate a queue as long as the one at the butcher's. As she waited she caught sight of a tall, fair-haired man, and for the second time in as many days, her heart did something painful in her chest as for the briefest of moments, she thought... was almost convinced... He was with a woman who was busily saying, in a pettish voice, 'For goodness' sake, Gerry, you've had your policeman's head on the whole time we've been here. We're supposed to be on holiday!'

Another tall, fair policeman! Dottie turned away, gripping the edge of the desk with white-knuckled fingers. At last the clerk gave her the form to sign, and she was free to go upstairs to her room, hurrying in the wake of the fast-walking adolescent who carried her bags.

She had a wash to refresh herself after the journey, changed her clothes then set off for Seaview Terrace following another brief consultation with the elderly man behind the desk. Mercifully there was no sign of the tall, fair-haired man.

Scarborough was in the grip of the new summer tourist season, and there were holidaymakers everywhere, in various states of casual attire, or sporting embarrassing sunhats and carrying beach towels or buckets and spades. Dottie was the only one there in normal clothes seemingly, and with a mission other than pure enjoyment. She pushed through the crowds all heading for the sandy beach, and made her way into the town, to one of the winding streets that ran uphill above the resort.

Seaview Terrace was just what Dottie had imagined: perched precariously on the cliff top, with one side of the street rising higher than the other, and here and there between the small homes and guest houses cramped there, a dazzling flash of bright sunshine and the blue sparkling ocean.

Number 71 had a weed-covered set of stone steps going up to the tall narrow entrance of a tall narrow house. The paint was chipped, the windows grimy, the lace curtains at the windows yellowish-brown with cigarette smoke and years of dust and dirt. Comparing it with the Gascoigne's family residence, a huge, ancient home set within acres and acres of park, Dottie couldn't help but feel uneasy about Diana being confined here.

Dottie found that the door knocker had broken off, so she rapped with her knuckles and stepped back to await an answer. After a full minute, the door was opened by a grubby teenage girl with a cigarette hanging from the corner of her mouth.

'What d'you want?' She looked Dottie up and down with a frown. 'You ain't collecting for the church?'

Dottie said no, she wasn't collecting for anyone, and added that she was trying to find Miss Diana Gascoigne. 'I understand Mrs Bessie Brown lives here and I believe Miss Gascoigne is visiting her?'

The girl stepped back, and with a shrug said, 'See for yerself.'

Dottie squeezed past her in the narrow hallway. The girl shoved the door shut with a loud bang, pushed open a door on the right, then continued down the corridor to a room at the back of the house.

Not quite sure what to do, Dottie peeked into the room on the right. By convention it should have been the front parlour, but it had been turned into a bed-sitting room. A small narrow bed was placed in one corner, with a commode-chair beside it.

By the grubby window Dottie had seen from outside, sat an elderly woman, rocking gently in a rocking-chair and gazing out at the world, though whether she saw what was before her or not, Dottie wasn't able to tell.

'Nanny Brown?' Dottie asked tentatively. The old woman turned her head to fix Dottie with faded blue eyes.

'I'm Bessie, I am,' she said, sounding like a small child, in spite of her harsh worn-out voice. 'I want my dinner. When's my dinner coming?' A trickle of saliva ran from the old woman's chin onto the front of her house dress, like a thread from a spider's web, and the dress bore the evidence of other meals already eaten.

The sound of a step behind her made Dottie turn. A woman of about forty stood there. She looked flustered.

'You're not from the church? Or the welfare?' she queried anxiously.

'No, not at all, I...'

'My daughter said something about a Miss Gascoigne. Auntie Bessie was with the Gascoignes for many years.'

'Yes, so I understand. I've heard that Miss Diana Gascoigne was staying with Nanny Brown to recover from an illness?' and in Dottie's mind, she heard William's words from the train—was it really only two days ago? I'm not sure we could still consider pregnancy an illness in this day and age. Those few simple words had brought Dottie's world crashing down. She bit her lip and forced the memory away, made herself attend to the woman in front of her.

'No one's staying here,' she said. 'We're not able to take anyone. It takes all my time to see to Auntie and get the meals and everything.'

Dottie hesitated. How much should she say? Diana would hardly want her situation to become widely known. But the woman, glancing over her shoulder as if there were eavesdroppers lurking nearby, lowered her voice and said, 'Look, you won't tell anyone, will you? Only she's no trouble really, poor old dear, and I couldn't have her locked up in one of those institutes, she was so good to me after my husband upped and left, and with what they do to them in there— why, it's in the Sunday Express every week about the awful things what goes on in them places. She's a bit doolally, but she's no danger to anyone, she's like a little child. I-I couldn't bear it if they took her away and locked her up in one of them places.'

'Of course not,' Dottie said, 'I wouldn't dream of saying a word. And I don't want to give you any trouble. Only it's a bit odd. We were told quite definitely that Miss Diana Gascoigne was staying with her old nanny. If she's not here, I'm not quite sure what I'm going to do.'

The woman thought a moment, then said, 'There was a young woman, well-to-do like yourself, but it was a couple of months ago. A young widow, a Mrs Dunne, she said her name was. In the family way. Could that be her?'

Relief flooded Dottie. 'Oh yes! That would be her.'

'Well I directed her to my cousin's hotel down on the seafront. Whether she's still there or not, if she ever went there, I couldn't tell you, as I don't speak to my cousin, not since... Well, never mind. It's called the Claremont Hotel and it's the last building on the prom. You can't miss it, it's painted bright pink. That's all I can really tell you.'

Dottie thanked her and said goodbye. Another long tramp—at least this time it was downhill—brought her back to the road that ran along the promenade. It was now mid-afternoon and Dottie had eaten nothing since breakfast-time. She ignored the rumbling of her stomach, promising herself a good dinner. She could see the little pink hotel at the far end for twenty minutes before she actually reached it, and what appeared from a distance to be an ordinary low-cost seaside hotel, proved at close quarters to be a crumbling ruin of a place, as filthy and unkempt as the house on the cliff where Nanny Brown was living out her days waiting for her dinner.

Dottie stepped up to the front door—which mercifully did still have a knocker—and as she let it fall, once, twice, she watched the flimsy door tremble under the weight of it. She suddenly realised she had no idea what she was going to say to Diana when she saw her, nor did she even have any idea whether Diana would welcome her arrival or If she would see it as an unforgiveable intrusion. What if she was furious with Dottie for discovering her shameful secret? Dottie began to think she shouldn't have come, but it was too late now. She took a few calming breaths.

The door was opened by a thin young woman in an overall. She bore such a strong resemblance to the woman at Seaview Terrace that Dottie knew this had to be the cousin.

'Ah Madam, come this way, do. A room? With a sea view and huse of a bathroom, of course...' the woman was already heading back inside, and her toothy smile beneath the cold eyes, coupled with the ingratiating, false voice grated on Dottie's already frayed nerves.

Dottie stepped into the long, narrow hallway but remained by the door. The woman, some six or seven yards ahead, turned and looked at her in surprise.

'I'm not here for a room, I'm afraid, I'm here to see Mrs Dunne,' Dottie told her.

'Mrs...? I shall have to see if that lady his staying with us. One moment, hif you please.' The woman ducked behind a miniscule counter slotted under the arch of the stairs. It was dark here; there was no bulb in the fitting that hung from the ceiling. As she waited, Dottie looked around her. The stair carpet was threadbare in places; there was thick dust on the window sills, skirting and stair rails. A huge cobweb was attached to the back of the front door like a hinge, sticking it to the wall. A fat spider sat in the middle of the web, busily rolling up a fly, still kicking, in its sticky threads. Dottie gave an inner shudder, and coming up to the counter, said, 'Your cousin at Seaview Terrace directed Mrs Dunne here, but that was more than two months ago. She may have moved on by now,' she added, mentally adding, I hope she's moved on by now.

The woman's eyes held a knowing look. Her obsequious manner vanished, her smile dropped as quickly as her aitches. 'She owes me two months' money, just so's you know. Oh, she's still 'ere all right. Where would she go, the state she's in? I've threatened her with the police. So genteel, but what good is that when you've not got sixpence to your name? And I'm not running a charity. I've got my business to think of. She's got a little room at the back. Almost her time to drop I'd say, but I've told her straight several times, she ain't having her little bastard here, bringing down my reputation. I run a decent place, and I don't want her kind under my roof. Coming here, pretending she's a young widow! Hah! Some posh boy's cast-off, that's all she is.'

'Just tell me where to find her,' Dottie snapped.

'You pay me, and I'll take you up.' She held out a hand, clicking her fingers impatiently. 'Money or the police, you take your pick.'

'Don't be ridiculous,' Dottie said. Then, 'How much are you owed?'

The woman thought a moment, all too clearly sizing up Dottie's worth. 'Fifty pounds.'

'Fifty!' Dottie glared at her, the grasping hand still outstretched.

'Fifty pounds,' the woman repeated. She set her jaw. 'And not a penny less. Or the cops. It's your choice.'

'I don't have anything like that amount on me. Very well, I'll get it for you and bring it with me tomorrow.'

'I could take some on account.'

'I don't have any money on me,' Dottie said. There was no chance of her handing over her last few pounds in cash. 'You'll have to wait; another day won't make much difference, will it?'

'You better bring it tomorrow, or I'll have the law on both of you. She's on the third floor, at the back. Room 302.'

Without another word Dottie turned away and headed for the stairs. The 'hotel' reeked of old boiled cabbage and the sewer. The sooner she got Diana out of there, the better. The carpet ran out after the first floor, and the dingy wallpaper and lampshades ran out after the second. From the light fittings—empty of electric bulbs—hung ancient fly papers, the wrecks of the tiny corpses still embedded on the filthy strands. Everything was thick with dust and cobwebs. On the third floor, the corridor was dark and narrow, the floorboards uneven, and the one window at the front was so grimed over with dirt that almost no light shone through. Looking out through the glass, it was impossible to tell if it was midnight or midday. Probably this was really the servants' floor from the building's Victorian inception. Dottie had to lean in close to each door to read the room numbers in the gloom.

She found the right door and knocked. Poor Diana, she thought, confining herself to this purgatorial place. Still, it should be easy enough to find a room for her at the rather nicer hotel where Dottie was staying, and if Diana had no money, well, her family certainly had plenty. There was a faint stirring sound from the room beyond the door, but no voice. No one came to open the door. Dottie knocked again. Still nothing happened. And yet she had to be in there, the woman had said so. Dottie tried the door. It opened. She stepped inside, unable to see anything much at first. She began to think it was a mistake, that this was nothing but an old storage space.

'Diana? Are you there? It's Dottie. Dottie Manderson.'

There was a soft gasp from a heap on a bed in the corner. The curtains, heavy and dark, were closed over the single window, blotting out all the light.

Dottie went forward and realised with a shock that the bundle she could see on the bed was in fact Diana herself, huddled, shivering, under a thin stinking counterpane.

Chapter Four

'Diana!' She caught her in an embrace, and was shocked by how thin, how insubstantial she was; there was nothing of her. Her hair hung loose, straggled and sweaty, her face glistened with fever. Her hands, burning hot, shook as she gripped Dottie's shoulders in a hug. Tears sprang into the eyes of both. Any last-minute doubts Dottie had about whether she would be welcome now vanished.

'Oh Dottie! Oh thank God, Oh...' Even her voice was thin and lacked any strength.

Dottie's words jumbled and fought to get out. She couldn't understand. 'Diana! Why...? Why are you here? Why are you so...? Just... why?'

'Oh Dottie! It's all such a mess. I've no money, my dear, that's the plain truth of the matter. I've been so ill. Oh Dottie, please help me. I'm so tired, I just can't do anything.'

Dottie could see Diana's belly was very large. 'How much longer have you got to go?'

Tears of exhaustion continued to run down Diana's face. 'No one was supposed to know. Mother and Father were so angry, so disgusted with me... They sent me to Nanny Brown's but...'

'Yes, I know,' Dottie said, 'I went there. But you can't stay here like this, you're getting sick. You need somewhere clean and decent...'

'Decent?' Diana's voice cracked with bitterness. 'No, Dottie, this is God's will for me, it's His punishment. I'm a disgrace, I'm a whore... that's what my father called me. I deserve to be punished. I shall die in my sin.'

'What rot!' Dottie said sharply. 'Now I'll help you to get dressed, then we'll get you to a proper hotel. I've got a room at the Grand...'

'Dottie, no, I can't do it, I'm just too weak, I'm not well enough. The baby—Dottie—I just want to see my baby, that's all. Then I can die happy.'

Dottie was dismayed by what she was hearing. She couldn't decide what to do, whether to call for an ambulance, or send for a taxi to take Diana to her own hotel. What should she do? Was Diana genuinely ill, or just depressed and guilt-ridden?

She put a hand to Diana's forehead. It was very hot. Diana sweated profusely but she was hugging herself, shivering. Dottie arranged the thin covers over her as best she could, pulling off her short jacket and laying that over the top.

'Diana, is the baby coming?'

'No, no, it's not due for two more weeks at least. Or it might be one week, I-I can't remember. I've lost track of the days. But no, not yet.'

That was something at least, though Dottie knew from what her sister had told her that babies came when they wanted to, and not when the doctor said they were due. But it should be all right.

'Have you had anything to eat or drink today?'

Diana didn't know. She tried to think about it, but she was muzzy-headed and not able to remember. In the end, she said in a questioning manner, 'I think I had some soup for dinner?'

'That would have been yesterday.' Dottie was alarmed to hear it, but not particularly surprised. Diana was no longer taking care of either herself or her child, and she was friendless here, with no one to help her. 'It's well past lunchtime now. I'll get some food sent up to you and call a doctor. Stay there under the covers and I'll be back in a jiffy.'

'Dottie dear, it's very kind of you, but I deserve this, I deserve to suffer, for bringing shame...'

'Diana, stop talking such damned nonsense! Think of the baby. You're going to need all your strength.' And she banged out of the room, slamming the door more loudly and with greater force than she'd intended.

Downstairs, to the woman who ran the 'hotel', Dottie said, 'I will give you an extra ten pounds if you take Mrs Dunne a boiled egg with bread and butter, and a pot of tea. Oh, and you must send for the doctor as a matter of urgency.'

Grumbling, but getting out of her chair, the woman called after Dottie's already-retreating back, 'Mrs Dunne! She better not have that wretch here! Bringing shame on my establishment!'

Dottie turned and made a show of looking around her. 'It's hardly the Grand, is it? Now get a move on, Mrs Dunne is very ill. You should have helped her, just out of common decency.'

She didn't stay to listen to any further complaints but ran back upstairs. Dottie went first to the filthy bathroom at the end of the corridor. She wet her handkerchief under the tap then returned to Diana's room. She pulled one of the lank curtains back to allow a little light into the room. The windows had been painted shut, so there was no chance of any fresh air. She turned on the lamp by the bed and set about gently blotting the damp cotton on Diana's face to cool her.

Diana was lying back against the pillow. She was horribly still. Her eyes were closed, and her face so ashen, that if it were not for the rise and fall of her breast, Dottie would have thought her dead. A terrible sense of foreboding came over Dottie, and she felt as though she was ministering to a dead woman. Fearfully she thought that even though there had been so many discoveries in science and medicine, it was still all too common for a woman to die in childbirth, and Diana was by no means robust.

How could a young woman from a wealthy and privileged background fall into such complete disaster? Dottie couldn't seem to marry together this scrawny sick woman with the lively happy girl she had last seen on New Year's Eve, talking so idealistically about a woman's sacred duty as a wife and mother. She held Diana's hand, sitting beside her on the narrow bed, waiting.

Where was that boiled egg? Dottie had an urge to go to the head of the stairs and yell her head off. And where was that wretched doctor, too? Why wasn't something happening?

Diana groaned and clutched her stomach. Dottie gave her a startled look.

'Is it the baby?'

Diana shook her head, slowly, as if it cost her all her strength to do so. 'I told you, the baby's not due for...' she broke off, crying out in pain, tensing suddenly then falling back against the pillow.

'Well I'm no expert,' Dottie said, 'but I do know babies don't always come when they're supposed to.'

Diana, panicked, gripped Dottie's arm. 'You will make sure a really nice family get my baby, won't you? I couldn't bear it if they didn't treat him or her properly. I want them to love him. Or her. And take proper care of him. It's not his fault...'

'Surely arrangements have already been made?' Dottie couldn't believe what she was hearing. 'Isn't there an adoption agency involved, or—or—something?' She knew nothing of how these things worked, she realised.

Diana's face contorted in another spasm of pain. That made three in less than four minutes. Dottie had no idea how to go about delivering a baby. Education at her highly-esteemed private ladies' college on such matters had been largely along the lines of, 'And when the doctor arrives, he will tell you what to do.' And for heaven's sake, where was that doctor?

'The baby's really coming, isn't it? But it's too soon...' Diana asked. Her face was bloodless, her hair stuck all round her face and neck. She looked terrified. Dottie knew she probably looked exactly the same.

'I'm very much afraid...'

'I know I'm not strong enough, but no matter what happens, you will stay with me, won't you? Oh Dottie, please don't leave me, I don't want to be alone. Please...' Diana's hand gripped hers.

'Of course I'll stay, but don't fret, you've a little time yet, and the doctor is on his way. He'll help you. He'll give you something for the pain, and he'll tell you what to do.'

'Dottie, if I don't—if I don't...'

'Shush now, everything will be all right. We will have time to work things out later. Save your strength.'

She heard the heavy sound of what could only be a man's boots clumping on the stairs. This had better be the doctor. The door opened and in came an elderly man with the obligatory black leather bag. He let out a rather coarse oath,

Dottie felt, as he caught sight of the woman in the bed, adding, 'How long has she been like this?'

Dottie fought her panic down. 'I don't know, I...'

'For God's sake, you stupid child, I should have been called hours ago! Out of the way.'

But Diana clutched at Dottie, who had therefore to stay put as the doctor began his examination.

'The child's breached, this is not going to be easy. Have you attended before?'

'Attended?' Dottie repeated, bewildered. 'Er, no, never.'

The doctor huffed, unimpressed. He bellowed out the door, 'Hot water, immediately, and clean towels!' Dottie doubted anyone would hear, let alone comply. He turned back to the bed. 'Who are you?'

'A friend,' said Dottie. 'I only got here half an hour ago.'

'I presume she's not married?'

'Er, no.'

'You?'

'I beg your pardon?'

'Are you married? Do you understand about this sort of thing? I don't want some useless debutante fainting on me.'

'I am not in the least the fainting type, thank you very much,' Dottie snapped back at him haughtily, and hoped it was true. Her heart was in her mouth. Diana's hand tightened on her arm as another contraction gripped her.

'Besides, I'm not leaving her.' She smoothed Diana's hair back from her face and murmured something along the lines of 'there, there', for the sake of something—anything—comforting to say.

The hot water and clean towels never arrived. In the end, Dottie had to go and fetch them herself, the precious time spent waiting for the water to heat on the stove weighed heavily and felt far too long. She was afraid she had been away too long, so long that...

When she finally arrived back upstairs, she helped the doctor wash and dry his hands and prepare his equipment, then she settled herself on the side of the bed, her back to him, and helped Diana to take a few sips of water.

For the next five hours the labour progressed, seemingly unending, yet Dottie knew five hours for the delivery of a first baby was a mercifully fast affair. There seemed to be nothing more to do than to continually urge Diana to take another breath, to try to stay calm, to breathe slowly and deeply. And later, to urge her to attempt one more push, to cling on for one more minute to her precarious thread of life. Never had Dottie felt so full of fear, nor felt so helpless in the face of an overwhelmingly inevitable outcome. 'Almost there, not long now...' How many times had she said that?

In the end, she wasn't surprised that it was all too much for Diana. The baby, finally arriving into the world, gave its first cry and Diana whispered, 'I want to see him. Or her.'

'It's a little girl,' Dottie said, and taking the tiny bundle from the doctor and wrapping her in her own jacket, she placed her by Diana's side. Diana slowly turned her head on the pillow to smile and press a kiss against the baby's cheek. 'Hello, my darling,' she said.

'What are you going to call her?' Dottie asked, entranced by the tiny fingers that gripped her own, and the wide eyes that seemed to regard her with ancient wisdom. There was no reply. She lifted her eyes from the baby's face to look at Diana, looking for the answer to her question. But Diana's face was a grey mask, her eyes staring at nothing, unblinking, unseeing.

'Doctor!' Dottie was on her feet, clutching the baby against her.

He shook his head gravely, felt for the pulse that wasn't there, and closed Diana's eyes. Turning away, he began to pack away his things, then pulled the filthy bedlinen up over Diana, covering her face.

'But...but...' Dottie couldn't form the words, too shocked for tears.

Already heading for the door, the doctor patted Dottie on the shoulder. 'I'm sorry, my dear, there's nothing more either of us can do for her. She was so weak with fever and malnutrition, I'm afraid this is just what I expected. I'll send a nurse over to do what's necessary and she'll take the child too, and see that arrangements are made. There's a respectable orphanage not far from here. They're used to dealing with bastard babies.'

Dottie clutched the baby even closer. Fighting for composure, she said, 'She's not going to an orphanage! And that's final!' Her voice sounded in her ears, her words had a fiercely defiant ring to them.

The doctor shrugged and left.

Beside her, under the filthy sheet, Diana lay unmoving. Dottie's hope that she would not really be dead, that the sheet would somehow miraculously rise with a newly taken breath, was a forlorn one. Dottie sank down onto a wooden chair to wait for the nurse. Every few seconds she cast an anxious glance down at the baby she held in her arms. The little one still stared contentedly at Dottie. How long would it before the baby needed feeding? What on earth did one do?

It felt like an age before the nurse bustled in, an older woman, probably a grandmother, Dottie thought, who had seen many babies born, and knew exactly what to do.

The nurse took one look at Dottie and said, 'My dear, what you need is a good strong cup of tea.'

With that she left the room again, returning five minutes later with a tray bearing a pot of tea, two cups, a jug of milk and a plate of bread and butter, neatly sliced and neatly spread. Her kindness brought Dottie to tears. The nurse put an arm round Dottie's shoulder, patting and tsking at intervals. At last Dottie's sobs subsided and she was left hiccupping but calm. And still the baby lay in her arms, quiet and staring.

'Good little thing, isn't she?'

Dottie nodded. 'And she's not going into an orphanage, either! I'm taking her back to my hotel with me, and—and...' she blurted out.

'Got family, has she? They'll take her in?'

'Yes,' said Dottie, and hoped to God it was true. She would take the child herself if she had to, not that she had a clue how to go about such a Herculean task.

The nurse indicated Diana's body. 'Next of kin, are you?'

Dottie shook her head. 'Just a friend. She's my—she was my sister's sister-in-law. My sister's husband's sister.'

'I see. Your brother-in-law's sister?'

'Oh yes.' Why hadn't she just said that to begin with, it was so much clearer. Dottie shook her head, but her thoughts were still scattered all over the place. She kept thinking... she kept seeing, and hearing Diana's voice... The nurse patted her again.

'Now my dear, you've had a nasty shock, and I don't doubt, looking at how young you are, that it's your first such. Now you just move your chair around this wee bit so you'll have your back to me whilst I just see to a few things about the poor lady. And you drink up your tea, there's nothing like a good strong hot cup of tea for steadying you down after a shock, I always say.'

'That's what my mother says,' Dottie responded, getting to her feet.

'Well now,' said the nurse, turning the chair to face away from the bed, 'Your mother sounds like a jolly good sensible woman. Now I'll take the baby, and just give her a check over, make sure she's perfectly healthy, though I daresay the doctor did that already. You drink your tea, my dear.'

Reluctantly, Dottie allowed the nurse to take the baby from her, the transfer done a little awkwardly on Dottie's part as she was still nervous, and uncertain of the correct way to handle such a tiny infant. The nurse lay the baby on the end of the bed, and began to unwrap the coat. Dottie resumed her seat, and drank her tea, shutting out everything except the hot tea going down her throat, a little too hot, but it began to revive her.

'Aren't there any things for the little one?' the nurse called over her shoulder.

'I couldn't find anything,' Dottie answered. Diana had few possessions in the room, and none of them was suitable for a newborn baby. Dottie wondered if Diana had even thought for a moment of surviving beyond this day. What would have happened if Dottie hadn't arrived? How had Diana imagined she could give birth all alone? What had she prepared for the arrival of her baby? Diana had surely not been in her right mind, but in the depths of despair brought on by guilt and grief.

The nurse said nothing, but wrapping the little one in the coat once more, she lay the baby on the floor. 'She's perfectly fine. Now you have your tea. Let the baby have a little nap.'

Dottie felt alarmed at the idea of the baby being on the floor, which was none too clean. 'Are you sure she won't roll away, or, or...?'

'Oh no, my dear, she's too young to do that. And there's no draught coming under the door, so you don't need to worry yourself about that. Once I've finished here I'll get my granddaughter to come over with some things. She can help you take the baby back to your hotel and stay with you tonight, as I'm sure you'll welcome the help.'

Dottie thanked her warmly, relieved beyond measure at the thought that she wouldn't be alone with the baby all night. Then hopefully, in the morning George would arrive, and take the baby back to Flora. Surely they would take the baby? Surely they would? She would ring them as soon as she got back to the hotel. They had to be told about Diana, and the baby, and... She shrank from the thought of what she would say to George. Poor George. His only sister, and younger than him by a number of years... At the nurse's reminder, she finished her tea, then poured another cup, realising now that breakfast had been a long time ago, and she was both thirsty and hungry. She ate some bread and butter very quickly indeed. She still felt upset, but she was calmer and steadier. The nurse had a cup of tea, chatting amiably about this and that, and watching Dottie closely for signs of shock. Then she collected her things in preparation to leave. Dottie experienced a moment of panic.

As if sensing this, the nurse turned to her with a smile. 'Now, my dear, don't you fret. Everything will be all right. My granddaughter will be with you in half an hour or so, and I presume your brother-in-law will be here tonight or tomorrow morning? And no doubt he'll bring his own nursery maid or nurse with him?'

Dottie had no idea, but it certainly made sense. If only he would come. What if he wouldn't, what if...? But no, no, he would come, she knew he would. George was sweet and kind, and a good man through and through. He would come immediately. With this realisation, she felt the sense of panic leaving her. The nurse came over and patted Dottie's hand. 'I'll be off now. I'll speak to the mortuary to come and take the poor lady. Then if you will be so kind as to just give my name and address to the family, I've written it down on this bit of paper, then they can make the proper arrangements, whatever they want to do.' She paused and looked at Dottie with sympathy. 'Well done, my dear, the doctor said you did very well. I expect it's your first time. When you have your own little ones, you'll have a bit of an idea of what to expect.'

'Death?' Dottie gave a bitter laugh that turned into a sob.

'You'll do very well, my dear, a good healthy sensible girl like you. Just don't get yourself into trouble. You find yourself a nice man and marry him first.' And with another smile, and a gentle pat on Dottie's shoulder, she left.

Silence settled about Dottie. The baby slept contentedly enough on the floor, wrapped in Dottie's jacket. Dottie waited for the nurse's granddaughter to arrive, counting the long minutes.

Chapter Five

A knock on the door woke Dottie. She called out, 'Come in,' and fumbled to look at her watch in the near-dark room. Almost half past nine. It had been forty-eight minutes since the nurse left, and Dottie felt guilty at the realisation that she had fallen asleep. A glance at the little bundle on the floor showed the baby was awake, staring at Dottie with those knowing eyes. As the door opened, Dottie wondered if it might be the hotel proprietor, coming to check on the damage done to her reputation, but it turned out to be a young woman carrying a great pack with her.

'Miss Dottie?' the girl asked shyly. Dottie leapt up, holding out her hand in welcome. 'My nanna sent me over, said you needed a bit of help.'

'I certainly do! Thank you so much for coming,' Dottie said with feeling. 'I don't know the first thing about babies.'

The young woman scooped up the baby and cuddled her. 'My, but she's a little poppet! What's her name?'

'She hasn't a name at present. She's going to my sister and her husband, and they will name her. Hopefully they should be here tomorrow. The baby's mother...' Dottie couldn't help glancing towards the bed.

The young woman followed her look and seeing the shape under the sheet, crossed herself. 'Lor, the poor lady! Got herself into trouble, Nanna said? Men are pigs, aren't they, use you and leave you. Mine were the same. The first two men were, anyway, though the third one, he's the dearest dad to all my kids, not just the ones we've got together. I'm Millie, by the way.'

'Pleased to meet you, Millie. I'm so grateful to you and your grandmother for all your help. I know nothing at all about babies, I'm afraid. How many have you got?' Dottie couldn't help asking, surprised, as she'd thought the girl no older than herself. She glanced back at the bed, biting her lip.

'Well I got the four, and another one on the way.' The girl patted her slightly plump belly with pride. 'One and two was gifts from Mr-I-thought-you-knew-I-was-married, number three was from Mr-I-never-said-I-would-marry-you, and number four and this 'un was from Mr-I-don't-care-about-the-other-men-I-love-you.'

'You don't look old enough...'

'I'll be twenty next month. That's plenty old enough. I'm glad I'll be married by the time I'm twenty. We gets married the week before it's due, so that's all right. Was beginning to think I'd be an old maid.' She chuckled heartily. 'Are you ready for the off, then? Nanna said I was to bring a cab to fetch us back to your hotel? He's waiting outside. It's my fella what drives the cab, so we're in safe hands.'

Dottie got up, feeling nervous. She couldn't seem to tear her eyes away from Diana's outline under the sheet. It felt so wrong just to walk out and leave her. Surely they couldn't—couldn't just...?

'Do you want me to carry the little one down them stairs, or will you do it, Miss?'

Dottie hesitated. She couldn't seem to decide. She looked helplessly at Millie.

'Shall I?' Millie asked.

Dottie nodded. 'I think perhaps you'd better.'

The girl said, 'Was there anything of the lady's that you might want to take? Otherwise I don't doubt it'll all get put in the furnace.'

Dottie looked around, taking in the few possessions Diana had in the room with her. Then she looked at the girl and shook her head. 'No, there's nothing.'

'If you're sure.'

Again Dottie hesitated. Millie touched her arm, and said softly, 'You've done all you could. It's time to go, duck.'

Dottie nodded, fighting back the tears, as she took that first, near-impossible step to the door.

Then they were going down the stairs, out of the hotel, where the proprietress glowered from the back regions of the hall, and out into the late evening sunshine. A horse-drawn cab was waiting for them, and the cabbie, a robust and handsome young man with wavy deep red hair came forward to open the door and help the ladies up into the cab. As the horse whinnied, Dottie got up first, then took the baby from Millie, who then got in and sat on the bouncing leather seat, and took the baby back again.

When they reached the hotel, and Millie had embarrassed Dottie somewhat with a rather over-long goodbye kiss with her 'fella', whose name was Noah, (and, Dottie thought, who was clearly applying himself in earnest to the Biblical command to care for and increase the population of the earth), they carried the baby into the hotel, Dottie leading the way up the stairs to her room, aware of the oddest sense of unreality, as she couldn't help contrasting the spotless plush carpets, potted palms and hushed, well-lit corridors with the 'hotel' they had just left, where even now, she fervently hoped, some gentlemen from the mortuary were preparing to remove Diana's remains and carry her to a new resting place. Here nothing was different, but for

Diana, and for Dottie herself, nothing was the same.

They reached the room just as the baby surprised them with her first gentle squalls for food. Dottie half-expected someone to knock on her door and complain about the noise, or demand to know what was going on, but no one came. Millie set the babe down in the centre of Dottie's bed and hurriedly began to pull apart the pack she'd brought with her, triumphantly pulling out a small glass bottle with a rubber teat, and settling Dottie into the armchair, she showed her how to feed the hungry infant.

It was easier than Dottie expected, and she was thrilled with the determined way the baby consumed the whole feed of a couple of ounces. Next, Millie produced mild soap and a soft wash-cloth and towel, and in the little sink in the corner of Dottie's room, she showed Dottie how to bath the baby, then they put a terry-towelling nappy on her and rubber pants to keep the damp in. Finally, they dressed the baby in a doll-sized knitted vest, bootees and a soft, much-washed babies' nightgown. By now the baby was almost asleep and Dottie was also yearning to go to bed. As she set the baby down to sleep on the plush seat of the armchair with an old but very soft and warm shawl wrapped about her, Dottie realised with pleasure that she was now far more confident about handling the baby. Even though she wasn't likely to need to do it, Dottie got Millie to explain to her how to make up the artificial feeding formula. With all this new information, Dottie felt as though she was a fully trained child's nurse. The contented baby slept, and Dottie couldn't believe what a little wonder she was, so quiet, so good.

Dottie made the most of Millie's company and excused herself for half an hour to go and make some telephone calls, and to order a late dinner for them both to be sent up to her room. Dottie stepped into the hotel manager's office to explain, in case there should be any complaints, that she now had a newborn baby temporarily staying in her room with her. The man was understanding and politely helpful, even though Dottie could see he desperately wanted to ask how the child came to be there, but didn't quite dare. He seemed quite relieved when she said that the child would shortly be taken to its new home.

Dottie's first call was to Flora and George. Cissie, Flora's maid answered, and Dottie asked for Flora. Dottie waited, feeling a little nervous. What would she say? How do you tell someone something so awful? It seemed like an age before Flora arrived, and as she came to the phone, Dottie could hear her sister laughing and calling something over her shoulder to a guest. They had visitors. Then Flora's voice, soft, concerned, came down the line.

'Dottie, dear, is everything all right? Father said...'

'Oh Flora, it's so terrible. It's Diana, oh the baby...' And Dottie, suddenly sobbing, and in a muddled way blurted it all out. Flora was silent.

At last, Dottie heard Flora call, quite sharply, 'George, dear, I need you! Now, please, darling!'

By the time the second lot of three minutes was up, a shocked George had been taken by Greeley the butler into his study to sit down with a glass of brandy, and Flora had promised to talk to him, and to her and Dottie's parents, then telephone Dottie back within an hour to let her know what had been decided.

Dottie returned to the room, relieved at the sharing of her burden. Her heart went out to George, as he dealt with not only his own sense of loss, but the decision made by his parents to send their daughter away. Flora had said he was incoherent with rage and grief.

Millie and Dottie ate their hot food, talking little, and with all their eyes on the little one sleeping on the chair. As soon as the food was finished and the plates cleared away, Dottie went back downstairs to wait by the telephone, even though she knew it would be another twenty minutes at least before Flora would be likely to call.

As she waited, she saw the man who looked a little like William Hardy walking along the hall to the lounge, and on his arm, his lady. Or wife? Or sister? He smiled and nodded at Dottie and she managed a stiff little nod in return.

It was her father who rang her back, not Flora. He was shocked and angry, but not with her. She was relieved to hear him say they would leave for Scarborough the next day. 'We'll be with you as soon as we can. We're not leaving until about nine o'clock: we've got to wait for an infants' nurse to arrive from Gravesend, then we shall be starting immediately. It'll be your mother and myself, and George, and the nurse of course, so could you reserve our rooms for us, my love?'

'Is George taking the baby back with him?'

'Yes, of course. He insists he and Flora will raise the child. Flora is in complete agreement, he said, which I admit I half-expected. George is naturally terribly upset, and he refuses to consider any other course of action, in any case. He's spoken to his father—and told him he never wants to see him again. No doubt, given time... But who knows. It seems barbaric, and George is furious. I've never seen him like this, he's usually such an amiable fellow. But that they could have done this to his own sister, to their own daughter.' Mr Manderson paused and took a steadying breath. 'Are you sure you're quite all right, Dottie dear?'

Dottie spent another minute reassuring him, then they said good night. Dottie went to see the manager again, this time to reserve the rooms, then she returned to her own room, relieved beyond measure.

She got ready for bed, and Millie settled herself to sleep in the other armchair, even though Dottie had pointed out that the bed was plenty big enough for two slim girls and that Millie had her own unborn baby to think about. But Millie was happy to sleep in the armchair. She had unpacked a few more nappies and had four more bottles of artificial feeding formula made up ready for the baby. She was keeping the bottles cool in the sink, which was filled with cold water.

'That should be enough to keep you going for a bit. If your sister's hubby and the nurse are delayed, we'll need to get some more made up in the morning. But if they are on time, I won't bother, the nurse is bound to have everything she'll need, I'm sure. She'll know what to do, and probably better than me. They can be quite scary, these nurses!'

As soon as Dottie put out the light to sleep, the baby started to wail. They took turns to shush her and cuddle her, they changed her again, and all was well until the light was turned off again. In the end, they left the light on, reasoning that it was up to Flora's nurse to develop a routine. At least, Dottie thought as she finally fell into an uneasy sleep, the little one had a good pair of lungs on her.

Dottie's parents arrived the next day in time for a late lunch. Her brother-in-law, George, was with them, along with Hudson, a hastily engaged but highly recommended infants' nurse.

Dottie had got up that morning feeling calm and reasonably well-rested. She and Millie took turns to go down to breakfast, at Dottie's expense—or rather, her father's—and Millie made Dottie laugh at her exclamations about the hotel's extensive range of foods. Then Dottie waited for what felt like an eternity in the entrance hall, glad to be able to leave the baby in

Millie's care. It was almost three o'clock when George's car halted outside the hotel. Dottie watched with perfect composure through the glass doors as they got out of the car and stretched the journey from their bones. But as soon as George came into the lobby, she faltered. She took a step forward, her smile turned into a half-sob, and she halted. Not caring about those around them, George snatched off his hat and crossed the room almost at a run and wrapped Dottie in a tight hug, tears streaming down his face. Dottie's fragile composure deserted her, and she sobbed openly on his shoulder.

Somehow her parents got them upstairs to Dottie's room where they could be private. Lunch was ordered, as her family had journeyed without stopping from London, a distance of some 240 miles, and were in need of something to eat and drink. Dottie introduced the new arrivals to Millie, and of course, the tiny baby.

It had been years since Dottie had seen her mother hold a small baby, and she was surprised by the tender confidence her mother showed as she took the infant from Millie and held her. The men crowded round, George wiping his eyes on a scarlet handkerchief, and blowing his nose vigorously. He was greatly embarrassed by his display of emotion, but Dottie had always adored him and felt that the emotion became him.

The baby was admired and cooed over. Everyone commented on her tiny fingers and dainty features, on her quiet composure and staring, interested eyes. It was a relief for Dottie, not just to see that they were so ready to accept and love the child, but that there was no inclination to reject or disapprove in spite of her unorthodox arrival into the world.

After a short consultation with the new nurse, Millie took her leave, receiving with astonishment a discreetly passed ten pound note and George's thanks for her trouble. He kissed her cheek and the young woman went away blushing and bursting to tell her family all about it. George's new nurse, Hudson, took over, tsking at the way the nappy had been folded. She busily unpacked her bag to supply one of her own choosing. The baby was quiet under her ministrations, and Dottie hoped that the nurse would be kind and gentle as well as efficient. It was true that she came highly recommended, but she was older than Dottie had hoped, and rather too bristling with the correct way to do things.

It took the best part of an hour for Dottie to tell them everything that had happened, but she was determined to hold nothing back. She had necessarily to explain how she came to know about Diana's predicament, so she told them about William Hardy, her conversation with him on the train, and this had to include his marriage proposal. She felt a little surprised at her own calm manner as she related the whole event, given that the very thought of it made her want to collapse in tears on her bed, but other than the trembling of her hands as she folded and unfolded her napkin, or twisted the button on the edge of her sleeve, she betrayed none of her feelings. She saw her parents exchange a look, but they said nothing. Neither they nor George seemed surprised to hear she had accepted Hardy's proposal. It was a relief to talk about the whole thing. Only now did she realise that for her family Hardy's proposal, and her acceptance of it, had been a foregone conclusion. Would they think her foolish for retracting her consent? She felt very foolish now, as she told them about her impulsive departure from the train at York and what amounted to a firm rejection of William Hardy and their engagement. She fought back a fresh flow of tears and tried to concentrate on Diana's story. What her family thought about her revelation was impossible to fathom, but they were kindness itself.

Her parents took charge, to Dottie's relief. The weight of responsibility fell from her shoulders. She felt lighter, more hopeful. She began to feel that things might turn out all right. George went down to the hotel lobby to use the telephone to call Flora, whilst her parents and the nurse settled themselves in their own rooms, the nurse carrying the infant off with her. After telephoning, George returned, bringing a portable baby's cot from the back of his car, and went directly to the nurse's room.

Dottie sat on her bed and looked around at the room, empty now except for her own things. She was so reassured that George and Flora had agreed to bring up Diana's baby as their own. All her anxiety and despair was at an end; now they could all grieve for Diana, knowing her little one was in safe hands. Dottie thanked God that the baby wouldn't grow up in some orphanage; the relief about that was almost overwhelming. She lay back on the bed and waited for her family to come and find her once they were settled. She fell into a light, dreamless doze.

When she awoke it was fast approaching dinner-time. Her mother was sitting in a chair near the bed.

'I thought it best to let you sleep, dear.' Looking down, Dottie saw that the coverlet had been pulled up over her. She got up and began to hurriedly wash her face and hands, then changed her blouse and skirt for a dress. Her mother relayed small bits of information to her as she did so, then as they were about to leave to go down and meet the gentlemen, she suddenly hugged Dottie tight and said, in a breaking voice, 'Darling girl, I'm so proud of you.'

Dottie fought back tears yet again. 'You don't blame me for getting involved with Diana? I know her situation was...'

'Not at all. It took great courage, Dorothy dear, and great compassion. I'm very proud of you. We both are.'

'Did you know?' She looked into her mother's eyes, thinking back to the day before her birthday at the end of March, when they had drunk cocktails at George and Flora's home with George's parents, and first heard that Diana had gone to the coast to recover from 'bronchitis'.

Mrs Manderson shook her head, but said, 'Well, I didn't know, but I admit I wondered. One hears rumours, and of course, it's a rather well-worn cliché, sending a young woman off to the coast for a few months to recover from some supposed illness. I wonder the Gascoignes' thought anyone would believe it for a moment. Though it never occurred to me that she would be so completely alone and friendless.'

'I never gave it a thought, I just accepted it completely,' Dottie said.

'Hmm,' said her mother, then, 'Of course I never dreamt the poor child wasn't being properly cared for.' She shook her head, her mouth a firm straight line of disapproval. 'It really is a terrible thing, to allow something like this to happen to a young girl in our day and age. How Piers and Cynthia could do such a thing to their own child... I shall never visit them again. No friendship could survive such behaviour, not even with all the years we've known them.'

'Diana wanted to punish herself. Perhaps she could have had help if she'd wanted it? But I think she wanted to die, she thought she deserved it for her wickedness,' Dottie said. 'Was she a member of the Daughters of Esther? From something she once said, I rather gathered that she was.'

'She had been, but she left before I got involved, in the aftermath of the murder of that man you found in the street. Is it important? Do you want me to find out?'

Dottie shook her head. 'The dead man was Diana's lover, Archie Dunne. No, don't trouble yourself to find out anything, I don't think it's important. It was just an impression I got from a few things she'd said. But it's too late now, it doesn't matter. Poor Diana is gone.'

Dottie's hand was on the door handle when her mother said, softly, 'Darling, I'm so sorry about William.'

Dottie sighed. Without turning, she opened the door, and stepping through, she said, 'Oh! Don't, Mother, please. I can't...' She felt her mother's hand just gently pat her shoulder.

'I know, my dear, I know.'

As dinner came to an end, their sparse conversation became fixed on recent events. Just before dinner, George and Mr Manderson had been to see Diana's body, now reposing at a funeral parlour whilst arrangements were made. George was pale but resolute as he told Dottie about a second telephone call he had made to his father.

'I told him in no uncertain terms exactly what I thought of him. And I told him he would have my sister properly laid to rest in the graveyard on our family estate, or he would never see Flora and myself, or any of our children ever again.'

George paused as the waiter approached. The waiter set coffee before them. When he left, George continued, 'Actually my parents are very upset, as well they might be, I told Father I blame him for Diana's death. It was he who insisted she was sent away. He told me my mother has left him, she had been against it from the start.' George closed his eyes momentarily, then added, 'She's gone to her sister's in Lincoln. He doesn't seem to think she will come back. I only hope it's a temporary separation, and that after a period of grieving, she will return home. However, we shall see.'

Dottie couldn't think of anything helpful to say. She patted his arm.

'Brandy?' asked her father. George shook his head.

'I'd better not. Wouldn't do to get plastered, and the way I feel right now, I doubt I could stop at just one. Anyway, so that's it. I've arranged for Diana's body to be driven home tomorrow, and there will be a small family funeral in a few days at Ville Coign. Cause of death will be given out as pneumonia—everyone seems to know that's why she went away, so... Small mercies, I suppose. I'm going home to Flora tomorrow, with Hudson and the little one, and then a day or two after that, I'll join my parents.'

'We'll be going home tomorrow too,' Mr Manderson said. There was nothing left to say; they were all too tired and too upset. They abandoned their half-drunk coffee and went up to their rooms.

At the top of the stairs, as George made to go to his own room, he suddenly hugged Dottie, and speaking through a fresh outbreak of tears, he said, 'I can't thank you enough, Dottie, dear. I'm really so, so very grateful that you... If you hadn't been so determined to see her, to make sure Diana was all right...' He couldn't continue.

She kissed his cheek. 'I couldn't help her, it was too late. You don't have to say anything...'

He turned and went away to his room. Dottie went to hers, and once undressed, she sat by the window looking out at the dark street and the sea beyond.

The next morning, very early, they waved off George, the nurse and the baby, who departed in George's car, then Dottie said goodbye to her parents at the railway station. Her mother had tried to persuade her to return home with them, but Dottie hadn't wanted to leave quite yet. Perhaps she ought to have, she thought for the dozenth time, as she strolled along the street to her hotel. There was, after all, so much waiting for her back in London. But she hadn't been able to face it. Her parents—and Flora and George— would be watching her like hawks to see if she was all right, and... oh, she just couldn't go back yet. She needed another day or two. She was completely drained, physically and mentally, and she just wanted to be quiet and to sit looking at the sea, and try to make sense of everything that had happened since she left Scotland, only four days earlier.

George and her mother had both promised to telephone her in the evening to let her know they were home safely, and she said she wanted to hear about the baby, and to speak to Flora. But it was now only half past nine in the morning, and the whole day stretched ahead of her. She felt a little adrift. The last few days had been overwhelming and suddenly it was all at an end; everything seemed empty and a bit pointless.

She returned to the hotel and went to her room to lie down for a while. She had no inclination to do anything else. She quickly fell asleep. For once, her sleep was dreamless, or nearly so, her mind refrained from taunting her with horror and grief. When she awoke, she was rested. And hungry. It was almost dinner-time so that was not entirely surprising. She tidied herself and went downstairs.

After dinner, she wandered along the hallway to what was the 'guests' lounge' according to a polished wooden plaque. In marked contrast to the room at her previous hotel in York, this one was a bright space filled with rattan furniture and large potted palms, rather as she supposed the deck of a cruise liner would be got up, or perhaps some conservatory in a hotel on the French riviera. Dottie went to sit at a little table near the large picture window that gave onto the street that ran along the promenade. She couldn't see the sea from here, but nevertheless it was a charming view. A lady sat alone at a table a little further along, Dottie thought she recognised her though couldn't immediately place her. A waiter approached, and Dottie ordered a pot of tea, not quite ready to be seen alone in public drinking alcohol as modern young women were wont to do in London.

The tall man she had seen in the hotel's lobby two days earlier came into the room, lean, broad-shouldered and fair-haired. He went to sit at a table with the attractive and elegantly dressed woman Dottie had just noticed. Yes, Dottie remembered the woman had said something about him being a policeman. Dottie tore her eyes away from him, and looked down at the hem of her sleeve. Would it be like this? Every man that was vaguely tall or nicely built, or fair-haired, would she always feel that little lurch inside and the hope that it was William? Her composure of an hour earlier had gone and she felt all the weight of her sorrow again. The waiter was returning with her pot of tea, and Dottie made a great show of stretching and yawning, surreptitiously dashing away a tear. She managed to force a smile and thanked the waiter. He bowed and walked away, and she leaned back against the chair.

Almost immediately she was called to the telephone. George reported himself home safely, said Flora was delighted with the baby, but he said little more, pleading weariness and the need for an early night. Not wanting to wait too long for her parents to phone her, Dottie requested a call to be put through to them, spoke very briefly with her father who assured her all was well, and that he would telephone the following evening to see how she was. Happy enough with that, Dottie returned to the Guests' Lounge.

A few other people had arrived: two men on their own, an older couple, and two elderly ladies, settled themselves at tables and gave their orders to the waiter. As Dottie walked by, the fair-haired man laughed at something his lady companion had said. Even his laugh wasn't the same. It wasn't William, she reminded herself. But why wasn't it? Why hadn't William got off the train? Why hadn't he come after her? Didn't he love her enough to follow her and try to put right what had happened? Or even to demand in a very forceful, masculine way that she give up this foolishness and return to London?

He had his job. She knew he had to go back for that. She knew too that he needed his job, that unlike her, he didn't have a wealthy indulgent father or a generous annual allowance from a grandmother's will, or any of the luxuries that enabled Dottie to more or less please herself. She knew all this, yet still a ridiculous, selfish, childish part of her demanded that he ought to have made a scene, that he should have shouted, insisted, proved his love for her by his very intractability and refusal to be reasonable.

But William Hardy was not like most other men. He didn't make demands, insist on his own way, didn't try to assume some role of entitled lordship over her that required her unquestioning obedience. He was considerate, accommodating, respectful of her views and opinions, and above all, he was conscientious in doing his duty as a police officer. Values that she had admired, that had meant so much to her, yet which were exactly the cause of this whole situation.

He had pleaded. Yes, she had to admit he had pleaded with her, in his polite, considerate manner. But in the end, he had just let her go. He didn't really love her, she told herself, quashing the image in her mind of his face when she forbade him the use of her first name. His expression when she had called him Inspector Hardy... He'd looked crushed, as if he wanted to weep.

She almost broke down again. Clearing her throat, Dottie made herself sit up very straight and poured herself a good strong cup of tea. She would think about what she should do next. She would be practical and make plans. William Hardy had got to be forgotten about. That was all in the past now, and there was no point in keeping on thinking about it. She wondered if he had heard all about Diana's baby, and that Diana had died? Surely he would know by now? She could imagine Janet telling the news to her Frank, and the sergeant would then definitely mention it to W—to Inspector Hardy. For a brief moment Dottie entertained visions of him getting the first train up to Scarborough to fling himself at her feet, or to sail in ready to protect and comfort her. But that would never happen. Deep down inside she knew these were just empty fantasies.

An eyelash poked her eye, and she opened her handbag to get her mirror and a handkerchief to deal with the minor annoyance, ignoring the slight redness of her eyes—hopefully no one had noticed that the girl sitting miserably all on her own had been crying—and as she was closing the bag, she noticed the little pasteboard card that Mr Bray, Mrs Carmichael's solicitor, had given her. Perhaps she ought to let him know she wouldn't be returning to London immediately?

When the waiter went past her to the people at the other table, she stopped him and asked for some writing paper and an envelope. Her rash detour had given her plenty to do. The waiter returned with the stationery a minute later, and Dottie quickly wrote a short letter to Mr Bray explaining that she had fulfilled his request in Scotland, and that she was taking a few days to fulfil a personal errand in Scarborough and would then return to London. She signed the letter, folded it, and copied his address from the card onto the envelope in her neat, if somewhat schoolgirlish hand, then she sealed the letter and gave it to the same waiter the next time he went past.

Now, surely, she had done everything?

Chapter Six

Next morning, she saw the familiar Lyons' Corner House sign moving in the breeze that ran up from the sea. She went inside, it wasn't busy yet, and she had her pick of the tables. She chose one beside the large plate-glass window and sat looking out into the street. Two couples followed her in, ordering their drinks almost immediately, and the everyday noises of conversations and movement bubbled around Dottie, a warm safe ordinariness that was comforting. She began to relax.

A smiling waitress took Dottie's order, and within a few minutes she had a pot of coffee and a plate of toast set in front of her. The sight and smell of the coffee and food brought a grumbling response from her stomach. It had been days since she had felt really hungry, and she devoured the toast, lavishing butter and marmalade on each slice. Feeling warm inside as well as out, she sat back to watch the world go by in the street outside, and sipped her coffee whilst trying to decide what to do with the rest of her day. But her thoughts turned again and again to recent events.

Sorrow was there, yes. Her heart still ached for Diana and for the tiny orphan who would never know either her true father or mother. Probably it would be years before she would be told the family secret. But there was hope, too—the baby would be cared for by a loving family, and live in a secure and comfortable home. It was the best outcome, considering the situation. Dottie felt a little thrill of excitement at the thought that she would witness the little one growing up, into a toddler, a child, an adolescent, a woman. She would always remember she had been the first to hold her, after the doctor of course. How she longed to know what George and Flora would call her. Surely Diana's name would be in there somewhere, as a kind of memorial? She did so hope it would.

And in time, she knew that her own feelings—now so raw and difficult to accept—would soften into sadness at the waste of a young woman's life. Whether she would ever stop telling herself she ought to have done more, was another question. At the moment she didn't believe she would ever stop thinking, if only I'd done this—or that—or something else. If only. Dottie sighed.

The bell over the door jangled. It had already heralded the entrance of several more people, but she hadn't really paid any attention to them. Now she turned and watched as the same man and woman from her hotel entered. It was he whom she had initially mistaken for William Hardy. Again, she thought, he's really nothing like William—Inspector Hardy—other than being a similar height, with fair hair, and very good-looking too.

Clearly he remembered her as he met her look with a broad smile and a nod. His companion looked to see whom he was greeting and she too smiled. They exchanged a brief word or two then to Dottie's surprise, they came over.

'May we join you?' the woman asked. 'It's a bit crowded in here—and we recognised you from our hotel. Is it too cheeky to scrape an acquaintance based on those two things?'

Dottie laughed. 'No, of course not! Do sit down. Although I was just about to leave.'

'Don't go yet,' the man said, 'or we'll feel as though we've offended you. Let me buy you another...er...?'

'Coffee,' Dottie said. 'Thank you, that's very kind.'

He caught the eye of the waitress—and most of the other women in the establishment—and gave their order. He reached across the table to offer Dottie his hand. 'I'm Gervase Parfitt, by the way, and this lovely lady is my dear sister-in-law Penny, Mrs Penelope Parfitt.'

Dottie was delighted to meet them and said so with great sincerity. She shook their hands. Her mother might belong to the generation of women who didn't shake hands, holding it to be a male behaviour, but Dottie was far more modern than that.

'I'm Dottie Manderson.'

'Are you on holiday, Miss Manderson?' Penny Parfitt asked.

'In a manner of speaking,' Dottie said. She didn't feel she could explain why she was really in Scarborough, but for some reason, her brain refused to function just when she needed some harmless small-talk. Her new friends looked at her, expecting her to clarify her meaning. Words failed her. She couldn't think of a proper explanation.

The waitress arrived with the teas and Dottie's coffee, and by the time they'd each attended to milk and sugar, the other two had forgotten—or politely ignored—Dottie's odd choice of words. Dottie raised her cup to her lips, glancing across the table as she did so. She met Gervase Parfitt's eyes regarding her with a very frank expression of admiration. She almost choked on her coffee, but managed to set the cup down without mishap and asked, with every appearance of composure:

'And are both of you here on holiday?' She made a point of looking at Penny as she said it but could feel his eyes on her. She knew she was blushing. It's ridiculous, she thought, I'm used to dealing with amorous men. How many times had she wrestled on the doorstep after an evening out with some young fellow who thought he deserved more than a quick peck on the cheek? So why did she feel so discomposed now?

'Actually,' Penny said, 'I'm here for a few days following the death of my husband a month ago.'

Before Dottie could murmur an apology or condolences, Penny added candidly, 'I just felt I had to get away. Arthur had been ill for some time, and I was quite exhausted. It was affecting my own health, so...'

'So as Penny's oldest and dearest friend, and practically a brother, I offered to accompany her to the seaside for a few days whilst the house is being decorated and some of the ghosts laid to rest.' Gervase said it with a broad grin, but patted Penny's hand tenderly. He seemed to be coping quite well with the loss of a brother. But if her husband had been ill for a long while, perhaps the family viewed it as a merciful release? If Dottie had wondered if there was anything more behind their friendship, this was disproved by Penny's sisterly playful slap and her laughing comment:

'Idiot. Oldest friend, definitely; none of my friends are as old as you! And I take issue with the use of 'dearest' too. But yes, it's true I'm having some of the rooms done out. It will be nice to go back to fresh rooms, and well, if not ghosts, there are quite a few memories which I suppose is inevitable when you've been married just over ten years.'

Dottie had been on the point of asking if there had been any children. But Penny continued, saying, 'We didn't have any children, so it'll be odd being in the house on my own. But my sister and her family are coming back from India in a few days. They'll stay with our parents, but it's quite nearby, and they'll visit me, of course, or I'll visit them, so I expect I'll get worn out with all the socialising and be glad to be alone again.'

By the time they'd finished their drinks, Dottie felt as though she was well and truly one of the party. They invited her to go with them to walk along the promenade and play mini-golf, which she hadn't tried before, and was delighted to find she excelled at.

Gervase was not shy about showing how much he already liked her. He seemed to take every opportunity to touch her arm, or put an arm about her shoulders as he showed her how to putt and swing her club. But it was all done so light-heartedly that she didn't feel any inclination to object. It was merely a casual flirtation, and was very soothing to her self-esteem. After lunch at the hotel, they went out again to listen to the band playing on the promenade.

By dinner-time she felt she'd known them all her life. They invited her to join them for dinner, and she gratefully accepted, not looking forward to sitting at her table all alone. Gervase set himself out to be very charming indeed, making her laugh with his tall stories, and Dottie found herself very willing to be charmed. It didn't have to mean anything, after all, it was just a pleasant light flirtation. He talked about his work, and Dottie was profoundly interested to hear that he was—far from being an ordinary policeman— actually the Assistant Chief Constable of Derbyshire.

'And the youngest in the whole country, too,' Penny told Dottie with great pride. Dottie couldn't but help be impressed, though he was self-deprecating and tried to make it sound as if all he did all day was read or write reports for Parliament.

'But surely you didn't start at the top, you must have worked your way up and earned such a rarified position?' she laughed.

'Oh I did, I was one of the country's first graduate detective sergeants, and I'm glad to say that the position brought me a number of unique opportunities so that my rise was both rapid and well-deserved!' They laughed at his pretence at polishing a medal on his chest. 'Of course, there are always a few blighted sorts who will cry 'nepotism',' he added, frowning, 'but I earned my rank, I didn't gain it through the old boy's club, or because my father is the Chief Constable of Nottinghamshire. The two forces are completely separate.'

'Of course,' Dottie said, hastening to soothe his irritated pride. 'And I'm sure anyone who knows you would never believe you gained your position by anything other than merit.'

'Thanks!' He shot her a smile. 'I like to think policing is in my blood, as I'm following in the footsteps of both my father and my grandfather. But it's good of you to say so, even though you don't know us very well at present. I do hope we have the opportunity to get to know you better.'

Dottie felt as though his looks and his words meant something rather more personal than the surface indicated. She smiled back at him, and felt her heart do a little tell-tale flutter.

The three of them lingered over dinner. Conversation was general, touching on what Penny and Gervase had done since arriving in Scarborough, and reminiscences of other holidays, other resorts. A small orchestra came in to play in the lounge which in the evenings doubled as ballroom. The staff pushed back the tables, chairs and numerous potted palms to create an intimate dancefloor. Dottie and her new friends opted to sit at a table near the orchestra and simply listen to the music and watch the few couples who got up to dance.

At ten o'clock the orchestra took a break, and Dottie excused herself, remembering she was expecting the telephone calls from George and Flora, and from her parents.

The call from her parents came first.

'Dorothy dear, are you there? Can you hear me?'

'Yes, Mother, I can hear you perfectly.' Dottie repressed a giggle, her mother was practically shouting. It seemed likely the whole hotel could hear her voice. Dottie had to hold the earpiece at least six inches from her ear.

'Well, dear, we're home. What a journey! But never mind, we got back all right, obviously. We got home in time for an early dinner yesterday, and today we've just been taking things gently, apart from a visit to Florence and George, of course. Once again dear, I just want to say how proud I am—we both are—of how you coped with such a grown-up situation.'

Dottie felt a tiny adolescent irritation at that, but said only, 'Thank you, Mother.' She teased her hair into place in the little mirror beside the telephone, then vaguely wondered why it had seemed the best place to put a mirror. Did callers always get bored and let their thoughts wander? Or was it an automatic requirement for ladies to fuss over their appearance, especially if talking with a gentleman? Her mother spoke of this and that, non-essentials, anything to fill the time, then rang off, with an urge to Dottie to, 'Have a lovely rest, dear, but come home soon. Your family miss you.'

With a smile Dottie said her goodbyes, rang off, and waited for the next call. It was just a few minutes later that Dottie heard Flora's voice. Immediately Dottie asked, 'Is George all right?'

'Yes, darling he's perfectly fine, just you know... so upset still. He's doing something manly in his study at the moment, goodness knows what. What with that trip up to Scarborough and back, and then he's been to see his father and back today, really he's worn out from all the travelling and grief, the poor pet.'

'And the baby?'

Dottie could hear the smile in Flora's voice. 'Oh Dottie, she's such a little angel, isn't she? Absolutely gorgeous.'

'She is. And what are you going to call her, have you decided?'

'Well we've thought of a few names, but I think the one we will plump for is Diana Dorothy Gascoigne. What do you think?'

Dottie smiled. 'I'm so happy you're calling her Diana. I'd hoped you'd put that name in there somewhere.'

'We might put the Diana first, we haven't really got it fixed yet. Dottie dear, about William...'

'No!' Dottie said, suddenly on her guard. 'Please don't... I can't...'

'Very well, dear. But you are all right?' Flora must have moved at the other end, for her voice sounded suddenly closer, warm and confidential.

Dottie felt as if her sister was by her side. 'Yes, Flora, I'm quite all right,' she said softly. 'And now I've got to go. I'll be home in a few days, and then we'll have a proper talk.' But not about William Hardy, she mentally added. 'Goodbye, darling, and kiss baby Diana Dorothy for me.'

'I shall. See you soon, Dottie dear.'

The orchestra had already returned and were well into the second half of their programme. Penny was on her feet, about to leave when Dottie rejoined them. Penny said goodnight, and Dottie wondered if she should say goodnight too, and go up to her room. Then Gervase smiled at her.

'Have I missed much?' she asked him. He had so politely got to his feet as she approached, and now as he smiled down at her, her heart gave another little lurch. She reminded herself this was just a little holiday romance, nothing serious. It was too soon for anything serious.

'This is only the third number, so not too much.' He stubbed out his cigarette and turned to hold out his hand to her, 'Shall we?'

She was beginning to notice that when Penny wasn't around, he was livelier and more romantic. Dottie stepped onto the little dancefloor. She loved to dance and something told her Gervase would be an excellent partner. She was right. It didn't matter whether the orchestra played a waltz or a quick-step, his actions matched hers and they moved in perfect tune. For almost an hour they danced. After a slow waltz, her head was drooping onto his shoulder, and he spoke in her ear, his voice low.

'Would you like a walk on the prom in the moonlight? I promise to be a perfect gentleman.'

She lifted her head to look into his eyes that teased her in the soft lighting. She laughed. 'Is there a moon? That would be lovely, and although I'm sure you're not a perfect gentleman, you do seem reasonably well-behaved.'

He laughed out loud at that, and giving her his arm, he led her out into the cool night air. She was glad of her wrap; a strong breeze blew in off the sea, and it was chilly after the warmth of the lounge, and the dancing. She hugged Gervase's arm. One or two cars were arriving outside the little parade of hotels facing the sea.

'Everyone's coming back after their evenings out.'

'Yes,' Dottie answered, but couldn't think of anything else to add. They crossed the road and went to lean on the railing and look at the sea. It was the perfect time of year. The long light evenings drew reluctantly to an end, the sun was still setting on the horizon, splashing the sea with red and gold. On the other side of the sky, in the deepest blue, the moon was full and bright, gilding everything with silver: the waves-tops, the posts along the promenade, glancing down Gervase's cheekbones and chin. If he kisses me now, Dottie thought, I shan't want to stop him. His eyes, deep in shadow, regarded her, and she knew he was thinking of kissing her. There was a long moment, then a stronger gust of wind ruffled her hair, a young couple went past arguing loudly, and Gervase, with a soft laugh, turned to pull Dottie's hand through his arm and they began to walk in the other direction. Dottie pulled her wrap tight around her.

'Cold?' Gervase, pausing in his stride, pulled off his jacket and wrapped it, still warm from his body, about her shoulders. They walked again, still in silence, but he kept his arm about her shoulders. People will think we're a married couple, Dottie thought, and the thought of marriage to this man thrilled her. It was true he was quite a lot older than her, but they seemed to complement each other so well. She sighed happily. Thoughts of a mere holiday infatuation were quickly fading. She was already imagining something far longer-lasting. Their steps had slowed, her head was almost on his shoulder. They walked on.

They were almost at the end of the promenade, and there was Diana's hotel, huddled in guilty shadow at the end of the walkway. No light shone at its windows. The garish pink of daytime was blotted out by the night, and it seemed almost as if it was trying not to exist. As they reached it, and paused ready to turn back, Dottie couldn't help but look up at the building. She shuddered.

'Are you still cold? Perhaps we should hurry back and get you inside? Don't want you catching a chill.'

She shook her head. 'No, I'm quite all right.' Then, longing to get it all off her chest, she poured out the entire story. Without names, of course, she told him everything.

His disgust and indignation were all for what Diana had suffered. He was modern enough in his outlook to say to Dottie, quite emphatically, 'Well I can't imagine the woman got into the situation all on her own—what of the man? If I was her father, I'd have horsewhipped him, and seen to it that he made an honest woman of her. There's too much of this sort of dallying with defenceless girls. We see so much of it in the police force. And from what you've told me, this poor woman was little more than a child. The parents were very wrong to lay the blame so entirely on her shoulders. The poor girl! She must have been in complete despair.'

'She was utterly guilt-ridden. She'd been starving herself and living in squalor. I think she felt she deserved to die.'

'You were marvellous to stay with her, to try to help her,' Gervase said. 'I'm terribly—and please don't be offended by this, Dottie dear—I'm terribly proud of your courage and determination. Not many young women of our class would have been so courageous, nor so compassionate. No, really, Dottie, that was quite astonishing. Such strength of character is so, so rare.'

Dottie was flattered, of course, but she was also embarrassed. But his praise pleased her, his use of the word 'dear', his tight hug as he spoke, it all pleased her. Already, she had to acknowledge to herself, she was half in love with him. She wondered if he felt the same, or if he was merely being gentlemanly. Yet he didn't treat her as a child, or even as the new acquaintance she really was; he seemed to be genuinely in earnest in what he said to her. He was so caring in his behaviour towards her. He seemed to like her, if anything, even more than she liked him.

They turned to head slowly back, and giving her a teasing glance, his eyes glittering in the moonlight, he kissed her fingertips before tucking her hand back in its warm place in the crook of his arm. He said, 'We're leaving for home tomorrow afternoon.'

Dottie's heart sank, and she felt suddenly tearful. It was awful news. 'So soon?' she said, trying to sound merely politely disappointed. 'What a shame.'

'It's a bloody disaster, Dottie, that's how I feel about it. I know I've only just met you, but I already feel...' He stopped and turned to look at her. 'Look I know it's all happening too fast, and this isn't at all conventional, but... Well I'd like to continue to get to know you. Would you consider a few days in Nottinghamshire? I'll be driving us back, there's plenty of room for a little thing like you in my car, and between ourselves, I think that Penny is a bit nervous about going back to the house on her own. You'd be doing me a huge favour if you could stay with her for a few days, help her get used to being in the house without Artie.'

Everything in Dottie wanted to thrust aside the brevity of their friendship and shout, 'Yes!' But she pretended to think about it. They walked on. After a minute or two she said, 'I would like that, but only if Penny really wanted me to go back with her. After all, we've only just met. And what about her sister arriving shortly from India with her family? I wouldn't want to be in the way.'

'They won't be arriving until the middle of next week. And in any case, they're not staying with Penny, they will be staying with Penny's parents, a mile or so away. I shan't be there,' he hastened to add, as if she was concerned about the impropriety of that. Dottie was simply aware of an acute disappointment. He went on, 'I have my own home, of course, but that's also only a mile away from Penny's, and I intend to make a nuisance of myself by visiting as often as possible.'

By the time they reached the hotel, and he said goodnight to her—excessively politely, to Dottie's mind: she had hoped he would kiss her—it was assumed she would be going with them. He had promised to speak to Penny first thing, but he was confident she would be pleased to have Dottie with her.

They planned to leave soon after lunch, and Gervase expected they would arrive in good time for dinner.

'I'm not going to push it,' he told Dottie over morning coffee. 'We'll take our time. There's an old mill where they do refreshments and light meals. It's a lovely spot, very picturesque, and we always stop there to break up the journey. Penny's not a very good traveller I'm afraid and she's usually glad of a bit of a breather.'

Dottie said she thought it sounded perfect. Gervase gave her a grateful smile when she added that she had an excellent line in small talk to take Penny's mind off the motion of the motor car.

'Of course,' he said, 'it's not just the journey itself, it's what lies at the end of it that is playing on her mind. She's been dreading going home and Artie not being there.'

She'd said the same to Dottie when they went to the ladies' at one point during the morning, adding that she was glad Gervase had invited Dottie to go back with them. Now, Dottie said simply, 'It must be so difficult for her.'

'Well, yes. To lose the love of one's life so young. I'd never recover, I'm certain of it.' He looked at Dottie, who blushed and looked away. But she gave a light laugh and said:

'You can depend on me to prattle on and on and not give her a second to worry or feel poorly.'

He took Dottie's hand, kissed it lightly, half-laughing, and released it. For a moment she thought he was going to say something, but in the end the moment passed and his original words went unsaid, replaced by the rather more conventional, 'Thank you. Now I must go and check that Penny's finally ready.'

They left a little later than intended and, Dottie noticed, Gervase was showing signs of temper. She saw that Penny was inclined to cling, and was in the habit of relying on Gervase to make every single decision and every single arrangement. She hadn't even packed her suitcases. It transpired that Gervase had arranged for this simple task to be done by a maid at the hotel. Then he had to arrange for someone to take the suitcases down to the car and strap them on the parcel shelf at the back.

When he asked Dottie what help she required, he was astonished that she had seen to her own packing, and even brought the suitcase, as well as her small overnight bag and her hat box down to the hotel's reception area.

'You really are such a breath of fresh air, my dear!' he told her. His smile was warm and just for her.

Dottie felt all aglow inside. Gervase had already begun to dominate her thoughts and inspire deeply romantic feelings. He was so... she couldn't think what he was. She had calculated, from something he'd said the previous day, that he was in his early to mid-thirties, and ordinarily she'd feel that a man twelve or fifteen years older than herself was too old. But it didn't seem to bother him, and from Dottie's point of view it only seemed to add to his appeal. He was mature, he was confident, experienced and capable. He was good-looking, appeared to be in good health, vital and vigorous. He was everything a man should be. More importantly he was single, and he was making it very, very clear that he liked her more than just a little.

If only they had been driving off together, Dottie had the scandalous thought, just the two of them, on some wonderful trip to the country. Perhaps they would have had a picnic, parking the car in some winding rural lane, beside a flower-strewn meadow. They could sit on a blanket surrounded by nothing but the beauties of nature and Gervase would lean across and kiss her, and...

'Golly, what is that awful pong?' Penny asked, suddenly nearby. She pinched her nose and looked about her. 'Oh, the dreyman's horse has just relieved itself. Golly, you'd think they'd close the doors, wouldn't you? No one wants to smell that in the hotel. Shall we go and get in the car, Gervase?'

Dottie, wrenched from her amorous daydream, made a face at the offending horse that had deposited the steaming heap just four feet away from her, and turned her attention to what she was supposed to be doing.

Gervase's car was a small one. The entire back was given over to the conveyance of luggage rather than people, and the three of them were squashed together in the front, with Dottie in the middle trying to keep her knee out of Gervase's way when he had to change gear. Once or twice—surely by accident—his hand had lightly knocked against her knee as he moved the gearstick.

They were on their way. She spared a few minutes' solemn thought for the awful events of her time in Scarborough. She was overwhelmingly relieved to be leaving. Poor Diana would soon be laid to rest in the family plot on the Gascoigne estate, but Dottie's memory would always be torn between Diana smiling and enigmatic, talking about a woman's duty at the New Year's party, and her lying there in the squalor of that room, punishing herself for her sin, asking with her last breath to see her new-born child. As the car left the coast road behind, the filthy pink façade of that hotel taunted Dottie, and her eyes prickled with tears. She would never, ever go back to Scarborough.

But as they headed inland, along field-lined lanes, winding towards the major road leading south, Dottie's mood lightened. It was done. It was over. New things awaited. And on that thought, she cast a sideways glance at Gervase. Seeming to sense her eyes on him, he gave her a brief look, and a wink, accompanied by a rogueish grin. She smiled and looked straight ahead. A little bubble of happiness warmed her on the inside, like a wonderful secret for just herself alone. Penny kept up a babble of chatter about anything and everything, and it took all Dottie's patience and energy to say at intervals, 'Oh absolutely', or 'You're quite right'.

Just after three o'clock they halted at the mill Gervase had mentioned. It was a little less picturesque than Dottie had imagined. In her mind it had been a watermill in a tranquil spot, surrounded by trees and the necessary river, and of course a lily-covered millpond.

But in reality it was a former cotton mill, a huge red-bricked edifice situated on a very busy street, surrounded by little shops and houses and all the busyness that modern life required. Admittedly there were plenty of flowers—in window-boxes, front gardens and even in tubs and pots along the front of the mill. And behind the mill Dottie could see trees and fields stretching away over a hill. She blotted out the roar of motor cars and horse-drawn vehicles, the shouts of drivers, delivery boys and shop-keepers, and followed Penny inside.

They were welcomed warmly by the host. A table had been laid for them on a shady terrace at the back of the mill, and here there was water, the narrow fast-moving stream that had once powered the mill, and all around were flowers and plants and the chatter and song of birds.

'Better?' Gervase asked her softly.

She nodded at him and smiled. He squeezed her arm as he held her chair out for her to sit. Looking across at Penny, whom he'd already seated, he said, 'Miss Manderson approves.'

'Oh good,' Penny said, but she was already looking about her for the waitress. It was only two hours since lunch, and Dottie had little appetite, but an early high-tea was served anyway. Gervase said he was starving and demonstrated that by piling up his plate, leaving the ladies to help themselves.

Penny continued her incessant chatter. Dottie had almost no chance to keep her promise to Gervase to distract Penny with conversation, as she'd barely managed to get a word in edgeways. At one point, as Dottie raised her teacup to her lips, she caught Gervase grinning at her and had to look away so that she could give a serious reply to Penny's remark, and not burst out laughing.

She had realised by now that Penny had little interest in the world around her, and was completely absorbed by her own affairs and those nearest to her. What Penny liked, what

Penny did, how Penny felt and who Penny knew were her only concerns. Try as they might, neither Gervase nor Dottie could shift Penny's thoughts from how dreadful it was going to be to return to her home, now bereft of Artie. And doubtless the decorators would have used all the wrong colours in all the wrong places, created mess and caused damage, and her home would be a home no longer. No matter what Dottie or Gervase said to try to cheer, encourage, reassure or console, Penny was determined to be gloomy. Only time would change this continual fixedness of her thoughts upon her loss.

By the time they arrived at the house, Dottie was exhausted. The afternoon had been hot, and she didn't know which was worse, driving with the roof up and being stuffy and hot, or driving with the roof down and being constantly buffeted by the wind and dust, but still being hot. Towards the end of the journey, Penny had become increasingly agitated and tearful, and Gervase had become increasingly irritable and monosyllabic. Dottie, literally between the two of them, had then to draw on all her patience to calm first one then soothe the other. For her, the journey couldn't end soon enough.

But at last they arrived. Gervase drove through a village, not especially pretty but at least it appeared quiet, and halted outside a large house, square and plain, in the middle of a short row which marked the end of the village. The house was surrounded by lawns with a few shrubs here and there, but otherwise had little to soften its square, hard features.

A maid bustled out to meet them. Dottie was surprised at how very pretty the woman was. She was not merely good-looking, but had a noticeably good figure, unconcealed by her uniform, and a calm, competent way about her that was appealing.

The maid introduced herself to Dottie as Margaret Scott. It seemed she was expecting the extra arrival. She immediately began to give Gervase a hand with the luggage.

'Go on into the house, Miss Manderson,' the maid said, 'I'll be just a moment, then I'll get the kettle on, I'm sure you'll be ready for a drink.' Dottie smiled and nodded. She was about to take her suitcase when Penny grabbed her arm in a vice-like grip and exclaimed, 'Oh Dottie, I don't know if I can bring myself to go inside!'

Dottie resisted the urge to say, 'Nonsense!' very firmly just as her mother would have done, but patting Penny's arm, she swallowed her annoyance and said simply, 'Come on, it will be all right, you'll see, I'll be with you. It'll be exciting to see the new colour scheme. And you'd like a cup of tea, wouldn't you?'

Behind her, she heard the low sound of Gervase's hushed voice as he said, 'My God, Margaret, you're a sight for sore eyes.'

Then Dottie heard a soft chuckle from the maid, and the woman said, 'You're not so bad yourself, Gerry.'

Dottie felt a pang. Was he one of those men who carried on informal intrigues with the maids? Or was it just the harmless teasing of long acquaintance? Aware of a sense of dismay, and unable to shake off the warmth in their voices, Dottie accompanied Penny into the house.

Chapter Seven

The house was charming, if a little gloomy and overfilled with ornaments and furniture for Dottie's taste. Penny's idea of a home was rather Victorian in that she had a tendency to cram every space with an object of some kind. Dottie found it a bit surprising that someone only ten years older than herself should be so inclined. Later, in an aside to Dottie, when Penny left them to go and fetch her photo albums, Gervase said, 'It's a bit claustrophobic, isn't it? All this clutter. Not my idea of comfort at all.'

Dottie had only time to murmur a noncommittal sound as Penny bustled back, slightly out of breath. Squeezing between the two of them on the sofa, she set down four or five sturdy albums on the coffee table. They'd already sat a long time over their evening meal, then Dottie had had a tour of the house. By now it was just after ten o'clock, and all Dottie really wanted to do was sleep. She felt rather depressed by the sight of so many albums.

'Dottie's all in,' Gervase said suddenly. 'Cut it short, Penny. Just show Dottie your wedding photograph and let the poor girl get off to bed. She can look at the rest some other time.' Dottie's gratitude at this went a long way to helping her to overlook his apparent intimacy with the lovely maid, Margaret.

Penny appeared surprised, though not, Dottie thought, offended. 'Of course,' she said, pushing aside all but the top-most album. 'Well here we are, my beloved Artie and I on our special day.'

Dottie leaned forward to look at the little scene. Penny—looking younger, lovelier and radiantly happy—in the fashion of the 20s, her white lace gown very white by contrast with the dark suit of the gentleman beside her. He was unmistakably Gervase's brother—the same fair hair, the same slightly too-large nose, the same deep-set eyes. He was tall but unsmiling, and coupled with his almost-black suit, had the air of someone attending a funeral rather than his own wedding.

'Artie did so hate to have his photograph taken!' Penny laughed.

'Even on his wedding day?' Dottie couldn't help asking.

Penny gave her a wise look. 'Well you know, dear, the wedding day is really for the bride, everyone knows that. And her mother, of course.

It's nothing at all to the men. Besides, Gervase and Reggie, and my brother Mike had got Artie horribly drunk the night before. As soon as the photographs were over, he ran off to be dreadfully sick in the roses. Mummy was furious.'

It didn't seem half so romantic now, Dottie thought.

Penny closed the album and set it down. She got up. 'Very well. Time for bed, then. I assume you'd like a nightcap before you go, Gervase?'

He grinned. 'Of course. I need something to keep me awake on the drive back to my place. I can have it in here if you like. Sleep well, ladies. I'll no doubt see you in the morning.'

Penny rang the bell, the cord of which was concealed behind the edge of the curtain. 'Not too early, I know I shan't sleep properly tonight. I shall probably have a late breakfast, or else have it in bed.' Penny patted his arm. 'Thanks for bringing us back, dear.'

He stood, kissed Penny on the cheek, pressed Dottie's hand, and said a very solemn goodnight. Feeling rather like a child of five, Dottie gave him a shy smile and followed Penny from the room.

At the top of the stairs, their ways parted. As they repeated the goodnights they'd already said downstairs, Penny turned and said, 'Dottie, dear, I know we don't know each other very well as yet, but I'm so glad of your company. I know I'm just a silly old woman, but I was—I still am—quite nervous of coming back to the house, with

Artie not being here. Your company is a huge comfort. Goodnight dear, I hope you sleep well.'

Dottie made a half-turn round the top of the stairs to head in the direction of her room, two doors along the hallway. A soft sound from below made her glance over the rail and down the stairs. She saw Margaret heading into the drawing room with a small tray. She heard Gervase laugh softly as Margaret entered the room, and Margaret made a soft response, and closed the door behind her.

As Dottie shut her door, she couldn't help wondering how long Margaret would linger with Gervase—Gerry!—and if the whisky and soda was all she was giving him.

Dottie slept badly and woke with a headache. A maid who was not Margaret brought her a cup of tea at eight o'clock, and she was tempted to send her away and go back to sleep. But she hauled herself into a sitting position, squinting in the bright sunshine that lit up the room as soon as the maid threw back the curtains. The maid bobbed and left. All very Victorian, Dottie thought.

Dottie was aware of a dull ache inside. Not a physical pain, but an emotional one. She dreaded going downstairs. She dreaded meeting Gervase again after what she had seen—or rather what she had thought, or suspected—she had seen the night before. Would he have an extra spring in his step when he next came to visit? A gleam in his eye? Had he even left, or had he stayed with Margaret the whole night? Or had it just been an hour of passion, rather than the whole night? She didn't want to see the look in his eyes whenever Margaret came into the room, couldn't bear the thought that this new man in her life—or almost in her life—might be of the sort to carry on illicit intrigues with the servants.

'How Victorian I sound!' Dottie said to herself. Clearly Penny's favourite era was a contagious one. She drank some tea. The sharp tannin revived her. And her next thought was, 'How very like my mother I sound!'

But she felt saddened. She had perhaps put Gervase on a pedestal; he had seemed so clever, so witty, he was so good-looking. Had she expected too much of him? Men had needs, she knew, something her mother had hinted at mysteriously, and her sister—married, of course—had vaguely alluded to. Dottie had never really considered how those nebulous, undefined needs might be met, and by whom.

She washed and dressed, still pondering these thoughts. In front of the mirror, trying to coax her hair to be both full-bodied and neatly restrained, she also acknowledged, impatiently, 'Well, we women have needs too! Even if it's not the done thing to admit it.'

Perhaps, she thought, if a man's needs were met by the right person, he wouldn't be forced to look elsewhere for satisfaction. This seemed only logical, and realising there was nothing more she could do about her appearance, she had little choice but to leave her room and go down to breakfast.

At the top of the stairs, continuing to mull these things over, she had the sudden understanding: 'But that's how Diana ended up in her terrible predicament.' She shook her head. No, she couldn't bear to end her days like that. Caution and abstinence were the only sane, and safe, courses of action.

No one was in the dining room when she reached it. But almost immediately, Margaret, looking fresh and lovely, came to the doorway and informed Dottie that Mrs Parfitt would be breakfasting in bed. Dottie thanked her politely, and agreed that she'd like some breakfast, and that she'd slept well. As Margaret went through a verbal list of alternatives, Dottie said that she preferred fried eggs to scrambled or poached, bacon to kidneys or kippers, and that she also preferred coffee to tea first thing in the morning.

Margaret gave her a condescending grin and returned to the kitchen. Dottie felt fed up, the brief improvement in her mood had vanished.

The house was quiet. It smelled of paint. It was cluttered. In spite of the new paint, or perhaps because of it, it was dark and gloomy, making the rooms seem smaller than they really were. Dottie longed to sweep all the ornaments and extra furniture aside and have clean empty space around her. Given the choice, she'd paint over the ochres and mustards with soft creams and pastel shades. She had to get out into the fresh air as soon as she'd finished eating. Even

London didn't seem so stuffy and airless as Penny Parfitt's home.

Margaret returned with a pot of coffee, and a plate containing Dottie's breakfast—overcooked, dried-up rashers of bacon, and eggs cooked so long the undersides had gone brown, the edges curly and almost black. By contrast the toast was limp and hardly more than slightly warmed bread. For some reason, Dottie felt compelled to thank Margaret for the meal. She thought to herself somewhat sourly, doubtless no one much cared whether Margaret could cook.

'Do you know what time Mrs Parfitt will come down? I was thinking of going for a walk.'

'I've really no idea.'

'Oh. Well, thank you, anyway.'

Margaret turned and walked out of the room. Dottie felt there was a bristling hostility in the woman's manner. It seemed as though she disliked Dottie as much as Dottie did her. Dottie wondered if it was for the same reason.

She ate a little of her food, poking at it on the plate. When she cut through the yolk of the egg, the knife came out clean, the yolk was so firm. All that stuck to the knife was a small piece of eggshell. The coffee was lukewarm and tasted of silver polish. It was admirable that the silver had been cleaned, and certainly the coffee pot was a beautiful piece of craftsmanship, but no one wanted to taste the ammonia in their coffee.

Dottie's headache had worsened rather than improved. The sun shone in at the window, glistening on motes of dust twirling gently through the air, and the room was growing warm. She had to get out. She wiped her mouth on the wrinkled linen napkin and got up. There was a garden door in the drawing room across the hall, where they'd sat the previous evening, she remembered, and went to see. However, when she tried the handle, the door was locked, and the key was missing.

She went out of the front door, and as she rounded the house to look at the gardens at the rear, she immediately saw the maid, sitting on a low wall overlooking a wide expanse of lawn, and smoking a cigarette. She jolted on seeing Dottie, and seemed on the point of leaving.

Seeing her so shaken, Dottie felt mean about her previous dislike. Perhaps she should try and make amends. She went over to sit beside her.

'Lovely day. It's so warm in the house, I just needed a breath of fresh air.'

'Me too,' Margaret said, adding with a wry glance at her cigarette, 'and of course, I'm not allowed to smoke in the kitchen.'

Dottie smiled. 'No, I suppose not. I expect it's even warmer in the kitchen.'

'Yes.' Margaret's face certainly looked flushed and damp. She pulled out a handkerchief from her apron pocket and blotted her face and neck. 'Look, I know your breakfast was horrid, by the way. I'm sorry. I'm a terrible cook, I just seem to get worse the harder I try. I know I'm not very good at my job, but I need the money, obviously, and I'm not in a position to be picky.'

'Oh?' Now that she'd heard Margaret say a bit more, Dottie noticed her refined tone. A well-bred woman, then, working as a servant, because she had to, not because she had some scruple that forbade her to live a leisured life.

'Well, you might have heard that I've got a little boy?'

Dottie shook her head.

'It's one of the top local scandals, I suppose. I'm a bit surprised you haven't already heard about it. 'Unmarried daughter of county family gets herself knocked up'.' Margaret raised her hand in the air to indicate the headlines of a newspaper.

'I'm sorry,' Dottie said, sincerely. She was wondering two things: should she tell Margaret what had happened to Diana, in the hope that it might make her feel better about her situation. And secondly, was Gervase the father of her child? That might explain...

'My own stupid fault,' Margaret said. 'But you know how it is,' a sideways glance at Dottie, taking in her neat feet primly together and her slender figure. 'Or perhaps you don't. But,' she sighed, 'It's like this. You meet a fellow. He turns on the charm, takes you about a bit, promises you the earth, tells you you're beautiful and that he's never met anyone like you before, then he ditches you at the first hurdle. They're swine, the lot of them.'

Dottie didn't feel she could find an appropriate response to that. Instead she said, 'And what are the other local scandals?'

Margaret looked at Dottie in surprise then laughed. 'You're a cool one, I must say. Well, let me see...' She stubbed out her cigarette on the brickwork of the wall, and immediately lit another. 'I suppose our biggest scandal was the suicide of a young negro fellow. That was a few years ago now, though. After the war, it was. I expect most people around here have forgotten it. Fifteen years is a long time. Though it's probably coming back to a few people at the moment.'

'Why?'

'It's the anniversary next week, and then of course, Mrs Parfitt's sister is returning home in a couple of days—and she was the fellow's fiancée at the time he killed himself.'

'Goodness!' Dottie said, then scolded herself silently but furiously for sounding like a twelve-year-old.

'Not that any of their friends or family knew about it at the time. No, they'd kept it a secret—obviously she knew her parents would never allow it. I mean, can you imagine?'

Dottie had to admit she could. After all, it may have been years ago, but even now there were so many people still holding onto these foolish prejudices. If Dottie had come home engaged to a black man, her parents—who were nicer and more intelligent than a lot of people—would go through the roof.

She said, 'But how awful that it drove the poor man to suicide! Mrs Parfitt's sister must have been devastated.'

'Oh, she was. There had been a ball the previous evening, to welcome home the heroes from the war—and even this negro chappie was honoured—amazingly, he'd become an officer in his regiment. Then the next morning, one of the servants found him hanging from a tree in the grounds. When Miranda heard the news, she fell onto the floor in a dead faint.'

'How awful.' Dottie could almost picture the scene in her mind's eye, it all sounded so vivid. 'Were you there at the time, then?'

'I wasn't there when he was found, but I had been there the night before, at the ball. We youngsters had our own little drinking party outside later, away from all the fuddy-duddies. Really it was just an excuse to get drunk and for the couples to neck.' Margaret stubbed out her second cigarette. Dottie noticed her hand was shaking. It had obviously all come back with the telling. It must have been dreadful, Dottie thought, someone you knew dying like that, and so young.

'His family must have been distraught, what with him surviving the war, then doing that,' Dottie commented. Margaret got up to go, and as she did so it seemed that the previous reserve had fallen upon them once more.

'No doubt. Well, do excuse me, I must see about lunch.'

Dottie sat there a bit longer. The sun went behind a cloud and a chilly breeze ruffled her hair. The hem of her dress rippled. She didn't feel like going back inside that gloomy house, but neither was there any point in staying outside. She wandered over to a flower border, sniffed a rose, and felt disappointed that it was all colour and no scent. She turned back to look at the house.

She felt rather restless and adrift again. She wished she had gone home with her parents. She should have gone home. She could have gone in to the warehouse and begun to take up the reins of the business today. She could have gone to see Flora and George, and Diana's baby. Yet here she was, shivering in the chilly breeze, and feeling completely in the way and unwelcome.

It was because of Gervase, of course. She had felt an immediate attraction to the man, although she knew it wasn't a serious attachment. He would not be interested in a girl as young as she—he was a worldly, experienced man. She had somewhat glossed over in her head what that might actually mean up until now, but now she was beginning to think. She had no real interest in falling in love with him, she felt too bruised and upset about William for anything of that kind. But she couldn't deny he was attractive, charming and had a way of talking her into things. And he made her laugh. She did wonder a great deal about just how well he and Margaret knew each other, though, and whether that 'friendship' was confined to the past.

But in spite of his excellent qualities, Dottie was ready to get back to her everyday life, and allow her normal routine to heal her wounds from 'the big row', as she now thought of it.

The garden door from the drawing room was swinging open. Penny Parfitt stepped outside. 'Good morning!' she called, and Dottie forced a bright smile. As Penny came closer, she said, 'I see you're the outdoor sort. My husband loved this garden. These roses were his pride and joy.'

In spite of her views on roses with no fragrance, Dottie said perfectly truthfully, 'I don't think I've ever before seen such bold colours.'

It was fortunate that Penny took this as a compliment. She spent the next hour telling Dottie in excruciating detail the names and habits of each plant, and where her late husband had acquired it, concluding at last with, 'And this one he found halfway up Mount Nubia, and almost broke his neck trying to dig it up and pack it safely to bring it back down the mountain. The natives had to lower him on a rope harness to reach it.'

The cause of all this trouble proved to be a tiny, daisy-like white flower that, without this new information, Dottie would have had no hesitation in plucking out and discarding as a weed. She managed to look impressed and nodded vigorously, words having completely failed her.

Penny, putting her arm through Dottie's, drew her away. 'As a matter of fact, I actually came out to find you as Gervase rang to ask us out to lunch. He's picking us up in about...' She broke off to glance at her watch. 'Oh my goodness, in less than five minutes!'

Dottie found herself being dragged in the direction of the house, Penny's sharp little fingers pinching her arm. Penny rushed upstairs; Dottie was about to follow her when Margaret came out of the kitchen.

'What's going on?'

'Mr Parfitt has invited us out to lunch. I'm afraid time has rather got away from us. He'll be here shortly.'

Margaret's face was a picture of fury. She flung away from Dottie into the kitchen, yelling over her shoulder, 'Oh, well then I'll just throw out the lunch I'm slaving over, shall I?' The kitchen door slammed.

With another wish that she had gone home after all, Dottie ran upstairs to change her dress and put some colour into her face.

Not that she needed the extra colour. The excitement she felt knowing she was about to see Gervase again brought her to life. She felt fluttery and restless, unable to settle her thoughts.

He arrived before they were ready, of course, but Dottie—the first to come down—found him lounging in the doorway of the kitchen trying to soothe the furious Margaret. Dottie again couldn't help speculating about their relationship.

She stepped off the bottom stair; her shoe tapped on the tiles of the hall floor. He heard her. Glancing over his shoulder at her, his face lit up with a smile. She chided herself. Obviously at his age, a man would have had past affairs, only an idiot would be surprised by that. But she knew she was the focus of his interest in the here and now, which was all that should matter to her.

With renewed confidence, she beamed back at him, and reaching his side, she was thrilled when, forgetting or perhaps, simply ignoring Margaret, he turned and swept Dottie into his arms, and kissed her with passion. She was blushing as he released her. She was aware of Margaret staring from the kitchen, and behind them, halfway down the stairs, Penny Parfitt was also watching, one foot halted mid-air as she stood there.

Dottie held her breath—no mean feat as she was so breathless from his kiss—waiting to see if anything would happen. Gervase still gripped her hand, his rough fingers warm and strong. Margaret simply turned and went back to the pan she was stirring on the stove, and Penny, continuing to come down the stairs, gave them both a broad maternal smile.

'Sorry to keep you waiting, Gervase dear. I'm so glad Dottie was able to–entertain you.'

She kissed his cheek, grinned at Dottie who was blushing happily and then, ignoring Margaret completely, she led the way to the front door. Gervase gallantly stepped forward to hold it open for her. Penny went out. Dottie was next. Gervase quickly dropped a kiss on her cheek. 'You certainly did that, all right,' he said, for her ears only.

Dottie giggled. Her heart felt light. An image of William intruded, and she pushed it away, along with a creeping sense of guilt.

In the car, she had little to do but listen to and laugh at the teasing banter between Penny and Gervase as they began to reminisce. She let it all wash over her, gazing at the countryside streaming past the window: here a little knot of cottages, there a horse; here a smiling boy with a dog, there an irritable-looking man on a tractor. She closed her eyes briefly. Beside her the conversation flowed gently back and forth.

'...I knew you had a soft spot for her...'

'...only for you, dearest Penny. You're the one that got away, my love...'

'Humph, I seem to remember chasing you one particular summer, only to be rebuffed...'

'Oh, but then I was just a child. Now I am a man and I have put off childish things.'

Dottie felt relaxed for the first time in a week. Everything was going to be all right. Everything would work out. She would get over William. Diana's baby would be loved and safe. Diana would rest in the family plot with her ancestors; and she, Dottie, would go back to London in a few days, rested and ready to learn everything she could about how to run a fashion warehouse. Life would go on.

She exhaled slowly and deeply and felt the last of the tension trickle away. Everything would be all right.

They were lunching, not at a restaurant or hotel as Dottie had expected but at the rather nice house that belonged to Gervase's brother Reggie. There were several people there already; Dottie felt a momentary shyness as she was presented by Gervase to the other guests, simply as, 'Our new friend, Miss Dottie Manderson,' though her hand through his arm, and his hand covering hers, seemed to indicate to everyone that 'friendship' was an understatement. As a result, surprised but pleased, the others all made a great fuss of welcoming her, crowding round to shake her hand or kiss her cheek.

The ladies bustled upstairs to dispose of hats, gloves and bags, and ensure the blustery drive had not ruined their hair or lipstick. Men were so inclined to forget that kind of thing when they decided to put down the roof on their cars. The men went into Reggie's study for something alcoholic and to argue about stocks and shares.

Lunch was a large formal affair in the dining room. They took their seats at the long, rectangular table. To her relief, Dottie was placed between Gervase on her left and Michael Maynard, Penny's older brother, on the right.

There was rather a lot of wine—red and white—and Dottie was glad to drink a glass of water to offset the effects of the alcohol on an almost empty stomach. The table buzzed with conversation. Everyone here had known one another for years and years, and Dottie felt rather overawed by their friendship. Reggie was very like Gervase in some respects, though he looked by far the older, rather than the two years younger he actually was. He stooped slightly in the shoulders, and his hair, already greying, was thinner than Gervase's. Dottie thought he rather resembled an anxious chicken, his long neck poking forward, a lone sparse strand of hair habitually flopping over his brow.

Next to Reggie sat Penny, talking nineteen-to-the-dozen and looking very flushed. Dottie wondered how much wine she'd had. Her brother Michael, on Dottie's other side, was boyish, charming, though a little inclined to make racy comments, and given to casual bad language. Not what her mother would call a true gentleman, but Dottie thought that he seemed pleasant enough, and no doubt when sober, he would be very nice indeed. He was talking to her about his other sister, Miranda, who Dottie knew was en route from India.

'It'll be wonderful to see her again. She went away after all that bloody awful business years ago—one couldn't blame her at all, had to get over it somehow, poor kid. So, she's been gone for fifteen years. Done all right out there. Damn well hitched herself to some major from some artillery company, and popped out a couple of sprogs.'

'Michael! Please!' Penny protested, but with an indulgent smile.

'Sorry sis, it just slipped out, as the bishop said to the chorus-girl.'

Across the table, Reggie spluttered his wine, and Deirdre, Reggie's wife tutted loudly. Dottie knew she was blushing. Gervase said, more sharply, 'Mike, for God's sake watch your language!' He surreptitiously patted Dottie's knee, and managed to lean close enough to bump her gently with his shoulder. She flashed him a smile, then turned to give her attention to the Maynards' cousin, Algy Compton who was seated on the other side of Penny and halfway through a very long anecdote about a newspaper article. He too seemed to have drunk rather a lot. Dottie was glad that the rather thin soup was out of the way and some more substantial food would soon be arriving to counteract the wine.

She felt a little bemused. All around her was the buzz of conversation and laughter. It was her natural environment, just as it had been Diana Gascoigne's. She couldn't help thinking about Diana now as someone talked about a radio show they'd listened to, and Dottie remembered the New Year's Eve party, when she and Diana had moved the big radio set into the downstairs hall of Diana's parents' home so that the guests could listen to the recorded sound of Big Ben striking the turn of the year. And now, here she, Dottie was, at a lunch party just six days after Diana's death, a mere six months later. It felt so wrong. She made a mental note to telephone Flora later, if Penny didn't object, and just see how the little one was doing, and if Flora and George were coping with their new routine, and whether they had made a final decision on her name.

Gervase leaned a little nearer. 'You look sad,' he said softly. 'Are you thinking about your friend?' His look was gentle and understanding. She felt the prickle of tears and hastily sipped her wine. She couldn't break down in public, and certainly not amongst strangers. She nodded quickly and felt his hand press hers for a fleeting second, then he said, more loudly, to everyone, 'What are we all doing for dinner this evening?'

'I thought we could go to that new place in town. They have a dance band there on Fridays and Saturdays. They're supposed to be very good,' Reggie said, leaning forward to catch his brother's eye.

Everyone agreed it was an excellent idea, and Gervase winked at Dottie. 'Coming from London, I'm sure Miss Manderson knows all the latest dances. She can teach us how to do them.'

Dottie laughed and protested. Algy warned her about Gervase's two left feet, telling her she had her work cut out. Mike then added that it was more his wandering hands she needed to be on her guard against. Reggie said that she had to dance with him first, and the chatter became generally loud and enthusiastic, amply covering Gervase's low comment to Dottie, 'I'm not sure I can spare you, you know. I might get jealous if you spend too much time dancing with the other fellows.'

She smiled again, and glancing across the table, noticed Penny exchange a knowing look over her wine glass with Reggie's wife Deirdre.

At last the meal was over and they all went out into the garden to sit in the shade and let their food—and drink—go down. There was some suggestion of setting up a net for tennis later. But no one actually got up. The lawn chairs were comfortable. Dottie felt pleasantly full. Bees droned amongst the nearby flowers, and soon she was finding it hard to keep her eyes open.

She came broad awake at Mike's loud comment, '...I don't see why, he was just a bloody Darkie. All this fuss! It's too much, if you ask me.'

Penny responded with a distressed-sounding, 'But Mike dear, she was engaged to him. Of course she wants to remember him.'

'She's married to someone else now. I wonder how he would feel, knowing she'd been planning to marry someone like that. I shouldn't care for it myself.' That was Reggie. His words were greeted with vague assents and murmurs of 'No indeed' from some of the others.

Dottie pricked up her ears, and saying nothing, managed to look politely interested. And she was interested. Immediately she'd realised they were talking about the poor man who'd killed himself fifteen years ago. Considering no one seemed to like the man very much, her impression was that they talked about him a good deal.

Gervase said, 'Dottie, we're talking about Mike's sister Miranda. She's coming home tomorrow after fifteen years abroad. She wants to have a little memorial service in the village church. Chap she was engaged to did himself in a few years ago, and she wants to mark the occasion. All us fellows knew him slightly. Sad case. I suspect it was due to the war. You know, some of the chaps weren't quite right in the head after what they'd been through.'

Dottie nodded. 'Margaret mentioned it...'

Penny gave her quite a sharp look, which Dottie couldn't account for. In fact, looking around, Dottie noticed they all seemed a little uncomfortable. But of course, she remembered belatedly, Margaret had been one of their set until she'd got 'into trouble'—and now she worked as a servant, and was very much treated as such. Except by Gervase, a little voice in her head commented. She ignored the little voice. No doubt it was hard for all of them to know how to treat her. She felt instinctively that they would find it difficult to remain friends with a servant. She said nothing, however, and waited to see if anyone would say anything further.

It was Mike yet again. Dottie thought he was one who could always be relied upon to say what no one else dared, or thought appropriate, usually in the most offensive way possible. 'Ah yes, the lovely Margaret. Always rather too free with her favours, as I recall. T.W.K. Rather Too Well Known, as we used to say back in the day. Damn shame, pretty girl, but there it is. Brought it on herself.'

Dottie hoped he wouldn't read the loathing in her face. But he hadn't finished.

'Yes, Miss Manderson, I'm sure she would take great delight in telling you, as an outsider, all our nasty little secrets. My sister was engaged to be married to a Darkie. A cowardly one at that, too. Hung himself from a tree in the grounds of our childhood home after a party one night. Disgusting business, if you ask me, and damned ungrateful after the way my father tried to include him in the welcome home honours. A good thing my sister did go away, she came to her senses in the end, didn't she? Married a decent white chap. Just as well. Damned difficult for our family to cut her out of our lives if she'd gone ahead with it. We'd have had no choice, obviously.'

'I see,' Dottie murmured, necessarily noncommittal. At last the conversation turned to pleasanter things.

By the time Gervase drove them back to Penny's house to get changed, Dottie was rather sick of Michael Maynard, Reggie Parfitt and his simpering wife. The only saving grace for the coming evening was the chance of dancing with Gervase again.

Chapter Eight

Dottie was relieved that she'd brought a nice dancing frock with her and her good wrap. As a Londoner, a single woman and the new proprietor of a fashion warehouse, she felt she owed it to herself to be perfectly turned out for any evening entertainment. As she surveyed herself in the mirror, turning this way and that, regarding the dress critically, she began to feel proud. And more confident. Because this was the first dress that Mrs Carmichael had sought Dottie's opinion over. Dottie had been the one to have the final choice of fabric—a deep emerald satin with a slight suggestion of gold in the weave as the wearer turned and the dress caught the light. Although she had liked the dark red also on offer, she had felt the green was so much more elegant.

It was also Dottie who had suggested the close-fitting skirt that skimmed the hips and flared from the knee to the ankle-length hem. She remembered so clearly their conversation, remembered saying to Mrs Carmichael with such passion and excitement, 'Oh it will flow out as you dance, and will be so much fun to wear, almost as if it were alive!' She practised a couple of quick turns now in front of the mirror and felt her spirits lift as the dress swirled about her legs.

When Gervase arrived to take them out, she knew she'd succeeded in her aim of looking her best. She was waiting in the drawing room, Penny was again halfway down the stairs, when Margaret let Gervase in at the front door. Dottie felt he was well-known enough in the house to let himself in, but she supposed Penny didn't see it that way. Dottie heard him greet his sister-in-law, then they came into the drawing room together.

Gervase's eyes touched on Dottie, he turned to make a remark to Penny, complimenting her on her outfit which Dottie privately thought uninteresting, then, his eyes wide and startled, he turned to look back at Dottie as if drawn by a magnet. He made a show of greeting her too, kissing her cheek in a friendly, brotherly way, though his expression, hidden from Penny, was one of passion. But he behaved impeccably, saying with a laugh, 'I pay homage to your elegance, I fear I wasn't expecting such—er—glamour. I'm not sure Nottinghamshire can compete with London.'

A sideways glance at Penny had made him hesitate mid-sentence. Dottie was sure he was about to say 'beauty' but he changed it to 'glamour' to avoid slighting Penny. Not that I am beautiful, Dottie thought, but I can give the effect of it with a bit of make-up and a nice dress.

Always over-sensitive, Penny did feel slighted, however, and stepping past Gervase to head out of the door, she said, 'I'm sure we could all look glamorous were we not in mourning.'

'Oh of course, Penny dear,' he agreed heartily and rolling his eyes at Dottie, ran to open the door and attend Penny into the car. Once Penny was established in the middle of the front seat, pulling together her many-layered black chiffon frock that to Dottie's knowing eye definitely pre-dated her bereavement by several years, and Gervase had adequately paid court to her mood, her manner seemed to soften, and she began to chat, her pouting look gone again.

They were to meet the others in the vestibule of the hotel in the centre of Nottingham. Gervase was saying, 'I told Reggie to go in and grab a couple of good tables about halfway back. We don't want to be right by the band, or we won't be able to hear ourselves think, but equally, we don't want to be out in the street either. Still, we'll see what he has got us. I'm sure it'll be wrong.'

'It's always up to him and he's terrible at making decisions. I can't think how your brother gained such a good reputation during the war, or his seat on the board of your father's company, He's never asserted himself once that I can recall, and he's such a ditherer.'

'Penny, you know that with Mike around, he hardly needs to assert himself. All he needs to do is just follow on behind—and that's exactly what he prefers to do. If you ask me, it's your brother who is too assertive, rather than mine not being assertive enough.'

They continued in this way until they reached the hotel. Gervase halted the car to allow the ladies to get out, then drove off to find somewhere to park. As it was a fine warm evening, Dottie and Penny waited outside for him. There were quite a few couples and groups going up the steps to the hotel, and Dottie was gratified to see a number of the ladies turned to cast lascivious looks at her dress. As did some of the men, though not for the same reason. The hotel itself was large, and modern-looking. Dottie hoped that meant pleasant ladies' rooms and an excellent dancefloor.

Gervase hurried towards them, running up the first few steps. They went in together, the ladies lifting the skirts of their gowns a little to negotiate the curving steps by the door. Bending close to Dottie's ear, Gervase murmured, 'Don't forget, I want all your dances!'

She only had time to say softly, 'Don't be silly...' but got no further as Penny, clutching her arm, called out:

'Oh Mike, we're here! Sorry we're a wee bit late. These youngsters aren't quite so good at being punctual, you know!' This was imbued with a slightly sarcastic edge as Penny made a point of glancing at Dottie.

Mike stepped forward to take Dottie's hand and pull it through his arm. 'All your fault, eh? You young girls, keeping all us chaps waiting. Good thing you're worth the wait.' And he bore her off into the ballroom, leading her through the gathering until they reached two tables right at the front by the band. Reggie was hovering, as if to ensure no one else tried to claim the tables.

The others were there, turned out in all their finery. They greeted Dottie warmly. Mike said, 'Dottie kept us waiting, what? Never mind, here now...'

Dottie was annoyed, as she suspected Penny had intended her to be, but she said nothing, and smiled good-naturedly. Algy leapt up to graze her cheek with his mouth, and she felt the sharp scrape of a stubbly chin and cheek as he did so. 'Definitely worth waiting for though, eh, chaps?' His eyes took a quick tour of her figure, and she stepped back from him feeling prickly and uncomfortable, her smile faltering on her lips.

'That's what I said,' Mike crowed.

She would have liked to explain that she had, in fact, been ready a good twenty minutes before Penny, mainly because she was so eager to see Gervase. But it would be petty and pointless to contradict Penny in front of everyone. However as she took a seat, she couldn't help smarting just a little from the injustice of it, especially as Deirdre Parfitt frowned at her.

No sooner had Dottie taken her seat than Penny complained about the position of their tables. Dottie had to admit Penny was right: they were much too close to the band, who were just warming up, but even so it added to her irritation. Penny called on Deirdre and Mike's unnamed lady-friend to back her up, and Mike and Gervase were dispatched to find a more suitable position. Within minutes Mike returned to say they'd found some better tables which Gervase was 'guarding', and the party moved.

By the time they were all settled in their seats and they'd gone through the difficulties of ordering drinks, the orchestra were striking up the first dance, to great applause. Gervase immediately turned to Dottie, but Mike's hand was on her arm, practically pulling her out of her seat. She accepted his 'offer' to avoid making a fuss, and allowed him to lead her onto the floor, her earlier opinion of him confirmed as ungentlemanly and coarse. Behind them, Mike's girlfriend—whose name Dottie still didn't know—took to the floor with Reggie, and Gervase took up a position nearby with Penny, who looked like the cat who got the cream.

Mike held Dottie rather too close for comfort, and she made a point of taking half a step back. She certainly hadn't wanted to be quite this close to him, and after all, they were in public, and his girlfriend—what was the woman's name?—was watching. She definitely looked out of temper.

But if he was disappointed at Dottie distancing herself, he didn't show it. As they moved around the floor with the other dancers, he bombarded her with questions about how well she knew Gervase, how they'd met, what her father did, and whether she and Gervase had 'an understanding', or whether she was courting anyone else.

By the end of the first dance Dottie felt exhausted from the interrogation. He led her back to the table commenting, 'I had rather hoped that, given time, Penny might be ready to make a match with Gerry. Don't get me wrong, you're a pleasant enough sort, and definitely easy on the eye. I don't blame him for fancying a bit of a fling with you, but it is hard to see one's little sister's hopes dashed, what?'

There was no time to reply to this. Which was probably a good thing, given how angry his words made her. Reggie Parfitt took her hand and again practically dragged her back out onto the floor for the next dance, much to her surprise, but she gave him a smile as she turned to face him, placing her hand on his thin shoulder. Did no gentleman ask a lady to dance these days? Irritated by the way she was treated like a doll, she paid him little attention, and they were halfway round the floor before she realised he'd spoken. Reggie was nearly as good-looking as his brother, but he was so thin and somehow, simply, less. He danced neatly and carefully, but without an ounce of passion or flair, as if he had learned to dance but never moved on from his lessons, never felt at ease. Under his breath she knew he would be counting the steps. She thought it was a shame he seemed content to let his brother—and all the other men—overshadow him. Confidence always gave a man an air that outweighed mere good looks.

'Mr Parfitt,' Dottie began, 'I wonder if I might ask you something?'

'Reggie, please. Ask away, dear lady,' he said solemnly, little knowing how that term irked her. But she'd counted on him being amenable, he was that sort.

'Would you say Gervase and Penny—Mrs Parfitt—are, um, fond of each other?' She hoped he'd understand what she meant. She caught sight of Penny and Gervase through the gaps between the other couples, circling the dancefloor for their second dance, smiling and talking.

Reggie looked a little shocked. 'My God! The poor woman only lost my brother a few weeks ago. It's rather soon for anything of that sort.'

'Yes, I realise that,' Dottie said, soothingly. 'I didn't mean any disrespect. Naturally I meant, after a suitable period of mourning. You know, old friends, constant companions. He helps her and looks after her. She relies on his judgement and advice. It wouldn't be unexpected if she one day saw him in a new light. In the fullness of time...'

Reggie executed a dainty turn, glanced briefly towards his brother then back at Dottie. 'I really—I really don't think so. I mean, yes, you're right, they've known each other a long time, we all have. But they've always just been pals. I really don't think it would ever come to more than that.'

Dottie nodded. He sounded sure, though she was less certain. But so often friendship did develop into something more romantic. And after all, Reggie didn't strike her as a particularly insightful chap.

She realised he was talking about lupins. It appeared he had a great fancy for them and was attempting to breed some new variety. He talked about it until the end of the dance. What with the late Artie and his roses and his rather dull daisy, and now Reggie going on about lupins... She wondered if Gervase had a secret passion for gardening too. Hopefully not. Dottie smothered a yawn.

Finally, she had her dance with Gervase, followed by another. Dancing with him was heavenly, and she was able to really relax and enjoy herself.

The evening wore on. She sat out a couple of times, but otherwise danced every dance. Algy Compton proved to be Gervase's equal in terms of his dancing ability, but there was something about him that made him unappealing. As well as his damp sticky fingers and his damp sticky face, always bathed in a light sheen of sweat, his manners were not particularly polished, and he had a salacious look in his eye she didn't like.

She managed to escape with only one more dance with Mike Maynard. He seemed to have abandoned his girlfriend for someone he had just met at the bar, dancing with her to the exclusion of all other partners. This new woman had long red hair and wore a low-cut black dress, which might explain his interest in her.

It was Dottie's third dance with Reggie, and she was determined they should have no more talk about lupins. It was for this reason that, as soon as the music had begun and he'd taken his first cautious leading step, Dottie said, 'Are you looking forward to seeing Penny's sister Miranda again?'

He stood stock still. Mike Maynard and the pretty redhead cannoned into them. Reggie didn't notice, however. But he frowned at Dottie and said, 'Surely you realise I'm a married man? Whatever you may have heard, I can assure you there's nothing improper in our relations now, nothing!'

With that he strode off, leaving Dottie standing in the middle of the dancefloor on her own, the other dancers awkwardly stepping round her. Gervase halted beside her, Penny in his arms. He looked amused, whilst Penny looked rather annoyed.

'What have you done to upset my poor brother?' Gervase asked. He gave her a broad smile.

'Well, I...' Dottie began, but that was as far as she got.

Penny impatiently threw herself back into Gervase's arms with a petulant look and a hurried, 'Oh, never mind all that now, she can tell you later. You said you'd dance with me!'

He shot her a rueful grin by way of an apology, and they swept on. With a heavy sigh, Dottie returned to their tables, edging round the outside of the dancefloor, stepping out of the way of the dancers and the occasional waiter, to flomp down into her seat, feeling ridiculous. She was the only one of their party sitting out at that moment. She sipped her drink, thinking how hot the room was, and watched the couples dancing: Mike being a little too friendly with the redhead, who was stiffening and leaning away from him slightly, her smile fixed and cooling quickly. Reggie's wife Deirdre was dancing with Algy, their steps in perfect unison, so well-matched, that a stranger might think he, not Reggie was her husband. Clearly she was getting a few things off her chest and Algy was saying nothing, just listening and nodding and casting thunderous looks at Reggie whenever he came in view, Dottie noticed with interest.

Then came Penny dancing yet again with Gervase, and yet again Dottie couldn't help but wonder just how close their friendship was. Gervase seemed to have a knack for developing friendships with women. What Dottie wouldn't give to have each of these neatly studied and labelled so she could understand what each woman meant to Gervase. She scrutinised them carefully, Penny liked to monopolise Gervase, Dottie had noticed, but as they went round the floor again, she also noticed that Gervase was moving back a little from Penny as they danced. He glanced across to smile at Dottie a couple of times, and each time he did so, Penny reclaimed his attention with a bump of hip or thigh, or bosom, keeping her eyes fixed on his face, and speaking to him whenever he looked away from her. Yes. Dottie's fears were confirmed. Penny was in love with Gervase.

Dottie became aware of someone nearby, and glancing up she saw Deirdre pulling out her chair to sit down. She glanced briefly at Dottie, sent a vague half-smile in Dottie's direction, then reached for a glass and drank the entire contents in a single gulp, then refilled the glass. Belatedly, she waved the bottle in Dottie's direction, but Dottie demurred. The cause of Deirdre's distraction was apparent: Reggie was propping up the bar on the other side of the room, gloomily drinking shorts.

Meanwhile, Mike and the redhead danced by, the redhead looking thoroughly fed up, and Mike, flushed and unsteady, was talking loudly at her. Dottie caught a few words above the music. He was telling her some kind of vulgar joke. Perhaps he thought he was in a billiard hall or at his club, Dottie thought. After about another ten minutes, Reggie swayed over to invite his wife to dance. But he made a point of not looking at Dottie sitting so close by, and she felt like a pariah. He was still offended, then, she thought. She felt a little dismayed that he could be so easily upset by something she'd not even put into words. And after all, she hadn't intended any offence, he was taking it to a ridiculous degree. What a thoroughly wretched evening it was turning into. She wondered how late they were likely to stay. The evening felt as though it would never end.

The current dance ended, the orchestra stood as one and took a bow to applause, then retired for their break. Chattering, laughing couples returned to their tables and waiters hurried forward to take orders for drinks.

Dottie made herself smile pleasantly as the rest of the party began to fill the empty seats around her. Penny sat beside Dottie, and after addressing one or two trivial remarks to her, turned to speak to Algy. Dottie, on the end of the row, was effectively blocked off. But Penny's plan—if it was a deliberate plan—was thwarted when Gervase returned. He insisted on everyone shuffling around so that he was able to put his chair next to Dottie on the other side, and along with Deirdre, he made sure she was part of the conversation. Mike and Reggie went off outside to smoke. Before they managed to push their way back through the throng, the orchestra was striking up again for the second half of the evening's programme.

Immediately Gervase grabbed Dottie's arm and almost dragged her behind him onto the dancefloor. Glancing over his shoulder back towards the table, Dottie could see Penny was watching them with an annoyed expression.

'I think Penny was hoping to have another dance with you,' she said.

'All in good time. I want to have fun too, you know!'

Dottie laughed at this and leaned into his arms. Unlike when he danced with Penny, Gervase held her close, his eyes on hers, or half-closed as he placed his cheek against hers in the way that gave her goose-bumps all down her arms.

Her dances with him always seemed far too short, however. And to her surprise—and a certain amount of dismay—she found Reggie cutting into the third dance and Gervase gave her a sorrowful little smile and stepped aside, only to be pounced on by Penny.

If she was surprised that Reggie wanted to dance with her again, she thought at least it might indicate that he was no longer offended. The first thing he said to her was, 'Sorry for acting like a chump earlier. Completely off, leaving you stranded in the middle of the floor like that. It was very wrong of me.'

'It's quite all right,' Dottie said, hastening to mend the breach. 'I'm so sorry for my careless remark. I certainly didn't intend any offence. I'm afraid I rather put my foot in it.'

'Not at all,' he said magnanimously. But she felt a little annoyed she was trying to soothe his feelings when she hadn't done anything wrong. He seemed keen to make amends, though, and she silently resolved to let him return to the harmless if dreary subject of lupins.

But he wanted to explain about Miranda.

'You're quite right, in a way,' he said. 'I mean it was, of course, many years ago, long before I met my wife.'

'Oh, of course.'

'And we didn't keep it up. We were rather keen on one another at one time, and I had hoped, but...' He let the thought drift away. He said nothing else for a minute or so, and Dottie had no doubt that this was mainly due to Mike Maynard dancing nearby with Penny in his arms. She looked like a woman who was marking time until some special event happens, Dottie thought. Beyond them, Deirdre and Gervase were dancing.

Once they were clear of them, Reggie continued as if he hadn't just been silent for the best part of ninety seconds. 'But there's nothing between us now. She's married, and I'm married. Happily. So, in answer to your original question, of course, as an old, and hopefully dear friend, I'm looking forward to seeing Miranda again. But that's all it is.'

'Of course,' Dottie commented yet again. 'I'm sure she's looking forward to seeing all her friends again. It'll be fun talking about the old days.'

'Hmm,' said Reggie, not at all convincingly. And then he was back on the subject of lupins. After another minute, Dottie felt she could write a treatise on the care and cultivation of lupins with no difficulty whatsoever.

Finally, the last dance came, a rather slower than usual waltz, and she was thrilled to find herself in Gervase's arms once more. He held her, like Mike and Algy, rather closer than was conventional. But unlike with them, she was perfectly content to permit it. She wished the dance would never end, she wanted to move with him in time to the music and forget about everything and everyone. Her cheek rested against his chin, and under the cover of conversation, he managed to nuzzle her neck with a suggestion of a kiss that sent flames through her whole being.

But the evening ended, as they do, and the party broke up and went their own ways. Gervase drove them back to Penny's house. In the car, Dottie sat by the window, Penny was once more in the middle, where she was able to monopolise Gervase and the conversation all the way back, complaining about this or that, or remarking about the music or the band, or the crowds of dancers, or the bumpy surface of the road. Gervase said little in reply, merely agreeing with her now and then and looking straight ahead at the road.

She had hoped that Gervase would linger, but he said goodnight as soon as he'd seen them to the door. He winked at Dottie as he turned away. It was better than nothing, she told herself, as she followed Penny into the gloomy drawing room. Not a lot better, it had to be said. She felt irritable.

They began to divest themselves of their gloves and evening wraps. Dottie prepared to gather them up to take them upstairs, but Penny waved a hand.

'Oh don't bother, Dottie dear. Margaret can do that. It is her job after all.'

She spoke so dismissively that Dottie was taken aback. Surely they had once been friends? Even allowing for Margaret's unfortunate situation, how had they grown apart to such a degree?

They sat on separate sofas, facing one another across a low japanned coffee table from at least fifty years earlier. It felt very formal, and gloomy in spite of the light from the lamp on the sideboard. But the sofas were too hard to be comfortable, and the backs were high to ensure any tendency to slouch was discouraged, and the sitter was obliged to remain bolt upright. The arms of the sofas were merely a continuation of the backs, and at the same height, so Dottie found she had to sit in the perfect, approved posture as taught at her private ladies' college in London. Without thinking she exhaled sharply, wafting her soft curling fringe up and down, and causing Penny to frown and say, 'I expect you're finding it all rather dull here with me. I'm too old and set in my ways for you youngsters.'

It was only good manners for Dottie to demur, and it seemed a bit ridiculous to her that Penny kept saying things like this when she was only ten or so years older than Dottie. It seemed she wasn't emphatic enough, for Penny continued, 'Oh yes, I realise now just how out of date I am. My clothes, for example, are at least two seasons behind. You are so up-to-the-minute in the lovely outfits you wear during the day—so comfortable and—well, fun. And tonight—that's a delightful little frock. I imagine it cost your father a great deal.'

Dottie couldn't help but feel as though she'd been insulted in some vague way. She murmured something indistinct, still puzzling over Penny's words and trying to pinpoint exactly what she'd meant by them. She found herself saying, 'I'm sure we're much closer in age than you might think.'

Penny said, 'Excuse me, dear.' She left the room, returning a minute or two later. 'I've just told Margaret to bring some coffee in. Really, one shouldn't need to ask!' Dottie was wondering why she hadn't simply rung the bell, but there was no need to speak, as Penny said, 'Now. Where were we? Ah yes—well I should think I easily have ten years' advance on you, dear. Not that ladies talk about their age, as your mother has probably told you. But in mourning, and of course, living out here in the country, one gets rather...'

The door opened, and Margaret came in with the cups, sugar bowl and cream jug on a tray. She set it down quite heavily on the brilliant surface of the coffee table, which made Dottie wince for the highly sheened finish. Her back to Penny, Margaret shot Dottie a grin, turned to give Penny an odd little bow and said, 'Ma'am,' then left the room.

Dottie felt so uncomfortable. A covert glance at Penny showed expression as one of satisfaction. That strange cat-that-got-the-cream look again. Dottie felt a creeping discovery that she didn't like Penny at all.

Dottie sat at the dressing table, plying her face and neck with night cream. She allowed the cream some time to be absorbed into the skin, bending forward to brush her hair vigorously the wrong way before sitting up again and brushing it back the other way. Then she took two facial tissues and carefully wiped away the excess cream.

As she did all this, she was thinking. She went back over the details of the long evening. She thought: Penny is in love with Gervase, and she is jealous of me; Deirdre is unhappy about Reggie. Mike is an outrageous flirt and possibly worse, and drinks like a fish. Algy and Deirdre dance really well together and complement each other perfectly, which is a shame as she is married to the lupin-mad, prickly Reggie; and lastly Reggie, so ready to take offence at the mildest question, is definitely still carrying a torch for the long-absent Miranda, no matter what he says to the contrary.

Dottie undressed and put on her nightgown. Wrapping a negligee about her, she wandered along the corridor to the bathroom. By the time she came back and got into bed, she had made up her mind that the long friendship enjoyed by the group was no longer something she admired or aspired to achieve. Dottie was now convinced it was stifling and claustrophobic, like ivy clinging too close about the branches of a tree, covering it until almost none of the bark showed through, cutting off the flow of life-giving sap and blocking out the sunlight.

Chapter Nine

Dottie woke to hear the telephone bell jangling in the hall below. She was on the point of getting out of bed to answer it, when the bell stopped, and she could discern the soft sound of Margaret's voice.

A few minutes later, there was a tap on Dottie's door, then Margaret came in.

'Excuse me, Miss, there was a telephone call from Mr Gervase. He wonders if you'd like to go out with him in his car today? If you're not busy? And are you ready for a cup of tea?'

'Oh yes! To both!' Dottie said. She got out of bed. 'Don't worry about bringing the tea up, I'll come down for it. Does Mr Parfitt want me to phone him and let him know?'

Margaret smiled. 'No. I took the liberty of accepting on your behalf. I thought you'd prefer it to sitting around here all day. He said he'll be here at ten o'clock, so you've got plenty of time.'

Dottie thanked her. If he wasn't coming until ten o'clock then she had time for a bath. She felt so excited—just to get out of the house, as Margaret had suggested—that she was almost running about the place as she gathered her things and went to the bathroom. She hummed to herself. Even when she realised, belatedly, that the invitation would be likely to include Penny, her buoyant mood wasn't dampened. Penny out of the house with Gervase would be far easier to manage than Penny at home without him. And far pleasanter.

But Penny was left at home. She hadn't been included in Gervase's invitation, and as she said goodbye to Dottie and Gervase, Dottie saw that Penny made no attempt to hide her resentment. As Gervase started the car, Dottie put a hand on his arm.

'Don't you think we ought to take her with us? It won't take her long to get ready.'

He took her hand in his, lifted it and kissed her fingertips. He laughed. 'Let her sulk. She'll only be in the way.'

And off they went, Dottie with an elated sense of playing truant. She spent the whole journey torn between looking out at the passing scenery and staring at Gervase's profile which, she decided was not only handsome but noble. Her heart sang, and William Hardy, so recently her one and only love, was very close to being forgotten.

Gervase began to tell her a little about the area—and once they'd left the green rolling hills behind, Dottie was surprised to see coal mines and sprawling red-bricked mills scarring the landscape.

'I had no idea this area was so industrialised,' she commented. 'I'm afraid I'm shamefully ignorant about the Midlands.'

'Well if you ask me, it's not a particularly nice part of the country. But I suppose we must have our coal, and our pottery, wool and cotton. I'd much rather live in a pretty location, but it's conveniently close to my work. In fact there are plenty of experts who tell us that it's due to industrialisation that we have so much crime and the criminal element, so I suppose I'm in the best place. Sorry I'm not one of your leisured class.' He sent her a teasing grin.

Dottie almost made the mistake of pointing out that for a fortnight he'd done nothing more than ferry Penny about—and for the last three days, herself too, of course—and indulge in leisurely activities. But she held back, not sure if he would take the teasing in good part or be utterly offended. She still didn't know him well enough. Then almost immediately he said, 'Of course, at the moment I'm taking some of my annual holidays, but tomorrow morning I'll be back there, with my nose to the grindstone, worse luck. So I shan't have quite so much time to enjoy your company.'

'What a shame you've had to waste all your holiday on being a gentleman!' This she did say in a teasing tone, and he gave her a broad grin in response, which melted her heart just that little bit more.

'For a man, it's always a pleasure to be at the beck and call of such lovely ladies.' He dropped a kiss on the back of her hand.

Ordinarily Dottie would have wrinkled her nose at a man's use of such an outmoded sentiment, but on this occasion she decided to overlook it, saying instead, 'Well, on behalf of lovely ladies everywhere, we are very grateful to you for your noble endeavour.'

He sent her another look, a frank, toe-curling look. 'Hmm. I hope that means I've earned a reward? Perhaps you might show your gratitude with a proper kiss?' His tone was bland, in contrast to his look.

Dottie, blushing but laughing, turned to look at the grimy mining village they were driving through. 'Oh, I don't think you've been quite that noble.'

'Damn,' he said softly, but he smiled as he said it.

Men stood on the corner of the street outside a public house. They turned to stare as the car passed them. There was not another car in sight. Nottingham lace hung at the windows of the small terraced houses. Even the lace appeared in need of a good wash. The men's clothes were dirty, and in some cases quite ragged. A filthy child played in a puddle.

'It doesn't look very prosperous,' Dottie said.

'Well, it wouldn't, would it? It's all working-class housing. The men all work in the mine. There used to be three mines here, but now there's only one, so they have shorter shifts, to keep as many of them in work as possible. But obviously if they're not working the same hours they used to work, they can't expect to get the same wages.'

'What happened?'

'Penny's father Norman Maynard sold all three mines to the government a few years back, but it was quickly discovered that it was cheaper to close two of them than to keep them working, so that's what they did.'

'Did the mines run out of coal?'

'No, silly, they just didn't yield enough to make a decent profit.'

'So, some of the men are unemployed? And the others are sharing their jobs, which means they all get lower wages?'

'At least they get wages. It's their own fault. They should have worked harder in the other mines and kept them profitable. What with all these demands for more money and better working conditions, and shorter hours! Maynard was a generous employer. Too generous if you ask me. He gave them a wage increase, and cut hours, but of course, that meant his overheads went up, and the pits became less profitable. The way these miners talk, you'd think they should be earning as much as me!'

'I suppose they have their children to feed,' Dottie ventured.

'Well if they can't afford to feed their children, they shouldn't have so many of the little blighters,' Gervase said comfortably. Dottie turned to stare at him in astonishment, but he simply said, 'Don't worry, dear, we'll soon be back amongst prettier scenery and nicer villages. We're almost there, actually. I hope you've got your passport handy.'

Dottie was bewildered. He laughed. 'I'm joking. We're crossing the county border into Derbyshire. There ought to be a sign up here stating, 'Beyond this point there be dragons.''

Gradually the landscape changed to green again, though with the occasional outcrop of limestone. Sheep grazed the fields, and streams twisted in and out along the side of the road. They arrived in the pretty little town of Matlock Bath, nestling in the gorge of the River Trent.

Dottie felt a certain amount of trepidation as she took Gervase's hand and stepped down from the car. She felt instinctively that she shouldn't have come. Because this was where William Hardy's sister Eleanor was staying with their aunt and uncle. Or if not here, then in the larger nearby town of Matlock, Dottie wasn't quite sure which. All she knew was that it was in this area somewhere. It was hardly likely that she would run into Eleanor, but even so, she looked very carefully at every young woman she saw, just in case it might be her.

A massive red-bricked mill squatted beside the river, whilst the houses and the other buildings of the town were further along the road, seeming to rise upwards rather than expanding sideways, following the twisting narrow lanes that twined along the cliffs of the gorge.

Gervase gave her his arm and they walked along, browsing the quaint little shops. They sat on the grass beside the rushing river, talking the whole time. She was surprised to find he was amusing—and if she didn't agree with some of what she privately termed his 'old-fashioned' views towards people of different backgrounds or levels of society, or religions and cultures, then at least she could acknowledge to herself that he listened to her views and didn't shout her down or dismiss her as a foolish girl. But he made her laugh, and that was so different, and so captivating.

They listened to the band playing at the bandstand, competing comfortably with the rushing of the river that powered the mill half a mile away. Then he suggested they took a slow winding walk up to the top of the cliff, to the Heights of Abraham, as Gervase told her that area was called.

It was such a steep walk. Here and there along the lane there were benches where people sat to recover their breath and enjoy the scenery. Dottie and Gervase paused here and there to look at the view. Gervase told her Byron had named the area, 'Little Switzerland' and she could quite see why.

At last they made it to the top, and across the gorge, there was the most spectacular view. Gervase pointed out the notable landmarks, including Riber Castle. Dottie was in raptures. They sat to enjoy an ice cream and look at the view. Then later, it was her idea to join the little queue of people waiting for the guide to take them down the rocky steps into the limestone caverns that lay waiting beneath their feet.

Gervase stood beside her in the dark tunnel, and as they halted for the first time to listen to the guide telling them all about rocks and minerals, the other tourists crowded about them, and pressed them close to one another. But Gervase appeared to be enjoying the proximity as much as she was. He gave her a grin, and his eyes, though grey and usually so cool and mocking, felt hot on her face, even in the diminished light of the caves.

He said, 'Have you ever been down into underground caves before?'

She responded gaily with, 'No, never!' The queue began to slowly shuffle forward as the guide led them on.

The crowd of visitors pushed forward, forcing them on, and at the same time the craggy narrow path took a sharp downward turn, and Dottie couldn't see where she was going. The air was cool, but stale and heavy, and the rock loomed above her head.

A man nearby said loudly, 'Just think of all those tons of rock above our heads right now. Why, there might be people walking above us and never know we were here! We could cry out and they'd never hear us.'

The headway slanted lower, the walls crept jaggedly in, and the floor seemed to dip and twist away from her in the darkness. The many other people pressed all about her, squashing her. Her smile faltered. Gervase gave her a look of concern.

She said, 'Oh!' and groped for his arm, her fingertips digging into his flesh. She shuddered and closed her eyes. She couldn't catch her breath. The air, there just didn't seem to be any...

'Dottie? Dottie, look here, don't faint, dear. You're perfectly safe. Nothing can go wrong. These caves have been here for centuries, the roof won't fall down on you.'

'Don't tell her that, mate,' said a helpful individual just behind them. 'Why, only last Autumn a bit of roof come down in that tunnel over there, and all twenty-seven visitors was crushed to death.'

Gervase stared at the man with hatred. 'Shut up!' The man looked hurt.

'I'm...' was all Dottie could manage. She couldn't tear her eyes away from the roof that almost grazed the top of her head and the walls that closed in on both sides. Gervase pulled her into his arms, regardless of those around them.

Some other young fellow laughed and said crudely, 'I must try that with that lass Edith. Reckon I could get my hand up her skirt and she'd never even notice.'

One or two other visitors tutted and looked disgusted by the man. Gervase shot him a dangerous look, and turned back to Dottie. A woman said, 'Aw, the poor lady,' and a couple of children jostled each other and jumped up and down to try to make the roof come down on them too, shrieking wildly as they did so. Gervase scooped Dottie up in his arms, and regardless of the guide's shout, turned to carry her back the way they had come.

Dottie buried her face in Gervase's shoulder, clinging to him, not caring about anything other than the need to get out into the fresh open air. She was every bit as astonished—and frightened—by her own reaction to the situation as she was by the physical aspects of the caves themselves. In her mind's eye she could envision herself, crushed like a leaf beneath the rock as the cave closed its mouth on her in the darkness. The vision of it was so strong she became terrified that her very fear could make it happen. She had never felt so irrationally afraid. She felt like a dumb wild thing caught in a trap, helpless and pathetic. If she could have fainted, it would have been a relief.

But every nightmare must end, and eventually they reached the top of the steps out of the tunnel. Gervase brought her into the open air, and set her on the firm ground, as weak as a kitten. She followed him a few steps, clinging to his jacket, her legs weak and wobbling, and as they stepped outside into the sunshine, thought returned.

She thought two things: I shall never again laugh at anyone who is afraid of heights, enclosed spaces, spiders, anything; never did I dream that I could react this way. And secondly she thought, Gervase must surely despise me now, I shall see disgust there in his eyes when I look at him.

It took all her courage and determination just to stand up straight, hold her head up and her shoulders back. She felt like crumpling into a heap and sobbing. She found Gervase was putting an arm around her waist.

'There's a tearoom over here. I think you could do with a drink.'

She nodded, silent, and allowed him to guide her inside. On the far side of the large open room was a huge picture window. He began to steer her in the opposite direction, to a quiet corner near the door, but she went to a table by the window and sat down. It was a magnificent view down to the valley of the gorge and the little town and the river. But she looked up at the broad blue sky.

Gervase gave their order at the counter and came to sit beside her. She immediately began to apologise for her behaviour, not daring to look into his face. He shushed her gently.

'Dottie, dearest. It's perfectly all right. You've had a fright, and you don't need to apologise for that.'

Had he just called her 'dearest'? She lifted her eyes to his, and saw his expression held nothing but concern. Her heart leapt. Nevertheless she continued in her attempt to explain.

'I had no idea—never—I just—had no inkling I could possibly feel so...'

'I know, Dottie, I know. But it's my fault. I never thought to warn you. I feel terrible for subjecting you to that ordeal.'

'It was my idea! I'm so sorry I humiliated you...'

He laughed and waved her apology away. A quick glance about him showed no one nearby. He leaned close and kissed her full on the mouth, a long, lingering kiss. 'It's quite all right,' he murmured softly, drawing back a little. 'I didn't care what anyone thought. My only concern was for you.'

The waitress brought their teas over. Dottie's was very strong and there were four sugar cubes in the saucer. When the waitress had given them a fond smile and gone back to her counter, Gervase turned back to Dottie. Relief flooded her whole being; tears smarted in her eyes. He pulled her against him as she fished for her handkerchief. He dropped a kiss on her hair.

'Darling Dottie,' he said.

'Bring Miss Manderson a brandy, Michaels,' Gervase ordered his butler. 'I took her to the Heights of Abraham and we went on the guided tour down into the Great Masson Cavern. She needs a stiff drink after that.'

The butler gave a delicate shudder and said, 'Cripes, Miss, you wouldn't get me down in them caves, not if you was to pay me a hundred pounds.'

Dottie smiled at him, immediately smitten with the genial old chap. 'I've learned my lesson, that's for sure. Never again!'

'Indeed, Miss.' He sent a scornful look at his master then turned back to Dottie. 'And I presume you don't really want a brandy, do you, Miss? In my experience it's really only the gentlemen who like that stuff.'

Seeing Dottie's hasty shake of the head and wrinkled nose, he added, 'Now I can offer you a nice cup of tea. Or you might prefer a sherry, Miss. Mr Gervase had an excellent stock of Dulce and also some Amontillado, according as you prefer.'

Dottie considered her options before saying, with a grin, 'D'you know, I think I'd just like a cup of tea.'

The butler nodded gravely, and with a glance at Gervase, he said, 'She's too good for you, sir!'

Gervase's mock outrage followed the butler from the room. When he had gone Gervase turned to her and said in a rueful voice, 'I'm afraid he may be right about that.' Dottie laughed, not for a minute taken in by his pretence at humility.

The butler returned ten minutes later, not just with a pot but with a full afternoon tea. He and a smiling young maid brought in trays of food which they deposited on a low table in front of the sofa. Dottie ate her fill of the daintiest sandwiches and the most appealing little novelty cakes. When the butler came in again with more hot water, Dottie asked, 'Who made all this wonderful food?'

'Ah that would be my wife, Mrs Michaels, what is cook here.'

'I suppose I couldn't lure the two of you to London, could I? Anyone who can cook like this must be worth their weight in gold.'

Mr Michaels appeared to consider Dottie's suggestion very seriously before finally shaking his head. 'I'm sorry, Miss. I don't think Mr Gervase could manage without us. Otherwise, I'd jump at the chance.' They exchanged a grin, and as he turned away, he winked at Dottie.

Once they were alone again, Gervase twined a lock of her hair around his finger. 'I must say, you've got a nerve, trying to poach my staff right under my nose. But there might be a way for us to both get what we want.'

She pretended not to know what he meant. 'Well I don't see how. After all, within the year you'll be married to Penny.'

'Penny!' He pulled a face. 'Heaven forbid! What on earth makes you think such a thing?'

'She adores you!' Dottie pointed out, laughing at his expression. She reached for another tiny Victoria sponge.

'I'm just useful to her, that's all. She likes having a man to make all the decisions for her. She'd have any man who would be prepared to dance attendance on her.'

'Hmm, you might be right. She seems to enjoy being the object of male interest.'

'Definitely.'

'She said she used to follow you around hoping you'd notice her.'

'She did. She was very annoying, actually. And a horrid, spotty kid at that. With a lisp.'

'Gervase! That's so unkind!' Dottie gave him a playful slap. 'I'm sure she wasn't that bad. Though none of us are at our best in our mid-teens.'

'I was,' he said smugly. 'I was already devastatingly handsome.'

Dottie did an unladylike snort at that. 'I'm sure you'd like to think so.'

'I bet you were every bit as gorgeous as you are now,' he said, nuzzling the hollow of her neck. She decided to put some distance between them before he got out of hand.

'How about a tour of your magnificent home?' she said. With a resigned grin, he got to his feet, and for the next hour he became a tour guide, showing her the many and varied points of interest of his home and telling her his plans for the garden. When they came back to the drawing room, it was time to go back to Penny's.

When they got back, Penny had already gone up to change for dinner. Gervase was, of course, invited to stay. He entertained them both with his wit, though most of it was directed at Penny who lapped up his attention. Then, just after nine o'clock, Penny went up to bed for an early night, pleading a slight headache, for which Dottie was most grateful. Margaret didn't seem to be around, so Dottie and Gervase were completely private in the drawing room.

She sat almost on his lap, and they kissed again and again. Gervase murmured all kinds of romantic nonsense in her hair and there was no doubt in her mind that they were both rapidly falling in love. There was conversation, all inconsequential: precious little of note was said. At last, at almost one o'clock in the morning, Gervase reluctantly tore himself away.

'I must go. If I don't go now, I shan't want to go at all, and I don't want to compromise you, Dottie my love. It's still more or less a respectable time of night!'

She was almost tempted to suggest he stayed but was sure her hostess would view it as an appalling abuse of her hospitality, Dottie helped him on with his jacket and after one last kiss, reluctant to close the door and shut him out, she stood there and watched him drive away.

She went up to bed, taking care to make as little noise as possible. She sat by the window thinking about what was developing between them and what it might mean. After all, even that very morning, she had told herself there was nothing more between them than a mild flirtation. Yet now...

She told herself she was happy, that she was in love, and happy. She knew Gervase felt the same—he hadn't said outright that he loved her, and she knew men didn't always find it easy to say the words out loud, but called her 'my love' and 'dearest', and two or three times he'd implied a future for the two of them, a future together. He was making plans. He clearly wanted to marry her. She must think about that, and presumably, consider alerting her parents to the fact that there was a new man in her life and that they needed to make his acquaintance. She went to bed light-hearted and happy.

Towards morning Dottie's romantic dreams of dancing in Gervase's arms at their wedding turned to darker thoughts, and she was clinging, by her fingertips from the side of the cliff above Matlock Bath, her green evening dress flapping in the breeze. She glanced down into the dizzying abyss to see her shoe fall from her foot. She watched it plummet through the air until it made a tiny splash in the river down below. The vertical cliffs of the gorge had become rocks at the edge of a hungry ocean, and the rising tide slashed at her feet, soaking her dress right through and weighing it down. Her hair was plastered to her face and neck by torrential rain, and when, as she was about to fall to certain death on the rocks below, a strong masculine hand came out of the darkness to grab her, hauling her up to safety, she looked into the face of the man who had saved her, whom she knew deep in her heart she loved as she could love no one else.

It was the face of William Hardy.

Chapter Ten

The image stayed with her all the morning, haunting her almost to the point of tears. She dismissed it again and again as nothing more than a mere childish guilt and grief for the loss of first love, or perhaps just the aftermath of her fright the previous day—she dismissed it repeatedly, but it persisted.

After lunch, they sat in the dreary drawing room, Dottie was listless, doing nothing whilst Penny busied herself with some embroidery that was giving her trouble. She kept either splitting the thread or having to unpick and rework the stitches she'd made. Dottie wondered why she bothered, she had neither pleasure in nor aptitude for the handicraft.

'Goodness, what a late night you must have had! I presume Gervase came in for a nightcap?'

Dottie couldn't be bothered to think up any excuse so she simply said, 'Yes, he did come in for a short while.'

Penny gave her a sly smile. Wagging her forefinger at Dottie in a mock lecture, she said archly, 'And I do hope he was the perfect gentleman, since you had no chaperone.'

Dottie forced herself to smile. 'Oh yes, of course he was.' She was praying that Penny wouldn't ask anything more, but Penny seemed to lose interest as she dropped her thimble and pricked herself at the same time. Dottie helped to fish the thimble out from under the coffee table, and by the time order was restored, Penny seemed to have forgotten the topic of conversation. After a few more minutes, Penny laid aside her needlework and strolled over to look out the window. An inane comment about the weather followed. Dottie wondered how she was going to make it through the rest of the day without screaming. All she wanted was to be in Gervase's arms. He would scare off those nightmares.

The photo albums were still there on the side-table where Penny had left them that first evening. She crossed to them now, and picked them up.

'Dottie? I've got an urge to look through these again. Are you interested?' Before Dottie could respond, Penny added with a sly smile, 'There'll be pictures of Gervase!'

Dottie felt a little annoyed by this. Over the last few days, Penny had developed a habit of continually referring to him, as if alluding to an understanding between Dottie and him. Ordinarily Dottie could laugh off that kind of talk, but it seemed to her there was behind it the hard edge she had noticed before with Penny's remarks: barbed, as if fishing for something, some weak spot or flaw she could use. She sensed a disapproval in Penny, too. Perhaps she thought Dottie was too young? Or perhaps it was only that Penny wanted him for herself? No matter what Gervase's brother Reggie might choose to believe, Dottie was convinced Penny had a romantic inclination for her brother-in-law. Once the mourning period was over, she might hope or expect Gervase to pay court. Whatever Penny's motive, Dottie was sure that she truly believed that in the 'affair' between Gervase and Dottie, the interest was all on Dottie's side. It really was starting to get on Dottie's nerves—as was everything else Penny did. And said.

Penny set the albums down on the coffee table, as usual taking no care to avoid scratching the lovely gleaming top. Dottie despaired of the table surviving the length of her visit. Penny gripped the table by the nearest leg and yanked it towards the sofa where she took her seat beside Dottie, scraping the albums closer, and throwing the cover open with a bang. Dottie couldn't help wincing at the sound. She had been so on edge ever since she'd come to stay with Penny. But she had already begun to plan to leave on the coming Saturday, and the day beckoned as a bright spot on her horizon. She'd have to wait until the right moment to tell Penny. She couldn't handle any sulks right now. At least with Miranda and her family back from India, Penny would have less free time to gloom about the house and miss her husband.

The first album was the wedding album that Dottie had seen so very briefly on her first night. Rather than looking at each page in turn, Penny had a tendency to flip over several pages rapidly to find the one or two photographs she liked best. Hopefully, Dottie thought, this shouldn't take too long.

Penny's object in this album was the wedding photo of herself and Artie Parfitt she had already shown Dottie. This time Penny pored over it for several long minutes, then she reached into her sleeve for a lacy handkerchief with a black border, and dabbed at her eyes and cheeks.

Dottie quickly said, 'And who were guests at the wedding? Have you got any pictures of them all together?'

Penny, distracted, hunted a few pages along for a photograph showing a small crowd. 'Here we are. Look at this, what a sketch we all are in those old fashions! You will think us so out-of-date! Look, there's Gervase, looking very young and handsome. He always does look very handsome, doesn't he? Quite the best of the Parfitt boys.'

He was in the second row of the photograph, standing behind the bride's shoulder, a smile directed at the lens. Beside him was Margaret, and on her other side was Reggie Parfitt.

'Is that Deirdre between Algy and your brother Mike?' Dottie asked.

Penny looked closely at the photo. 'Oh yes, it is. Yes, if I remember rightly, she came as Algy's guest but ended by being taken home by my brother Mike. It wasn't as though they were engaged, but even so, Algy was furious. And Mike's fiancée broke off their engagement. Threw the ring across the dining table at him, and it scratched the surface of the table. Mummy wasn't at all pleased.' Penny smiled fondly at the memory. 'And that led to a falling out between Mike and Algy, though they made it up eventually, of course.'

Penny went through all the guests one by one, detailing each person's life history and their relationship with herself or Artie in excruciating detail. Any attempt of Dottie's to move Penny on to a new photograph came to nothing.

'Of course,' said Penny, looking over her shoulder and dropping her voice, 'this was long before Margaret—disgraced—herself. She was still part of our set back then. She was actually my chief bridesmaid, or matron of honour, if you prefer the term. Little did any of us realise just how soon after this that she would become an actual matron!' Penny laughed at her own wit, then cleared her throat and said, 'Yes, well. You mightn't think it now, but she was more or less my closest friend back in those days, after Miranda had left. Though some people—

including my parents—thought she was a bad influence. Rather too free and easy with her charms, always running around with the men. Not that I had any idea just how free and easy she was. I always thought she was just an incorrigible flirt. But virtue was not a word she knew the meaning of.'

Penny got up and went to ring the bell. For a mad moment, Dottie wondered if she was calling Margaret in to give an account of herself but when Margaret appeared, Penny simply said, 'Tea please, Margaret.'

Once Margaret had gone, Penny said, 'You'd never think, would you, to look at our happy smiling faces, that tragedy was waiting in the wings for us. How innocent we all were back then. I mean, this was June 1925. By Christmas of that year, Margaret was an unmarried mother, and now, just nine years later, I'm a widow and poor dear Artie is lying in his grave.' Suddenly overcome, Penny murmured something indistinct and hurried from the room.

A moment later, the door opened and Margaret came in with the tea tray. She set it down on the end of the table next to the album that lay open.

'Looking at the old photos, I see,' she remarked to Dottie.

'Er—yes.'

'Is she getting all weepy about Artie?'

'Yes, she's just gone upstairs, she was rather upset.'

'Hmm,' said Margaret. She bent to look at the photo. Her cynical manner fell away, and she shook her head sadly. 'How young we all were. You just never know how things are going to turn out, do you?'

It was essentially the same sentiment that Penny had just expressed, but more lovingly done, and with a lot less self-pity.

With a sigh, Margaret went to the door. Looking back over her shoulder, she said to Dottie, 'Don't believe everything she says about her precious 'poor old Artie'. It wasn't a happy marriage, and the best thing he ever did for her was to drink himself to death.'

Dottie was shocked. But whether by the sheer spite in Margaret's voice, or what she had revealed, she didn't know.

She leaned over the photo. Was Margaret leaning closer to Gervase than to Reggie? Staring at the photo, Dottie couldn't quite make up her mind, though it looked horribly as if... Had one of these two been her escort? Or perhaps it had been someone completely different. But no, Dottie realised. If Margaret had been the chief bridesmaid, she would have been part of the wedding party, so wouldn't have had an escort. Even so... It was a bit of a cliché, but the bridesmaids were often pursued by the groomsmen. Who had been the best man? That was almost the only thing Penny hadn't told her.

Dottie flipped the page over to look at the next photo. It was so similar to the first that for a moment she thought it was simply a copy. But then she noticed one or two differences, and looked closer to find each subtle variation. To begin with, not everyone was looking straight at the camera and smiling. Also a small child had wandered onto the scene and was standing in front of the bridal couple, its image blurred as if it was still moving as the picture was taken. No doubt that was the reason for the subsequent photo. But there were other differences.

Arthur wasn't smiling. His face, slightly shadowed due to him turning to his right and away from his lovely bride, looked serious. Penny's eyes were fixed in a most determined manner on the photographer, her smile as fixed as her stare, the first fresh impulse of joy having become set in her chin and jaw. There was tension in the way she held her neck and shoulders. Still, Dottie thought, everyone always said how exhausting and worrying it was to get married, in spite of the happiness of young love.

Behind the bride was the answer to Dottie's question. Margaret was laughing, looking into Gervase's eyes, her hand on his sleeve. And he laughed down at her in response, his head bending towards her in an intimate way that almost brought his mouth level with her cheek. It was a scene that you couldn't look at without feeling intrusive. It was the way he looked at Dottie herself when he was with her.

'Shall we go for a walk?' Penny said suddenly from the doorway, and Dottie, concentrating on the photo, jolted in surprise.

'What a good idea!' Her voice was over-bright, she knew. She jumped up. In a moment she had run to change her shoes. They went straight out, the unpoured tea quite forgotten on the table beside the photo album.

'Were Gervase and Margaret ever involved romantically?' Dottie knew it was foolish to ask Penny of all people about Gervase, but she just couldn't stop herself. She knew that Penny had a malicious streak that enabled her to enjoy the weakness or the misfortunes of others. Nevertheless there was no one else Dottie could ask.

As they turned off the main street of the village to head towards the church, Dottie's words were blurted out before she had a chance to think about the wisdom of saying them.

Penny laughed. As if Dottie's future happiness might not hang on her answer. Dottie could have kicked herself. Or Penny. But she kept her hands folded neatly behind her, and her feet moving slowly forward in a ladylike manner. She fixed her eyes on the lovely pale yellow roses spilling over the wall of the vicarage garden, filling the air with their rich scent.

'Of course! I mean, surely you've realised by now that over the years, Margaret has run through the lot of them: my brother Mike, Cousin Algy, Reggie, Gervase, and as you've probably guessed, my own poor dear Arthur. And God knows how many others besides. I'm rather surprised that she has only one bastard to show for it. In fact, I think she and Gervase have had a couple of affairs.'

Dottie couldn't think of anything to say in response. She was shocked at Penny's biting use of the B-word, and although she knew none of it might be true, she felt there was pain behind the words Penny seemed to so carelessly throw at her. Dottie fought to find something to say about the roses or the pretty little church, but no words presented themselves. She felt as though she was going to choke. But pride—the only thing she really had left—kept her from reaching for her handkerchief. She would not let Penny know how her words had hurt. But now some words did come, and she said them, firmly. A little too firmly, perhaps.

'By the way, I've decided to go home on Saturday morning. Thank you so much for your kindness in having me to stay with you, it's been a delight, but sadly I must be getting home. There's my work,' she added, with a ring of pride in her voice, 'And of course, my sister's baby will be arriving soon, so...'

'Of course, Dottie, dear, I completely understand. It's been lovely having you here, but we all know that holidays can't last forever, don't we?' She prattled on for several minutes in the same vein, pointlessly repeating the same sentiments in a variety of ways. Dottie agreed with her from time to time, but otherwise blocked out Penny's voice, taking a long time to admire the vicar's roses.

Penny and Dottie settled back in the armchairs with their cups of cocoa. Dottie felt relieved that she had made the decision to leave, and that she had told Penny. She realised now that Gervase had exaggerated how much Penny needed company in the house. Thinking back to that first day, when Penny had been so agitated, Dottie was convinced he could have managed her on his own. Penny was definitely perfectly content to be in the house.

Penny said, 'Now I'm on my own, I'm wondering about letting Margaret go.'

Dottie gave her a surprised look but said nothing.

Penny seemed to take her silence as disapproval, however, and rushed to explain: 'Well, there's so little to do about the house, especially when I'm here on my own. I can do some of it myself, of course, and the daily woman can easily manage the rest.' She halted. Dottie waited once more, sensing Penny wanted to say more. Dottie endeavoured to look suitably attentive and interested. After another minute, Penny said, 'The thing is, Artie hasn't left me so terribly well off as I'd expected. I may need to consider some economies.'

Dottie clicked her tongue sympathetically and shook her head. Penny, leaning towards Dottie and dropping her voice, went on, 'And really, I can't bear to have that woman under this roof a moment longer.'

Dottie said nothing, but in her head, a few separate ideas clicked into place. Penny continued, 'With how much Artie has left to her, she's almost as comfortably off as I am. It's beyond bearing.'

Dottie ventured to say, more in the way of testing the waters, 'But then she has the child to educate, I suppose he had to think of that.'

Penny shot Dottie a sharp look, and Dottie had a brief moment to wonder if she'd overstepped the bounds of their short acquaintance, but then it was as if continued concealment was too much for Penny. She sighed heavily, passing her hand over her forehead.

'Exactly so,' she said. 'And I suppose I can understand, even approve of, his somewhat belated sense of responsibility. Many men wouldn't do half so much.'

'Very true. As my poor friend discovered,' Dottie said.

Penny nodded and sighed again. 'I've always been thankful that Miranda showed such restraint.' Dottie was puzzled by this. How did it fit with their conversation? Penny added, 'Because of—you know—the man she was engaged to. The one who killed himself.' She ended it on a whisper.

'Ah!' Dottie said. Suddenly Penny's meaning was all too clear. 'You mean...'

'Well, honestly, Dottie, can you imagine—a half-caste child. She'd never have held up her head again. But thankfully they had the good sense to wait. He was a very moral man, in spite of his—er—background.'

You mean his colour, Dottie thought, appalled once again by Penny's attitude. Not that Penny was alone in this. It was the same bigotry displayed most of the rest of Penny's circle of friends, including Gervase, Dottie was ruefully forced to admit. And it was the same bigotry displayed by most of so-called 'civilised' British society.

'Yes, his grandfather was a vicar or something, I seem to remember, so that's doubtless why Richard had very strong moral values. More so than perhaps...'

'Do you think they'd have gone through with it?' Dottie butted in suddenly, speaking purely out of curiosity. 'With the marriage, I mean. If he hadn't... you know...?'

'Hanged himself? Goodness knows. My parents would have thrown her out if she had persisted with the engagement. Or they would have made her break it off. But of course, they didn't know about it until later, after he was dead. Otherwise...'

'Otherwise?' Dottie prompted.

At least Penny had the grace to look a little uncomfortable. 'My father would probably have had him horsewhipped. And shipped off back to wherever it was he came from. Most of them went back anyway once the war was over. I mean, it was all right in a crisis, having them here, or sending them off to fight, but once the emergency was over, well... it seemed only natural to send them back again, back to their own country. They didn't fit in here, after all. No one wanted them to stay here, and obviously there was the risk of them not sticking with their own kind, of marrying into English society, or of getting girls into trouble and leaving them to cope with the results. They weren't like us, after all. So they weren't really welcome.'

'And yet he was a respectful, moral man.' Dottie couldn't help pointing out. How could Penny say such things about a man she had already said was morally upright and a nice man?

Penny turned on her quite quickly, a frown forming a deep ridge between her brows. 'What makes you say that?'

'Well you said yourself, he was the grandson of a minister, and had high moral values, and that he hadn't persuaded Miranda to—you know—be intimate...' Dottie was annoyed with herself that she couldn't help blushing over this allusion. '...before marriage. So it shows he was both respectable and respectful, and that he had regard for her reputation.'

Reluctantly, Penny nodded. She sank back into her chair. After a few moments' retrospection, she said, 'I know he was a black, but in many ways, Richard was the handsomest man I'd ever met. I mean, I was just a child, but he was so good-looking. And kind. He was a very charming young fellow. He was really Algy's comrade and friend. Mike and Richard didn't really get on. Mike had no time for darkies, as he called them, he still doesn't. But even though he was an officer, it wasn't easy for Richard to find anywhere to stay, so he stayed with us twice when he was on leave, and then again at the end of the war. Although, when my father had the 'Welcome Home Heroes' ball, Daddy found lodgings for Richard in the village. My father has always been very fond of a celebration, and he spent a lot of time and money planning the ball. He was M.P. for this area at the time, it was shortly after he got his knighthood, and obviously it was important for him and my mother to be seen doing things for the community, and you know, glad-handing. Daddy had great hopes of High Office.'

Dottie poured them both more cocoa from the shining silver pot that Margaret had brought in earlier. At least this didn't taste of polish, she thought. She wanted to encourage Penny to keep talking, sensing that there was a story here. 'When was that party, you know, when the young man...'

Penny gave a slight smile as she looked down at her cup. 'Oh that. It was 1919. Fifteen years ago. The war had ended the year before, but it took such a long time to bring all our troops— and our wounded and dead—back from the different theatres of war. Gervase will tell you all about that, I'm sure. Months later, almost a year in fact, young fellows were still being demobbed. My father wanted to welcome back my brother Mike, and my cousin Algy Compton, and the three Parfitt boys who were our friends.

'And Richard came too—as he was a great pal of Algy, and as his family were all the way over in

Jamaica, it seemed only decent to invite him to come along with Algy and be part of the celebration. Not that my parents—or any of them—treated Richard very well. But he took it all in good part or at least he seemed to. I think he mostly just let it all wash over him. He used to be very sweet to me. Protective, sort of big-brotherly, even though he was only six and a half years older than me, and I didn't think that was an especially big age difference, and after all it was only a month before my sixteenth birthday. We'd got fed up with the ball—the grown-ups were all so stuffy, and seemed so old to us young ones then—and we went off with some bottles and had our own little party out at the pavilion— the summerhouse—in the grounds of my parents' house.

'It was the most perfect summer evening. You know how it is this time of year—warm, breezy, the long, long light evenings, the flowers. Everything is just so lovely. It seemed so...' She struggled to find a word to capture that moment in time, but ended, with a frustrated shake of the head, back on the same word again. 'It was perfect. So perfect. The perfect summer's evening.' Her lower lip trembled and her voice died away.

Dottie put out a hand to her, and Penny took it, squeezed it, and let it go. She said softly, wistfully, 'We feel these things so keenly at that age, don't we? Everything is life or death when you're not quite sixteen.' She sipped her cocoa. Then with a stronger voice, said, 'Of course, it didn't last. The boys were all drinking far too much and getting rowdy. Mike took liberties with Margaret, and she slapped him. Then Arthur kept sniping at Richard, they didn't like each other at all. At the time, I wasn't really aware of anything, you just accept things are the way they are, don't you? But now, looking back, I realise how tense it was that night, and that there were undercurrents I was too young to understand. I was trailing around like a love-sick puppy after Gervase—poor Gervase! Reggie Parfitt was clinging onto Miranda's very shadow, and at every opportunity Miranda was doing the same with Richard. Mike and Artie didn't like that at all, and kept trying to separate them, or trying to annoy Richard so much he'd just up and leave.'

She took another sip of her cocoa, and cradling the cup, sat staring into the fire. At last she sighed heavily and sat back. Her eyes still held the distant look of reminiscence. With a sad smile she said, 'Oh, Dottie, my perfect evening was nothing of the sort, was it? I just didn't realise. It was like waiting for a bomb to go off. All the tension and the youthful emotions. But in the end, the evening simply fizzled out. The boys all drank so much they passed out or were ill in the shrubbery. Miranda and Richard quarrelled at some point then didn't speak for the rest of the evening. Later he walked me back to the house, and everyone else drifted off home.' She paused for a moment, and when Dottie turned to look at her, to see if she was going to say any more, Penny added softly, 'And in the morning, one of the servants went out to the pavilion to clear up after our party, and found Richard hanging there, from the lowest branch of the big old copper beech tree.'

Chapter Eleven

Dottie slept badly again that night. She had a lot on her mind. She was captivated by the wistful story of the night Richard Dawlish killed himself, and Penny's sorrow touched her deeply, even though they didn't especially like each other.

And Dottie was certain she knew why—they were in essence rivals for the attention of everyone who came to the house—not just Gervase. Penny loved to be the centre of attention, Dottie could see that now. With Dottie in the house, well, that was one more person to take the attention away from Penny.

Besides which, Penny had her sister and sister's family to take up her time and attention, and any outsiders would just be in the way. Dottie was most definitely de trop at this time that was reserved for family and close friends. Like Richard Dawlish, she had served her purpose, and now she was no longer either needed or welcomed.

Eventually Dottie slept, glad she had only three more full days to get through.

Penny's sister Miranda arrived with her family from Southampton via London, travelling from London by car to the family home in Nottinghamshire. Major Percival Parkes, Miranda's husband, oversaw the loading of their luggage into the front of the car and the luggage space at the rear, and elected to do the driving himself, in the main so he could ignore his wife and squabbling children all squashed into the back seat, and fix his mind on the road ahead. Thus Major Parkes arrived at the Maynards' in a mood of relaxed contentment, whilst his wife and children were all furious with one another.

Dottie felt that, in Miranda's shoes, she'd have rather had a day or two in London to recover from the long journey from India, but the Maynards collectively appeared to feel that the perfect time for a long-awaited reunion with family and close friends was the very afternoon of the homecoming. Consequently, Gervase called to collect Penny at three o'clock and drove her, chattering and excited, to her parents' home to meet the new arrivals.

Dottie was not invited to accompany them on this occasion. She didn't particularly mind, but

Penny seemed uncharacteristically embarrassed at this enforced neglect of her guest.

'Of course, you will be very welcome to the formal dinner tomorrow. But this afternoon, we did just want it to be a gathering of the family and dearest friends. I do so want you to meet my sister, you've heard me talk so much about her.'

For the fourth time, Dottie assured Penny it didn't matter in the slightest, that it was perfectly all right, and that she absolutely understood. Even as Gervase, his patience already worn thin, was holding the front door open for her, Penny continued in this vein, apologising and promising in equal measure. Dottie was relieved when they finally drove off.

She had a letter from Flora to read. She curled up in an armchair in the little morning room that overlooked the garden—a much pleasanter room, in Dottie's opinion, than the overstuffed and dim drawing room at the front. Ripping open the envelope she began to read the letter that had been burning a hole in her pocket since it arrived at twelve o'clock.

First of all, Flora assured her they were all well, and that they'd finally settled on the name for Diana's baby that they'd been pondering: Diana Dorothy. Flora wrote:

'And she is the most darling little thing, and quite a little beauty. I'm sure she's already grown, even though she's only a week old. Hudson tells me I'm imagining it, but I know I'm not—I can see that her clothes are already getting a bit small, the sleeves too short and the buttons pulled tight across her chest. Hudson is proving to be something of a bully. Oh yes, she's so, so efficient. But it's a bit scary—I feel as though I'm part of some kind of scientific experiment—everything is so very carefully measured and weighed. I know one needs to be careful with tiny babies, but really, she takes it all too seriously. There's no fun, and no enjoyment, and everything is done by a timetable. I'm not even allowed in my own nursery unless she says it's the right time of day. In all honesty, I don't know if I can put up with her much longer. Even Mother is a bit scared of her: and that should tell you all you need to know! George says it's up to me. I think I will try to persuade her to be a bit more human, if at all possible, and if not, well, I shall have to find someone else. It may be the modern method to bring up one's babies as scientifically correct as possible, but that's not how I see motherhood at all.'

Flora went on to say a good deal about what George had said to his father, and detailed all the funeral arrangements. There was some news about the members of staff, and then, right at the end, Flora ventured some remarks about William Hardy. Dottie supposed it was hardly a surprise that their mother should pass on what Dottie had told her about that morning on the train. Dottie sighed, and acknowledged it had been inevitable that Flora would hear all about it. Flora said, 'Oh Dottie darling, I understand why you did what you did, and thank God you got off that train to go and find Diana. But are you completely certain you can't ask William to forgive you and take you back? He is perfect for you, and I know the two of you would be so happy together. Think about it, Dottie. Don't let mere pride ruin your whole life.'

After that Flora signed off, sending love and good wishes and begging for news. But Dottie read these last few lines with misty eyes. Did Flora think she had done something so very terrible? Clearly she did if she advised Dottie to beg William's forgiveness. Did her whole family think she was in the wrong? But it wasn't about pride, Dottie told herself. It was all about trust.

'Is something wrong?'

Dottie leapt out of her skin, dashing away her tears and forcing her lips to smile at Margaret. 'Oh, I'm sorry, I didn't realise you were still here. I was just—er—reading a letter.'

'Upsetting news?' Margaret came to perch on the edge of the sofa opposite Dottie, a thing which surprised but pleased her, knowing Margaret would never do it if Penny was at home. Here in Margaret, Dottie felt she had the start of a friendship.

She tried to laugh it off. 'Oh well, you know how it is. News from home always sets me off.'

'You're quite sure you're all right?'

Dottie nodded.

'Want a cup of tea? Or something stronger?'

'Tea would be nice, thank you.'

'Why don't you come and sit in the kitchen? It's warmer in there. Even in the summer this room gets chilly in the afternoons sometimes. Or I could make up the fire for you?'

'Oh no, don't. I'll come into the kitchen. Thanks.' Dottie followed Margaret out and across the hall, and through the swinging baize-covered door to the kitchen at the back, situated in the wing opposite the morning room.

A small boy was sitting at the table drawing. He was long-limbed and fair, with blue eyes and something unmistakably reminiscent of the Parfitt men in the shape of his nose and chin.

Dottie couldn't help wondering about his paternity again. She pulled out the chair next to him and sat talking to him about his drawing. As Margaret made a pot of tea, the boy, who told Dottie his name was Simon, invited her to help him with his picture. He was working on the mane and neck of a chestnut horse. Dottie began to supply stable doors and a nosebag hanging on a nail, to Simon's delight.

When the tea was ready, Margaret brought it over to the table, and sat down with them. Leaning across the table, her head almost touching that of her son and contrasting her dark locks and his fair, she also took up a colouring pencil and set to work creating a small dog in the corner of the picture. The three of them drew and shaded in a companionable silence. When the picture was finished, they all admired it, and Margaret wrote Simon's name on it in the top corner, the way they did at school, then pinned it on the wall with drawing pins.

Simon ran to play outside, and Dottie and Margaret resumed their seats at the table.

'Does he have friends in the village?' Dottie asked.

'One or two, though I don't really encourage it.' There was a pause, and Dottie knew she was about to be taken into Margaret's confidence. Margaret said, 'Actually I'm thinking of moving away. Artie—Penny's husband—left me something in his will. It means I can afford to send Simon to a proper school and get a nice little cottage somewhere nearby. I'm just waiting for the probate and everything to go through, it takes a while, doesn't it? Then, well, I'll leave. I probably won't even give my notice. Penny treats me so badly I shan't feel any compunction about leaving at short notice.'

If Dottie was astonished at this, she said nothing, merely regarding Margaret over her cup.

Like Penny, Margaret seemed to read a criticism into this, and her tone became defensive. 'Well, what's the point of staying here? I mean, it's not as though my former friends want anything to do with me, and I hate the way I have to bow and scrape, and smile when she treats me like dirt.'

Dottie set her cup down. 'It will be a new start for you—a wonderful opportunity. And a proper education for Simon will ensure his future. He will be able to get a profession and earn a decent living. It sounds like a good idea. Do you know how soon...?'

Margaret's shoulders lost their tension. She smiled. 'I don't know. As soon as the money comes through. The solicitor said it should only be another month or thereabouts, it's been going on a while already. Sorry I snapped. You've no idea how horrid I've become. You do, you know, when you feel as though everyone and everything is against you. And when people you've known since the nursery turn against you, or throw accusations at you.' She looked out to the garden to where Simon was executing some complex manoeuvre with a football. 'Yes, a fresh start. That's just what we need. Simon's future will be provided for, and I can settle down somewhere and not feel like everyone is looking down their noses at me. I've got to get away. I plan to call myself Mrs Scott. No one will ever know I was never married. I can't tell you how I long to be respectable again! I'm sick of being judged all the time.'

Dottie nodded. 'I imagine you are.'

'Please don't say anything to Mrs—to Penny. I haven't told her yet. I'm waiting for the right time. She's going to be so busy with Miranda coming back. In any case, she's not talking to me because she's heard from the solicitor about Artie's will. I know she thinks it was significant that he left me money, but it wasn't. He just felt sorry for me, and they had plenty to spare. Anyway, I'll tell her in a few days. I know she'll go off the deep end, and she'll make my life hell, so the longer I leave it, the better.'

When Penny arrived back from her parents', there was only just time for her to change before the car came to take them to Gervase's home for dinner. She insisted on Dottie accompanying her upstairs so that she could impart the information she was practically bursting to tell her.

Dottie helped her to smooth down the navy-blue dress that had caught on her bun of hair at the back. Penny was too impatient of everything, her words almost stumbling over each other as she scrambled to give Dottie an account of the afternoon.

Dottie persuaded her to sit at the dressing table and began to arrange her hair in a 'different', in other words a more becoming, style. As Dottie curled and combed, Penny prattled on, revelling in the attention.

It became clear that she was reaching the climax of her story when she grabbed Dottie's arm, and with a giggle in her voice, said, 'But you should have seen Reggie Parfitt's face! When Mummy was making the introductions, poor old Reggie came forward at last and said, 'Hello old girl!' and Miranda said—oh, Dottie dear, you'll love this—Miranda said, 'Oh I'm sorry, I don't think we've met." Penny broke off in gales of laughter.

Dottie, who had only been half-listening, was confused. 'But I thought...?'

'Well yes, of course! She'd just forgotten him for some reason. But his face! Oh my dear, you should have been there. He actually looked quite ill. If he'd been a woman, I think he would have burst into tears. Oh Dottie, I could have died laughing!' And she proceeded to laugh again.

Dottie thought it was very cruel. Not for the first time it was clear that the Maynard sisters had malicious streak that delighted in the misery of others. She smiled politely, so as not to offend her hostess, but felt a deep sympathy for Reggie, who seemed to have been the target of their malice for the afternoon.

'At any rate,' Penny concluded, 'poor old Reggie got put in his place. But he should have expected it from Miranda. She threw him over for Richard fifteen years ago, and now she's a married woman, so it's like she thrown him over, all over again. We girls can't let these men just walk all over us!'

'Hmm,' Dottie said. She hoped her non-committal response would satisfy Penny's idea of female solidarity. She couldn't help feeling it was a good thing that dinner this evening would be a small affair, with just Gervase, Penny and herself. Dottie wasn't looking forward to meeting Miranda Parkes at the dinner the next day.

But she just said, 'And how was your sister? It must be wonderful to see her again after so long.'

'Oh it is! Thank you for asking, Dottie dear, she is quite well, as are her family. A little tired, of course, that's only to be expected after such a long journey. But such dear little children. It's so delightful to hear the sound of children's feet scampering about the house, up and down the stairs, in and out of every room, and of course there's nothing like the wonderful laughter of little ones that can be heard everywhere, no matter how far away they are. And so playful and energetic—kicking the ball in the hall and on the stairs, and running in and out constantly. Really they never seem to tire, do they?'

Dottie almost laughed. Clearly Penny hadn't enjoyed her nephew and niece as much as she claimed. But now Penny was blotting her eyes with her handkerchief. 'Arthur and I were never blessed with children.'

Dottie managed not to roll her eyes. 'What a shame.' She needn't say more, Penny could talk for both of them.

'Indeed. Such a high calling. How I should have loved to be a mother.' The way she said it made Dottie imagine a capital M for Mother. She made a vague sound of agreement. Her thoughts were back in the room with Diana, watching as she placed her first and last kiss on her baby's cheek. Her small knowledge of motherhood didn't quite chime with this sentimental drawing room version. She certainly couldn't picture Penny panting and groaning as she pushed a baby into the world.

'Alas it is too late for me!' Penny said. Dottie was in two minds whether she should either agree or contradict. She could imagine Penny wanting both her pity and commiseration at her supposed advanced age and lack of a husband. But Dottie felt she might also be expected to say to Penny that there was plenty of time for that, that she could in due course, marry again, and of course, a vehement denial that Penny was too old. Doubtless in Penny's mind she already had Gervase lined up for that. Conversing with Penny was like walking a tightrope. In the end Dottie opted for a sad smile, and simply waited.

Yet after a pause Penny said, 'I'm afraid I've had rather a falling-out with Gervase. It's his own fault. You know how he can be sometimes— so sure he is right all the time.'

Dottie was rather surprised by the vehemence of Penny's words. She certainly still looked quite annoyed. 'What did he say?' Dottie asked, genuinely interested in Penny's conversation for the first time that day.

'Oh, it was nothing really. It was more in the way he said it. Of course, you weren't there, and you'll probably think I'm just being silly.'

'I'm sure I won't,' said Dottie, feeling guilty about telling such an outright lie.

'Well, he said to me on the way back, 'Miranda hasn't changed a jot, still treats everyone around her like dirt.' Not that he said dirt. I shan't repeat what he did say.'

'How rude,' Dottie said, hiding a smile.

'Wasn't it? And so like him. He always thinks he is in the right.'

'What was it that your sister said to make him attack her like that?' Dottie wondered for a moment if she'd been too strong, but it was clear her choice of words exactly coincided with Penny's resentment.

'Oh, it was just that stupid thing with Reggie, when she hadn't recognised him, that's all. But of course, Reggie was offended, and kept going on about shaking his head and saying, 'After all I've done for her'. So that meant Gervase was annoyed with Miranda. Not with his own dear brother, mind you, oh no! No, he decided it was entirely Miranda's fault. Really, as much as I adore Gervase, he can be quite ruthless and cruel.'

Seeing Dottie's look of surprise at this, Penny said, 'Oh yes, my dear. He has quite another side to him than you, as a casual acquaintance, will have yet seen.'

Dottie felt like slapping her, seeing the calculated, crafty look in her eyes as she made a show of hesitating to speak so frankly. Penny dropped her gaze to her hands, playing restlessly with her dress button. 'Oh yes,' she added, softer still, 'He has a very different side to him in private. You probably don't know this, but he and I were once... but as soon as I saw how he could be, I turned to Dear Arthur. It's true Arthur was never quite as dynamic as Gervase, nor as good-looking, but he was such a gentle soul, a truly good man.'

It was quite a performance; Penny was certainly an accomplished actress. Dottie privately dismissed it all as rubbish. In a second, she thought, Penny will beg me not to mention any of this to Gervase.

Even before Dottie had finished this thought, Penny put a hand on Dottie's arm and said, 'I-I'd be grateful if you didn't say anything to Gervase. I'm sure you can keep a confidence. We girls need to stick together, don't we, and I wouldn't want him to be angry with you.'

'Of course,' Dottie said smoothly. 'I completely understand.'

Mr Michaels, Gervase's butler, greeted Dottie like an old friend, which Penny immediately noticed. She pursed her lips but said nothing. Dottie knew it had been filed away to be brought out later, probably at a time when it would cause embarrassment to either Dottie herself or to Gervase.

She was glad Algy was there, though not quite so glad that Mike was there too. But fortunately, both men appeared to be more or less sober, and neither seemed in the mood for ribald jokes and offensive remarks. She wondered if Gervase had warned them about their language beforehand. To Dottie's great surprise, it was a very pleasant evening.

After dinner they went into a little room at the back of the house, a kind of billiard room and study combined. Mike and Penny partnered Algy and Dottie at billiards, which Dottie had never played. So long as someone told her which ball she was supposed to be aiming for, she was all right, as it turned out she was quite a good shot. Penny became a trifle sulky as she failed to gain as much admiration as Dottie and in the end, Dottie felt it would be diplomatic to let Gervase take her place. Immediately Penny pouted to have her way and become Gervase's partner against Algy and Mike. Dottie sat in an armchair nearby, dividing her time between cheering them all on and looking through Gervase's books.

Once the billiards was over, the others came to sit down with Dottie, and Michaels came in with a tray of drinks. At some point one of the men, following on from a discussion about a book Gervase had recently read, introduced the subject of space travel and the possibility of men journeying to the moon in spaceships.

'Nonsense,' Penny said, dismissing the subject out of hand. 'It is an insane idea. Who knows what could happen if men travelled beyond their own planet?'

The men enjoyed a good-natured debate, going from travelling through space to the notion of time travel. After a second round of nightcaps, they were each saying who they'd like to go back in time to meet. The men of course chose military figures. Penny wanted to go back and meet Cleopatra, which Dottie wasn't particularly surprised to hear. When it was Dottie's turn, she wasn't quite sure what to say. She had no interest in meeting old soldiers and war-mongers. It was purely on a half-joking impulse aided by too much sherry that she said, 'What about Richard Dawlish? After all, I've heard he was terribly good-looking. Penny said she adored him, and obviously Miranda was engaged to him, so...'

'So what?' Gervase's tone was quite sharp, she noticed. She realised she must be a little tipsy, but it was too late, she'd introduced the subject.

The air about her was tight with strain, and she knew it was the topic that caused the sense of everyone being on the alert.

'So... perhaps he gave the rest of you some unwelcome competition?' She tried to keep her tone light and teasing.

'But he was...'

Dottie held a hand up to Gervase. 'If you're going to insult him purely because of his skin colour, I'm not going to listen to you.'

'You're so liberal,' he grumbled, but he smiled at her. Penny was watching her closely. Mike and Algy were also simply watching, not saying anything, which she found a little odd.

'Yes, and proud to be.' Dottie said in reply to Gervase. She thought for a moment and added, 'I wish I could have met him, he sounds like such a nice interesting fellow.'

'As a matter of fact, he was,' Gervase said, grave now, a cleft between his brows as he frowned, remembering. 'It was all very sad. I wish he had talked to me—or to Algy, he knew Algy better than the rest of us.'

On an impulse, Dottie said, 'How wonderful it would be to go back in time to that night and stop him from doing what he did to himself.'

'Yes indeed.'

She reached out her hand to Gervase, and he caught it and brought it to his lips for a soft kiss right in front of everyone. In a slow, meditative voice she said, 'I wish I could have been there. I so wish I knew what happened that night.'

'You do know,' Penny pointed out. 'I've told you all about it.'

'I mean in depth,' Dottie said. 'Because really, when you think about it, it's very odd. Everyone says how very moral he was and all that. Yet he killed himself. How did he go from one extreme to the other like that? It's a complete mystery. Did the police never think it could have been simply an accident? Some kind of joke that went wrong?'

'No. That was quite out of the question.' Gervase said, his tone brooking no argument, but Dottie sent him a querying look.

Algy said, 'He was a jolly good chap, as a matter of fact. I was frightfully sorry about what happened. Still am, actually.' He looked down into his almost-empty glass. 'I'd like to go back in time to see him, too. Feel like I let him down, letting him kill himself like that, and not being with him.'

'Just to know what was really going on in his mind, what he was thinking,' Dottie said. 'I'd just so like to know.'

Chapter Twelve

'What on earth is this?' Dottie asked, staring down at the manila folder Gervase had just dropped onto her lap. It was just before lunch and she was rather surprised to see him at this hour. He stretched out on the sofa beside her, reaching an arm round her and craning his neck to nuzzle behind her ear. She slapped his knee. 'Behave yourself and pay attention!'

With an exaggerated sigh, he withdrew arms and lips and sat up straight. It was as well he did for just then Penny came into the room and sat down, looking very interested in the folder on Dottie's knee. Gervase said, 'Well, you were interested in Richard Dawlish's death, so I brought you the original case file to look at. Strictly between us, of course. I thought it might interest you, though there were some pretty ghastly photographs...'

'Were?'

'I removed them, of course. Not at all the sort of thing a young lady would want to see.'

'Hmm,' Dottie said. Then, 'Gervase, dear, surely you're not allowed to just take police files away with you?'

'I'm the Assistant Chief Constable, I can do what I like, more or less.' He gave her a self-satisfied smirk and received another slap. She had an overwhelming sense of impropriety, yet her curiosity was so strong, she just had to take a peek.

Regarding the folder critically, she said, 'My first thought is, I'd expected the file to be a lot fatter.'

'Well, it was just a straight-forward suicide case, after all, not a juicy murder.'

She opened the folder and began to look through the sheaf of documents. There was the coroner's report, tersely to the point: 'verdict: open' was the phrase near the top that just jumped out at her. There were the statements from about half a dozen witnesses, a full medical report, a police report, and along with a few other bits and pieces, that was just about the entirety. It made Dottie feel so sad to think that everything Richard had been, and all his achievements, could be boiled down into this thin folder of legal papers. She looked at Gervase.

'May I read it?'

'Of course. That's why I brought it to you.'

'But I mean, do I have to read it right now, or can I keep it for a few days?'

'Keep it as long as you like, dear. It's of no value now. Although, of course, I shall need it back at some point, to go back into our archives.'

'Thank you.' She was quiet, reflecting. 'It's not much to show for a life, is it?'

'Oh, I don't know. Like I said, it was a cut-and-dried affair, not some lengthy enquiry. I suppose next you'll be wanting to see his effects? Clearly you mean to conduct your own investigation.' He was laughing at her now, but she stared at him.

'What effects? May I see them? Do you have them with you now?'

'No of course I don't, you goose. But it's just a few items in an envelope, and I could fetch them for you, your worship.' He bowed in mockery but she could tell he was pleased by her interest. She nodded, delighted, and he promised to get the items for her the following day.

Dottie ran upstairs to put the folder away in a drawer, bearing in mind it was a confidential police file, and not something that ought to be left just lying about. She so longed to sit quietly and read through everything right now, but she had to go back downstairs. Gervase finished his cup of tea then reluctantly said he must head back to work, which made Dottie laugh. He seemed slightly annoyed by that and she didn't dare tease him about how little actual work he appeared to do. At the door, she reminded him about Richard Dawlish's effects, and he promised to bring them round.

Penny was expecting Deirdre for lunch.

'But Dottie, dear, I will perfectly understand if you would prefer not to join us,' Penny said, 'as you really hardly know Deirdre, and we'll spend so much time talking about people you don't know at all.'

Dottie took this to mean that they didn't want her company, and she hardly minded. It would be restful to sit quietly in her room and read through the case-file on Richard Dawlish's death without feeling guilty about not making conversation. If anything she was a little surprised that Penny hadn't tried to get a look at the folder herself.

Therefore, on the stroke of twelve-thirty, as soon as Deirdre's knock sounded at the front door, Dottie headed for the stairs, exchanging a smile with Margaret as she ran to let Deirdre in.

Dottie could hear the sound of their voices, of course, but she was too far away to make out what they were saying. It was quite pleasant to hear voices but feel no pressure to respond. She fetched the folder and went to sit by the window, taking the documents out one by one and laying them out neatly on a nearby little table.

The ink was blue-black, and still as fresh as when it had first been applied to the cover of the file. Fifteen years old and almost no dust or wear. No one had looked at this file since it had first been laid to rest in the store-room. No one cared what happened to Richard Dawlish, then or now, she thought. It was easier for everyone to believe he had been a social inferior, a nobody, who could be completely disregarded and forgotten about, consigned to an obscure shelf in a back room in some rambling old building.

She picked the papers up one at a time and began to read.

The police report was brief to say the least; Dottie read it twice through from beginning to end in less than a minute. The dismissive tone displayed only too clearly the bias of the police who had looked into Richard's death.

'A negro male was found to have hanged himself in the garden of the Honourable Norman Maynard, M.P. on the night of Saturday 7th June 1919. There were no signs of a struggle. No suicide note was found, but as it is commonly known that negroes are often illiterate, this is not surprising. The deceased was identified by members of the Honourable Norman Maynard's household, specifically his son Group Captain Michael Maynard and Captain Algernon Compton, Hon. Maynard's nephew. There may have been some depression or mental crisis following the deceased's war-time experiences, or from his approaching deportation to the Caribbean as his service was now at an end.

'The medical officer arrived at the scene at 8.10am precisely and confirmed death. Photographs were taken of the scene. The body was then cut down and upon examination a preliminary time of death was reported to be between six and ten hours prior to discovery, so the man had hanged himself somewhere between ten o'clock on the night of the 7th June, and two o'clock the following morning. The coroner has been informed and a date for the inquest has been set at Tuesday 10th June 1919. Next of kin will be informed as soon as details are acquired.' This document was signed by an Inspector A. E. Reed, and countersigned by Chief Inspector Edwin Parfitt, and dated Monday 9th June 1919.

Dottie took a piece of writing paper and began to make notes:

1. It was assumed from the outset that the death was suicide, even though there was no note.

2. It was assumed that Richard Dawlish was depressed or had suffered a mental breakdown.

3. They only gave themselves two days to carry out the investigation, which means they had no intention of carrying out a proper enquiry into Richard's death. Because they had already decided what the cause of death was.

Next, she picked up the medical report. This was, of course, more in-depth, but somewhat technical and unpleasant. She confined her attention to the covering summary.

'The deceased is a well-nourished adult West Indian male in good general health. The age is given as twenty-two. Following examination, death can be attributed to one of two causes, being either: asphyxia due to hanging, or due to the contusion on the front left temple which occurred either at, or immediately before death, causing bleeding into the brain. The wound yielded splinters of beech wood, which is consistent with the location where the deceased was found. It is possible the deceased bumped his head during the process of hanging himself, perhaps by attempting to use the seat of the swing as a means of reaching the noose, as the seat was broken and lying beside the tree trunk. The deceased had eaten a light meal some hours prior to the time of death, and had drunk a quantity of beer, possibly as much as two pints of beer in addition to a small amount of champagne, enough to slightly impair the senses and mental faculties.'

The coroner's report surprised Dottie. The verdict was an open one and not, as she had assumed from what everyone had said, a definitive one of suicide whilst of unsound mind. The coroner had little to say other than that it was his sad duty to give a verdict but in view of the deceased's exemplary war record, and the alcohol in his bloodstream, he was recording an open verdict on the grounds that the deceased may not have intended to take his own life but had perhaps been indulging in some boyish horseplay under the influence of drink. The coroner offered his condolences to the late Lieutenant Dawlish's fiancée and family in Jamaica.

Dottie sat back and thought about this last part. The wording was a bit odd. Did it mean he had another fiancée back in Jamaica, or was it supposed to refer to Miranda?

At least the coroner had tried to be kind, she thought. Everyone, including the police, had to have known there was a party on that night, and that the young people had been out at the pavilion to have their own celebration. That was surely widely known. So the coroner seemed to have allowed for the alcohol and the possibility that things had got out of hand.

Yet at the same time, it was perfectly clear, from what Dottie had been told, that the party had already broken up before Richard had died. But the medical examiner said sometime between ten o'clock, when presumably both the main party and that of the young people, were in full swing, and two o'clock in the morning. Even two in the morning wasn't excessively late for a party, in Dottie's experience. Especially such a special one. It seemed likely that there were still people around at that time. So how was it that no one had seen him die?

Or had they? Dottie stared into space. It seemed inconceivable that anyone could have known what was on Richard's mind and yet have done nothing to try to help him or dissuade him. Was it possible that it was after all just some stupid game that had gone horribly wrong and been hushed up?

But everything she had heard about Richard made him sound so sensible, so responsible, not at all the kind of person to get involved in rash exploits under the influence of drink. Besides, two pints and a bit of champagne wasn't a lot. She was willing to bet those around him had consumed far larger quantities of alcohol, if their present day drinking was anything to go by. Yet he had been decorated twice for valour. That required a special kind of daring, didn't it? A scant regard for one's own safety that was essential in times of war. She shook her head. She didn't know what to think. She pulled out the sheaf of papers and extracted the witness statements.

The first was that of one Gervase Parfitt. Dottie immediately began to read it.

'I am Second Lieutenant Gervase Parfitt. I am twenty years of age. I was a guest at the party given by the Honourable Norman Maynard on Saturday 7th June. After Mr Maynard had made his toasts to the returned officers, a number of us including Mike Maynard, Miranda Maynard, my two brothers and a few others, decided we would take some drinks out to the pavilion in the Maynards' garden and have our own party away from the older people.

'It lasted until about half past twelve. I think Richard Dawlish was one of the first to leave. We had all been sitting on the steps of the pavilion. We had a lot to drink and I think all of us fellows and a couple of the girls were pretty well drunk. We were just laughing and joking around. The girls had been playing on the swing earlier but it got broken at some point, so the ropes were hanging down from the tree, but there was no seat.

'At one point, Richard went off into the bushes with Miranda, and we all teased them and laughed. I think we all assumed they were necking or something, although when they came back, it was obvious they'd had a row. Richard only stayed a few more minutes, then he walked Penny, Mike and Miranda's little sister, back to the house. As far as I recall, that was at about half past ten.

'Some of us stayed back drinking, but I think the next to leave was Algy Compton who walked Deirdre Myers home from the party as she had to be in by eleven. Algy returned about a quarter past eleven. I didn't see Richard again that night. We went home at half past twelve, and Mike and Miranda went back up to the house. Everyone else had gone by then. When we left there was no one outside the pavilion, we were the last.

'I never heard Richard say he wanted to kill himself or talk about being unhappy, or talk about hanging, even as a joke.'

Then there was Miranda's statement:

'I am Miranda Maynard. I am nineteen years of age. I was present at my parents' house on Saturday 7th June for the Welcome Home Heroes party. After the speeches my brother and his friends suggested having a party in the garden. It was a warm and pleasant night and we thought it would be fun.

'But the boys were all drinking far too much and were getting rowdy. Some of them were teasing Richard because he was so serious, and they laughed at him. Richard and I went into the shrubbery. In the middle of the rhododendron bushes there's a tiny clearing and a tree trunk that makes a bench. I wanted to talk to him in private.

'He had asked me to marry him the day before, and I'd said I would, but I wanted him to understand that I had to find the right moment to tell my parents. They would be shocked at the idea of my marriage to a negro. So I had to wait until the right time. Richard was upset though, because he wanted to tell everyone right away and have it out in the open. He said it was wrong to be ashamed. I'm afraid we argued. He was upset, and I think he was afraid I would change my mind about marrying him, and that he would have to go back to Jamaica as my father had promised him a job in one of his offices.

'We returned to the others then Richard took my younger sister back to the house as our group were getting a bit too much for someone of her age. He said he would walk her back. I never saw him again. It breaks my heart to think I made him so desperate that he felt the only way out was to kill himself. I shall never forgive myself.'

The other two statements were from Penny and Mike Maynard.

Penny said simply, 'I am Penny Maynard. I am fifteen years of age. I didn't know Richard very well but he seemed nice but a bit sad. When I asked him why he was sad, he said I was too young to understand. He took me back to the party in the house, but I don't know where he went after that. I thought he said he wanted to be alone to think, but I'm not sure if that is what he said precisely.'

Mike's said almost exactly what Gervase's said.

There was nothing else in the file. Dottie went back to the beginning and read it all again.

She jumped as a knock sounded on her door, and Penny looked in at her. 'Gervase has just arrived. We'll be leaving in about half an hour.'

Dottie gathered everything together, saying as she did so, 'My goodness, where does the time go? I shan't be long getting ready.'

Penny withdrew, but not before her avid eyes had taken in the papers.

Chapter Thirteen

Dottie didn't know quite what she was expecting when they arrived at the home of Norman Maynard for the dinner to celebrate his eldest daughter's return from India. Certainly, she hadn't expected Miranda to be a mousy little woman in a gown five years out-of-date, and with badly-done make-up. She looked the same age as her mother. For some reason Dottie had half-expected to meet a confident, worldly, modern woman, a beauty; or at the very least, perhaps, a domineering, powerful woman, or... she didn't quite know, it was just that when she met Miranda, she was surprised by her, and felt she had to lower her voice and talk gently to this faded little person.

As soon as Dottie had been introduced, Miranda's eyes strayed beyond Dottie to smile benignly upon Gervase, and behind him, Reggie and his wife. They came forward and kissed Miranda and hugged her as if they hadn't only seen her the previous afternoon, although Reggie, perhaps understandably, appeared to hold back a little. Everyone had assured Dottie that she was welcome but she already felt as though she were intruding upon a private family party. A butler paused at her elbow and offered her a tray of hors d'oeuvres. Another moment later, and a maid offered her a glass of champagne.

A small chamber orchestra was playing in a corner, softly, discreetly. There wasn't much room in front of them, but Dottie suspected there would be dancing later, there was enough room for perhaps a dozen couples, plenty of room for such a small company. She only wanted to dance with Gervase, the other men were either uncongenial or insipid as dance partners. But at an intimate party such as this...? Surely it would have been better to dispense with the orchestra and just allow everyone to mingle and talk; surely Miranda, her family and their friends had so much to catch up on?

Dottie stepped to one side to allow the guests some space to talk to the Maynards, their daughter and her husband, Major Percival Parkes, who looked as though he would sooner be anywhere than here in this ballroom, making small-talk with a bunch of people he knew only as names on a Christmas card. He was deeply tanned and spare of frame, oozing energy and impatience. His petite wife was dwarfed by him, and he looked away with a frown as she gushed and simpered as friendships and acquaintances from her youth were renewed.

She looked much faded from her fifteen years in the East. The sun hadn't so much tanned her as bleached out all her colour. Her hair—once famously chestnut and curling, according to Gervase—now was a limp kind of indeterminate dull brown heavily accented with grey. Her face was quite badly lined for a woman only in her early or mid-thirties, especially around the eyes. Too much sun, Dottie thought, and not enough use of a shading hat. Her figure was slightly bent, her bust small and easily overlooked, her hips and middle somewhat spread by a life spent mainly sitting down. And yet the men congregated round her. She had—something. A kind of magnetic appeal, perhaps? Or was it just that she seemed so fragile, so in need of manly protection?

'Not wearing any of her new frocks,' a male voice said in Dottie's ear. She turned to see Major Parkes beside her, frowning in the direction of his wife who was smiling and leaning close to catch a whisper from Gervase. 'We spent tedious hours shopping for new duds before we left, yet here she is wearing that old thing she's had for years. Makes her look dowdy and behind the times. Women! Incomprehensible!' He sipped his glass of champagne, made a face, and set it down on a side-table.

'I'm sure the butler will be able to bring you a glass of beer, or something else,' Dottie said. The major's eyes lit up.

'D'you think so? Not really a champagne man, myself.'

The butler was on the other side of the room, but he immediately saw Dottie's attempt to catch his eye and bustled over. 'Can I get you anything, Miss?'

Dottie indicated the major. 'This poor gentleman is in urgent need of something that isn't champagne.' She grinned at the butler, who grinned at the major, and became completely human.

'Is he, now? Can't say I blame him. I'll see what I can do, sir.' Within two minutes he was back, his tray bearing a generous glass of whisky. Dottie wasn't too pleased, but the major grabbed it like a lifeline.

'I believe this is what you enjoyed last evening, sir?'

'It is indeed, thanks a lot.'

The butler melted away and the major raised the glass to Dottie in a toast. 'Jolly decent of you, m'dear. Never trust a man who drinks champagne, what? Well, tally-ho.' He downed the drink in one and caught the butler's eye again.

Dottie smiled politely. She turned to the cluster of people just inside the doorway.

'Have you met your wife's family before?'

'No, we met and got married in Karachi, then I was sent to Calcutta. Been there ever since. This is our first trip home.'

'And are you back here for long?'

'It's permanent. I'm taking up a new post at the end of the month. Felt it was time to come home, what, and see the old country again. Got to get the children into school, you know. Get them civilised. Can't have them growing up like savages out there.'

Dottie couldn't think of anything to say to that. Not without causing a scene. She had been at school with a number of people born and raised overseas, and had always found them to be equally well-bred, if not more so. Certainly they had a greater respect for other people than was generally found in what was termed 'polite' society in this country.

Lack of inspiration led her to ask, 'And how many children do you have?'

'Just the two. Had two more. Died from the heat. And the water. They do, you know, over there. Almost everyone we knew had lost at least one infant, and it wasn't unusual for it to be several. Miranda didn't want to lose any more. That's really why we're back. I was doing well enough out there, but the life doesn't suit the womenfolk.'

'Indeed.' She was casting about her for something else to say. 'And will you take a house in this neighbourhood, or...?'

Gervase was making his way over, and Dottie's heart lifted. She smiled, but not for Major Parkes.

'Damn well hope not,' the major said beside her, but she'd already forgotten what she'd asked him. Gervase stood beside her with a conspiratorial grin, but it was the major he engaged in conversation. Penny drifted over in Gervase's wake and positioned herself between Gervase and the major, almost leaning on Gervase's arm, to Dottie's mind for all the world as if to give the impression that they were a couple. In fact, almost immediately Gervase was forced to clarify their relationship with the slightest of frowns, by explaining that Mrs Parfitt was the widow of his brother Arthur and not his own wife. Penny pouted slightly but was unable to deny it.

Soon Gervase and the major began to discuss politics and Dottie drifted away. Penny stayed for a moment but as the men appeared to forget her, she followed Dottie, grabbing her arm as if they were best friends, and pulling Dottie across the room, saying, 'Have you seen this? Come and look.'

'This' proved to be a photograph of her parents with no lesser personage than His Majesty the King. It was one of a number of handsomely framed photographic prints that covered a wall in a kind of snapshot of the life and times of Norman Maynard, M.P.

'That's Daddy getting his knighthood in 1917.'

Dottie made all the right noises. She was far more interested in the photo next to that one. It was a picture of two men smiling at the camera and holding aloft a silver cup. To judge by the golf caddies beside each man, Dottie assumed it celebrated the winning of a tournament.

'That fellow looks awfully like the Parfitts,' she commented.

'Oh yes, well he would do, that's Edwin Parfitt. Their father. He's the chief constable of Nottinghamshire. He and his wife are here somewhere.' She looked vaguely around then said, 'Oh yes, there they are, look. Gervase will introduce you to his parents at some point, I expect.'

Dottie was aware of an anxious knot in the pit of her stomach. But Penny turned back to the photo and said, 'He and Daddy are best pals, have been since school. We've always seen a lot of them. Of course that's also because Mummy and Evangeline Parfitt are cousins; only second cousins, but they've always been close.'

'So Gervase and Reggie are also a kind of distant cousin to you, Mike and Miranda?'

Penny wrinkled her nose. 'Well, ye-es. But very distant. I mean, if the relationship had been too close, Artie and I would never have dreamed...'

'Oh, of course not,' Dottie hastily agreed. Not that there was ever any danger of Penny and Artie producing any children, if what Gervase had told her was anything to go by, she thought, but said nothing of that to Penny, who liked to keep up the pretence of a happy, loving marriage. 'And Algy?'

'Oh Algy's from Daddy's side of the family, so he's not related to the Parfitts at all by blood.' Penny turned back to the photos. 'Daddy and Uncle Edwin love their golf, and as you can see, they've done very well at it too, over the years.'

'Wonderful,' Dottie said with her best social smile. Penny talked her through the other photos on display. But in Dottie's head, wheels were beginning to turn. How interesting that the Honourable Norman Maynard, M.P. and the Chief Constable of Nottinghamshire were so closely associated. Dottie kept a watchful eye on Edwin and Evangeline Parfitt, whilst Penny continued to chatter.

It quickly became clear that she was not happy with her sister's appearance. She spent some time telling Dottie how beautiful Miranda had once been, and how her clothes had always been of the fashion of the moment. Penny speculated about her sister's health. Did her lacklustre appearance denote some illness as yet undiagnosed? That would certainly account for the way Miranda had ceased to bother about how she looked, Penny suggested with a slight smile. Dottie was beginning to think it was odd, if Major Parkes was to be believed, that Miranda had decided against wearing a new outfit. Did she actually want people to feel sorry for her, or concerned about her health?

As they made their way to the dining room in response to the gong, Miranda was in front of them, her arm through her father's, and Penny was forced to cease her assassination. Augustine Maynard, slender, fair, and elegant, was almost a carbon copy of her cousin Evangeline as well as Evangeline's two sons. She directed the guests to their seats.

'I'm afraid there are only twelve of us now, since poor dear Artie... And so there are not quite enough ladies to go round, and some of the gentlemen are next to one another. I can't remember quite how it happened but we've ended up with thirteen at table, I do hope no one is superstitious about such things? But as it is more or less a family party, we didn't want to include any outsiders to make up the numbers. Oh apart from you, dear,' she said with an awkward smile at Dottie, belatedly remembering her presence, and the reason for the inauspicious number of guests. 'There's always room for a friend of Penny's.'

'It's fine, Mummy,' Penny said, 'You don't need to worry, or explain. No one cares about that sort of thing nowadays.'

Dottie was seated between Mike Maynard and Algy Compton. But although she was disappointed not to be next to Gervase she did at least know Mike and Algy a little better now, and felt certain that between them they would entertain her. Unless of course they drank too much, in which case... Quite the worst thing about the seating plan was that Dottie had to endure the sight of Miranda lolling all over Gervase on one side and Deirdre all over him on the other, directly across the table from her. It had dawned on Dottie over the last few days that Gervase was much sought out by all the ladies; even those who were married enjoyed flirting with him, and basking in his attention. Getting him away from all of them would be quite a task. Penny didn't look any happier about the seating arrangements than Dottie.

As the meal began, Deirdre asked Miranda, 'So how did you like India?' Miranda began a rather long and lukewarm response. On Dottie's right, Algy struck up a conversation with Gervase's father about some recent fishing rights debacle.

Mike turned to Dottie, and his voice lowered, he said, 'Good thing for Miranda to have got away all these years. I only hope it doesn't all come flooding back, now she's returned. We don't need any hysterics. She's talking about getting up a memorial service for Richard. Poor taste under the circs, I should say, but we'll see what happens. Might not come off. Percy seems like a good chap, I only hope he puts his foot down.'

Dottie was surprised. 'Oh dear. I shouldn't think your parents would like it either.'

'Exactly. Poor taste. Raking up the past. Been married to another chap for—what? Ten years? Twelve years? He'd hardly want to be reminded of his wife's past loves, would he? And a black at that. I know I shouldn't. I mean, even if it was Richard. Not as if anyone knew at the time. Miranda kept it all hush-hush, I can only suppose they'd planned to elope. Present us all with a done deal, then we'd have to just lump it. Probably the only way to bring it off. I mean, a black man. Can you imagine? But Miranda was always one to go her own way and damn the consequences. Good thing it all went to blazes, if you ask me. Percy Parkes is much more suitable fellow.'

'I'm sure they are very happy,' Dottie said primly.

'Bloody hope so. He's a cracking fellow. Can tell a joke. Plays billiards. Enjoys shooting. Going out together tomorrow to bag a few.'

'These early attachments don't always come to anything, anyway,' Dottie said, feeling very old and wise. 'Quite often the girl realises she's about to make a huge mistake. It's not always a good thing to follow one's heart.'

'Hmm, well I don't know about that,' Mike said, 'I'm still waiting for the right woman to come along. Though if anything happened to Reggie, I'd have Deirdre back like a shot. Oh yes, she was mine, originally.' He had the grace to look sheepish. 'Well, I suppose originally she was going about with Algy, but that didn't last long, then she and I were an item for some time after that,' he added in response to Dottie's look of surprise. 'Reggie used to tease me about her. Dreary Deirdre, they all called her. She was just a bit shy, that's all. Sweet girl. One that got away. I don't have a lot of luck with the ladies. Not very good at all that flirting and joking around and paying compliments.'

Dottie murmured a kind of catch-all phrase, thinking that if Deirdre ever had cause to turn to anyone other than her husband, it was very likely to be Algy, with whom she clearly still had a strong bond. Poor Mike seemed to be completely clueless as regards the opposite sex. But she said none of this, instead giving all her attention to her salmon mousse. After a moment she said, 'It must be rather nice to have so much history, all of you. Every chief event in your lives has been shared with all of them over the years. You've known each other forever, and you will always have those memories to look back on. I don't have any friends like that, apart from my sister.'

'Hmm. It's not always a good thing. Too much in one another's pockets, I sometimes think. I sometimes wonder if we oughtn't to have gone our separate ways a bit more.'

'Do you all still live locally, then?'

'Oh yes, all within a mile or two of here. Reggie's probably the one that lives the furthest away, and that's only, what three or four miles?'

'How did Penny's husband die? I haven't liked to ask.' She didn't mention that Margaret had already alluded to alcoholism. Mike's response was to the point.

'Artie? Drink.'

'Oh!' Dottie was scandalised by his bluntness. If two people said it, surely it was true?

And she couldn't help glancing in Penny's direction. Penny was staring at her sister with something like disgust. Dottie, engrossed in her conversation with Mike, had missed what had happened to cause that look. But it quickly became obvious that she was miffed over the intimacy displayed by Miranda and Gervase as they talked and laughed together. Right at that moment, Gervase was speaking softly in Miranda's ear and she laughed heartily at his words. Dottie felt like glaring at the pair of them too.

Further down the table, Reggie was looking at Miranda with scarcely veiled hatred. It seemed he still hadn't forgiven her for her slip the previous day. If indeed it was a slip. Dottie somehow doubted it. He was drinking steadily and eating little. Dottie fervently hoped there wouldn't be a scene. She wondered if her own face showed her feelings too, as she saw Miranda pawing at Gervase's arm, then her hand dipped beneath the table-top, no doubt to caress his knee. Along the table on Dottie's side, Percy Parkes was downing his wine and signalling for another.

Beside her, Mike continued: 'Yes, poor Artie used to drink like a fish. I mean I know we all drink a bit more than is good for us, but Artie... Poor fellow was half-cut most of the time. His liver just gave up on him.'

'How awful for Penny,' Dottie said. 'She must have felt so helpless, watching him suffer like that. I expect she pleaded with him to stop? Banned drink from the house? That sort of thing?'

'Oh er, probably. I don't really know, to be honest. Though from what I hear, it wasn't the happiest of marriages. Artie wasn't really the marrying kind. Damned hard luck on Penny of course, but there you are. A word to the wise, my dear. Those Parfitts are excellent fellows in their way, and the best friends a chap could ask for, but I'm not sure they make good husband-fodder, if you see what I mean. Too inclined to go their own way and damn the rest of us.'

Dottie felt herself stiffening against his words. 'Well I'm sure you know them better than I, but...'

'Keep my long nose out of it? Of course. Sorry to offend, my dear.'

'No, no, it's all right, I'm not offended, but, well Gervase and I are just friends, that's all, nothing more.'

Mike sat back and threw his napkin onto his plate. 'I'm glad to hear it, my dear. That's always the best way to keep it with old Gerry.'

A light iced dessert was brought in, and cheese and biscuits with it for those who didn't care for the sweet dish. Dottie was grateful that Mike, unlike Reggie, didn't go in for the sulks after she had rebuffed him, and his open friendliness was beginning to appeal to her. He wasn't quite as boorish as she had at first thought, though he still used the worst possible language much of the time. She decided to satisfy herself about a matter that had made her curious. Leaning a little closer to him, she asked in a confidential voice, 'I expect you knew Margaret in your younger days? She was one of your set back then, wasn't she?'

He gave her a startled look. 'Margaret? God yes, she was always around back then. By rights she should be here now too. She was Miranda's best friend. They were practically inseparable. Penny used to be so jealous, following them around all the time, trying to get them to include her. But poor old Penny was just that little bit too young in those days, a good few years younger than the other girls, more than a few younger than us fellows.'

'Age gaps make a huge difference when you're young. Though she was Penny's chief bridesmaid, so they obviously became closer friends at some point.'

'Very true. Although I think that had more to do with Penny not really knowing very many girls of her own age, and of course, Miranda had gone to India by then. Margaret and Miranda were at school together, and Margaret's parents lived locally, so it was inevitable those two would become buddies.'

'But she never married?' Dottie already knew that she hadn't, but she wanted to draw more from him.

He pulled a wry face. 'Well I imagine you've heard the scandal. Got herself into trouble. She refused to give it up for adoption, but then her parents threw her out, wouldn't have anything to do with her, so she was forced to earn her living. The fellow wouldn't stick by her, of course, said it was nothing to do with him. Not that she was the sort of girl to...' He looked down at his empty plate. 'At least... I mean, there was always a lot of talk, but... That is to say, I never really thought she was as bad as they said.'

This was completely different to what he'd said about her a few days ago. Dottie was in an agony of curiosity. She risked a further comment: 'What a shame her parents couldn't put pressure on the young man, insist upon him marrying her.'

'Bigamy is still a crime, you know.'

'Oh!' Dottie couldn't think of anything else to say. That put a different complexion on things. She had always assumed... Of course, there was nothing to suggest that the man was one of the Parfitts at all, other than all the hints everyone kept making. But it wasn't impossible that it was all entirely false. The child's father could have been some acquaintance from a completely different area. Yet Dottie had assumed... Even Penny had seemed to indicate... All Dottie could think of saying next was, 'Poor Margaret, though. Women always seem to suffer for their reputation as men never do.'

'So you and Gervase are just friends?' Mike asked again. There was a question in his eyes.

She smiled. 'Yes, I'm not even of age yet, so I'm too young for anything serious. And I could never marry someone my parents didn't know and approve of.'

'No indeed,' he agreed. He sat back a little from her and began to look around the table. It felt like the termination of the conversation.

The Honourable Norman Maynard got rather unsteadily to his feet, tapping a spoon against his glass as he did so. How these people did drink, Dottie thought. The servants ran forward to top up everyone's glasses with champagne, nimbly stepping in and out of the diners. Dottie surmised toasts were about to take place. She glanced at Major Parkes and saw him frown at the pale liquid being poured into his glass. He seemed even more drunk, in spite of all the food, rather than less so, and she spared a moment to wonder just how much he'd had and whether it was a habit. Military men were rather known for their heavy drinking. At least, according to her mother they were.

The Honourable Norman began to ramble. His wife frowned at him once or twice, but there was little to be done other than fix a smile on one's face and just wait it out. Eventually he came to the point, slightly slurring his words.

'So I'd like you all to raise your glarshes to my daughter and her hush-hushband, Major and Mrs Parkes.'

There was a general murmur in response and everyone took a sip of their drink, some more than others. The Honourable Norman resumed his seat. Dottie felt everyone begin to relax again. Then Miranda Parkes got to her feet. Immediately the room felt tense and oppressive. It was clear she'd had more to drink than was good for her. She swayed. She raised her glass, holding it crookedly. Champagne slopped over the edge and ran down the front of her dress.

'Next week,' she began, and Dottie had a sinking feeling that she knew what Miranda was about to say. Her words were slurred. 'Next week, marks the fif-fifteenth anniversary of a very special occasion. Very speshal. For it is the annivershary of the death of a great man, and one who deserves to be remembered. Thusly, I have deshided to celebrate the life of that great man by honouring him in a—by celebrating him in—what was I shaying?' She swayed again, and for a moment Dottie, watching this with her heart in her mouth, thought she was going to fall. But Miranda rallied, crossly shaking off Gervase who tried to persuade her to sit down again. 'No, Gerry, shtop it. I have shumthing to shay.' She flapped her free hand at him in a shushing motion, slopping more champagne down herself so that her glass was almost empty. Dottie saw the maid with the champagne bottle send a questioning look in the direction of the butler who shook his head very slightly. Around the table everyone was looking embarrassed and annoyed, except for Gervase, who looked rather amused by the whole thing, and sat leaning back in his chair with his arms folded.

Miranda's mother began to get up, saying in a twittery little voice, 'And now perhaps it is time for the ladies to withdraw, and allow the gentlemen to enjoy their cigars.'

Dottie was the only lady who got to her feet, everyone else had their eyes fixed on Miranda. Who had found her voice again, and now said, very loudly, 'It is time everyone acknowledged what a wonderful pershon Richard Dawlish was, and that we remember him appro—appro—right. And sho, next week there will be a shervice for him in the chapel in the village, and prayers will be said to comem—com—comememorant his...erm...'

At this point, Miranda Parkes vomited all down herself and fell into a heap on the floor.

Chapter Fourteen

Penny and her mother helped Miranda upstairs, followed by one of the maids. Everyone else had been more or less evacuated from the dining room: the men to the Honourable Norman's billiard room, and the remaining three ladies to the drawing room.

No one quite knew what to say, and although the coffee had been poured out, no one seemed to feel like drinking it. Dottie, Deirdre Parfitt, and Gervase's mother Evangeline, sat about on the sofas, smiling at each other and looking at the carpet. Dottie had not been looking forward to meeting Gervase's mother, uncertain how she would be received, in the capacity of Gervase's 'friend'. And at first glance she appeared quite daunting: tall, fair and poised. She had not been overly friendly towards Dottie thus far. But even

Evangeline Parfitt seemed to find this particular occasion an ordeal.

'What lovely weather we're having for the time of year,' Deirdre ventured at last. The other two ladies hastened to agree with her. Dottie tried not to laugh as she thought, it's the second week of June, early summer, and the weather has been quite summery, so in fact, it's exactly what one would expect for the time of year. But she said none of this. At least Deirdre had made an effort. Originality counted for nothing at times like these. Suddenly inspired, Dottie felt that she might have a go.

'Have you lived in the area all your life, Deirdre?'

Deirdre turned to Dottie with obvious relief. 'Oh yes, since I was a little girl. Mama and Papa moved into the area when I was a baby. They had been living in London, but the city is so bad for one's chest, don't you find?'

Between the three of them they managed to keep the banal conversation alive until the men came back an hour later, followed shortly after by Penny and her mother. They had decided to concoct a scenario whereby Miranda had been taken ill following her long journey and had been delirious with fever. Everyone seemed only too glad to go along with this version of events. Gervase said something about the dangerous bacteria one met when travelling in hot countries, and Mrs Maynard made one or two comments about the uncertainty of the female constitution, and said that in her opinion,

Miranda would doubtless be completely recovered in a day or two, once she'd had a chance to really rest properly.

Major Parkes exhibited no outward interest in his wife's health, but continued to steadily drink his whisky, topping it up from time to time from the bottle he had brought with him from the billiard room. He ignored everyone else in the room.

Mike and Gervase kept up a conversation with Deirdre and Evangeline Parfitt. Penny sat next to Reggie and tried to engage him in conversation but for once even lupins couldn't seem to draw him out of his preoccupied state. Reggie looked so pale and drawn, Dottie couldn't help wondering if he was ill. Norman and Edwin conversed loudly and boringly with Algy about golf and cricket. Augustine and Dottie smiled at one another politely from time to time and commented on the weather for the time of year.

Reggie and Deirdre got up to leave and everyone seemed to take that as a cue for the party to break up. Standing in the entrance hall waiting for the various cars to be brought round to the front door, Dottie caught Reggie alone for a moment, and under the cover of the other, louder conversations all around, she put a hand on his arm and looked into his face. 'Are you all right, Reggie? You don't look at all well.'

Up close, she was even more shocked by his changed appearance. His face was thinner, his skin lacked its usual healthy glow, and he looked as though he had been without sleep for days, though she had only seen him a couple of days before. His black wool evening suit made him look as if in mourning, which didn't help at all. He gave her a rueful smile and patted her hand. 'Thank you I'm quite well. Just a few-er-business worries, nothing serious.'

Clearly he was lying, but if he didn't want to say more, she couldn't force a confidence. She nodded. 'Of course, well I'm glad it's not serious. Is it something Gervase can help you with? Or even just by listening...'

But he just smiled, and said, 'Bless you, my dear. No, really it's nothing.' Then, his wife calling to him, he left.

Gervase's car was the next to come. With relief Dottie followed Penny and Gervase down the steps. Once they were seated and under way, Dottie felt she could at last relax. The ordeal was over. Forgetting for a moment how closely connected they all were, she only just managed to refrain from saying to either of the others, 'What an evening! And what people!'

But she thought it to herself. It had been twelve years since Dottie had been to a party where one of the guests was actually sick all down themselves right there at the table. She still couldn't believe it. What had been behind Miranda's attempted speech? Did she still have feelings for her dead lover? It looked as though her husband thought she did, and he wasn't at all happy about it. And what on earth was wrong with Reggie?

Dottie wasn't entirely surprised that Miranda visited them early the next morning. Well, perhaps she was a little surprised by how early Miranda visited. Margaret opened the door to admit her at half past eight, and went to hang up Miranda's wet coat, for it was raining. After all their talk of the good weather the night before, Dottie thought. Miranda came into the dining room, where Dottie was having tea and toast at the table. Penny, as usual, was still in bed.

Miranda looked around curiously. Of course, Dottie thought, this was the first time she'd been to Penny's home. Margaret brought another cup and Dottie poured Miranda a cup of tea. Miranda didn't even spare Margaret a glance. Dottie couldn't help wondering if she didn't recognise Margaret, in the same way she had 'failed to recognise' Reggie Parfitt, or whether like all her friends, Gervase excepted, she simply thought Margaret beneath her nowadays. Yet they had once been best friends.

Miranda drifted aimlessly about the room touching this and picking up that and generally being irritating. She so obviously wanted to talk to her sister. Why didn't she simply go upstairs and wake Penny if it was all so very urgent? Dottie decided to finish her breakfast quickly and go to her room, leaving Miranda the privacy she needed, when—or perhaps if—her younger sister should come downstairs. But just then Miranda took a seat at the table, and said, 'What must you think of me? I'm so sorry for the spectacle. Honestly, I never usually drink that much. I certainly never disgrace myself in that way. I'm utterly humiliated.'

'Oh don't worry about it,' Dottie said, 'I'm sure everyone will have already forgotten all about it by now.' As soon as she'd said that she realised no one would ever forget the time when Miranda Parkes nee Maynard was sick all down herself and spouted on about her dead boyfriend in front of her husband. With a rueful smile, Dottie added, 'Well, at least it was among friends. Everyone will be very forgiving, and keen to overlook what happened.'

'Perhaps. Though I've had an almighty row with Daddy this morning. And with Percy. He's furious. Says I've made myself a laughing stock, and humiliated him in front of virtual strangers, and...'

Dottie couldn't help a little frown as she interrupted with, 'Oh I really don't think it was quite that bad...'

'Oh it was, it was! He said it was tantamount to infidelity and that he is disgusted with me. And now he's taken the children to stay with his mother in Sussex.' Miranda broke into floods of tears, her face buried in her hands. 'He says when I've come to my senses, I can go down to Horsted Keynes and beg his forgiveness. Until then I can't see the children, or... And my father...'

At this point, Penny entered the room, tying her wrap about her as she came.

'What is it? What's happened?'

Between sobs, Miranda poured it all out again. Margaret came in, and with unconcealed interest listened to the tale as she brought in Penny's breakfast and some limp pale toast for Miranda, who now finished what she had been about to say. 'And Daddy says I've brought shame on our family, and that I've made a disgraceful exhibition of myself over this whole episode. He said I did it fifteen years ago and I've done it again, and that I should never have come back from India.' She turned to Penny, her arms thrown out in a dramatic plea for help. 'Oh darling, I can't go back to Mummy and Daddy. Please, please, please can I stay here with you? Otherwise I don't know where I shall go.'

She collapsed into a chair, sobbing. Dottie almost rolled her eyes. Thank goodness I'm going home tomorrow, she thought.

In London, Inspector William Hardy had just returned from Scotland for the second time in ten days. At least he was finally making progress with the case. He turned his latch-key in the lock and pushed open the front door of his lodgings. His boot stepped onto the mat, scuffing a quantity of envelopes that lay there from the late delivery. He stooped to pick them up. Three items were for the other lodgers, two were for himself: a letter from his sister, postmarked Derbyshire, and a picture post-card of the south of France. He frowned over this, standing there in the open doorway to look at it. It was definitely addressed to him. There was no return address. He read the short greeting on the left side of the back:

'Dearest William,

We arrived safely. Thank you so much, dear boy, for your help in getting to the train on time. The weather here is very nice, and the boarding house is pleasant with a lovely view of the harbour. Take care of yourself dear, love to Dottie. Fond regards,

Your devoted Uncle Bill and Auntie Anna.'

After the signature there followed several large Xs. For a moment he stood there dumbfounded. Then a fellow lodger arrived and shoved past to get into the house, and William came to life again, walking upstairs to his room. By the time he unlocked his door, he had a broad smile on his face. Then he read his sister's letter.

The three women lunched at the Reginald Parfitts. It was an invitation that had been issued several days earlier, before Miranda had so completely offended Reggie. Dottie felt vaguely surprised that neither Reggie nor Deirdre had managed to think of an excuse to cancel the arrangement. She was even more surprised that it was Penny who drove them in her own little car, and it was just as well for the fine summer weather had given way to rain, as it so often did.

Dottie was relieved to see Reggie looking a little better than the previous day, if still noticeably 'off' with Miranda. He greeted Dottie as though she were his favourite person in the whole world, and even Deirdre seemed so glad to see her, squeezing her hand and saying with particular emphasis how glad she was to see Dottie, and that they would miss her terribly when she went back home.

While it was just the ladies, no one mentioned what had happened at the Maynards' dinner, and conversation was dull, dull, dull. Dottie would never have believed Reggie's continual waffle about lupins would be the most interesting thing about a lunch party, when he finally left his study and came to join them at the table. Time and again Deirdre tried to head him off, but then it was as if she just ran out of energy and let him carry on. Dottie was almost grateful to him for his stubborn way of turning every topic of conversation to his favourite plants. It was rapidly becoming a subject she knew a great deal about. And with Penny smirking and simpering but saying nothing of interest, and Miranda still wallowing in her disgrace, and constantly apologising for her gaffe, there was nothing much worth listening to, as far as Dottie was concerned.

That Reggie was embarrassed and uncomfortable with Miranda in his home was clear to Dottie, and she felt sorry for him, as Miranda still treated him with no consideration at all. She had to know it was making him uncomfortable to continually refer to the incident of two days earlier as if it were a humorous anecdote. For Reggie it was still too recent an embarrassment. For about the sixth time, Dottie thought, why hadn't Deirdre cancelled the invitation? It was a mystery.

They endured a most uncomfortable afternoon. Dottie was looking forward to getting back to Penny's and packing her things for her journey home in the morning. She longed to get away from all these people with their secrets and their past loves and hates. Gervase had promised to take her into the railway station at Nottingham so that she could get an express to London. She fully expected to be home just after lunch.

She sighed under her breath and forced herself to smile. Only another twenty-four hours and she would be gone. Though the thought of leaving Gervase had her almost inclined to cancel her plans. It was odd that she felt so much pain at the prospect of leaving someone she'd only known for just over a week.

Deirdre excused herself to check on something in the kitchen, and Dottie went after her to gain directions to the bathroom. When Dottie looked back from the door, Reggie looked quite alarmed to be suddenly left alone with Miranda and Penny.

If only she didn't have to go back to join the others, she thought, as she came back down the stairs again two minutes later. But surely they would be leaving soon? A lunch couldn't last the entire afternoon!

Her wish was granted. As she entered the room, Miranda appeared to be sulking, and Dottie just had time to hear Reggie saying, 'You

ought to remember who your friends are,' but he
fell silent as she came back into the room. The
atmosphere was distinctly chilly. Penny
announced it was time to leave, whilst Deirdre
just looked as though she wished the ground
would open up and swallow the lot of them.
Reggie could barely bring himself to say a civil
goodbye. As they got into Penny's car, Dottie saw
him shake off his wife's hand and go back into
the house, leaving her alone to wave them off
from the shelter of the porch over the front door.

As soon as they reached Penny's house, Penny
and Miranda excused themselves to go to their
rooms for a nap—too much wine and a heavy
lunch, coupled with the warm though wet
summer's day had made them sleepy, they said.
Miranda was now occupying the room next door
to Penny's, the one that had been Artie's until so
recently.

   Dottie didn't mind being left alone to entertain
herself, quite the opposite. She went to her room
and began to pack. She felt excited at the
prospect of going home, though a little nervous
as it would mean a return to new
responsibilities. But she had been away for
almost three weeks: a week in Scotland, and
twelve days divided between York and
Scarborough then Nottinghamshire. That was
quite long enough. She was ready to go home.

   She slipped the last blouse from the hanger in
the wardrobe, folded it, and placed it into her
suitcase. She had laid her travelling suit across

the back of the chair ready, along with a blouse, her stockings and underwear; and her shoes, neatly polished by the kind daily woman, were under the chair. All she needed to do was to leave out her night things and her other bits and pieces for the morning, and she was finished. She changed into her evening dress rather early so that she could pack the things she had been wearing all day.

She decided that she would take a leaf out of Penny and Miranda's books and have a short nap; she had slept so badly since coming to the house. When she awoke, she looked out to see it was still raining. Not that it mattered, she thought, at least it was still fairly warm. It was almost tropical, so humid and damp yet warm.

Then she had an idea and went downstairs. She put a call through to her sister, and immediately said, 'Flora? Do you remember Catherine Merritt-Gable?'

Dottie leaned against the coats on the pegs at the back of the hall as she spoke into the telephone receiver. One of the coats was wet from the rain, and she hastily repositioned herself away from it, brushing the water off her shoulder as best she could before it seeped through the fabric of her blouse.

'From school? Yes of course. She was terribly good at hockey.'

'Have you got her address by any chance? I think she married, didn't she, last year? But I can't remember his name.'

'Oh, she married a young fellow named Walter Sherbourne. He's a church chappie, isn't he? A curate, or something?'

'Probably,' Dottie said, 'because she was very religious, wasn't she? I think her father was a clergyman, too.'

'He became a bishop! It was in the newspapers, ooh, two or three years ago? I remember he came to school once on open day, just before I left, and he won the 100-yard dash! She said he'd been a great sport at school and could have been in the Olympics, but he went into the church.'

Dottie could hear Flora at the other end of the line, tapping her teeth with a pencil or something similar. It was extremely annoying.

'Flora!' she said sharply. 'That's a horrid sound!'

'Sorry. Just thinking. I believe that Jemima Goodman knows them. She was at some do or another and ran into Catherine not long ago. Do you want me to ask her if she an address or anything?'

'Yes, please.'

'Why? What made you suddenly think of Catherine?'

'I was thinking about how hard it is to be West Indian in this country, and how very unpleasant a lot of people are. I wanted to ask her a bit about that.'

'Oh!' Flora sounded surprised but interested. 'There were a couple of teachers in particular who were really unpleasant to Catherine, I remember. As a child myself, it never occurred to me I could say anything to the teachers. And some parents even complained about their daughters having lessons with her. It must have been a miserable time for her—and her home was so far away. She must have been so lonely. Not like us. We were so lucky to go home every afternoon.'

'Yes, we were. I'm so glad we didn't board.' Dottie said. They talked for a couple more minutes, then Dottie said goodbye.

She missed Flora so much. She had to get home soon.

It was to be her final dinner at Gervase's house, on this visit, at least. She would have liked to dine tête-à-tête, but it was not to be: Gervase had invited Penny too, and therefore more or less had to include Miranda. Perhaps that was all for the best, Dottie thought as she felt inclined to be sentimental. Having other people around would force her to be sociable and not think too much about going home and leaving Gervase, or how much she would miss him. She didn't want to be bursting into tears again. She had cried too much of late.

Before they went in to dinner, they had a sherry in the drawing room, and chatted. Gervase drew Dottie to one side, and reaching into his jacket pocket, brought out a little package for her. For one wild moment she thought he was about to propose, but as soon as her heartbeat slowed back to normal and she could think again, she saw it was a brown envelope. On the front was marked 'Richard Dawlish—effects from jacket pocket'. Of course.

She opened the flap of the envelope and peeked inside. It contained just four items: a battered leather wallet, half a book of matches, half a packet of cigarettes and a small reference book. Once again, she was struck by a sense of, 'Is this all there is?' But then a thought occurred to her, and with something like relief, she looked up with a sudden smile and said, 'Of course! How silly of me. Obviously, the bulk of his belongings will have been sent back to his family in Jamaica. Phew, for a moment, I thought this was all that was left of Richard's life!'

Gervase was frowning. Not with annoyance, this time. She recognised it as a sign he was thinking. 'I don't think there was anything to send back,' he said. 'As far as I can recall, there was nothing else.'

It was Dottie's turn to stare. 'There must have been,' she insisted. 'Surely he had clothes, shoes, and I don't know, books? Or personal belongings of some kind? What about his medals and things from his war service? Don't army fellows usually have a big kit-bag or something? Surely that would all have gone back to his family?'

'Oh Dottie, do think, dear child!' Miranda put in. The other two had drifted over to see what was going on. Her rather sarcastic way of talking to everyone, especially Dottie, made Dottie feel like putting her tongue out at her.

'What? Think about what exactly?' Dottie asked, exasperated.

'Well, I was his fiancée, if you remember, so naturally his belongings came to me. What few there were, that is.'

Dottie stared, appalled, and even Gervase looked uncomfortable.

'Miranda, I'm... I do beg your pardon, I'm afraid I completely forgot...' Dottie began, but Miranda waved her words aside and with a martyred air, said:

'Of course, it didn't matter to me that he hadn't much to leave. It was he who mattered, obviously. But I kept his things. They're probably still there, up in the attic at Mummy and Daddy's house. No one's likely to have thrown anything out, Mummy and Daddy are such hoarders. His clothes I didn't bother with, I gave those all to our maid, and I believe the stuff that was any good was given to some local mission run by the church, and the rest were burned. Oh and of course his little Bible. I think that got handed on to some charity or another. There wasn't a lot else apart from those.'

Dottie was wondering whether to ask if she could see the items. Would Miranda—or her parents—think she was displaying too ghoulish an interest? But before she could even broach the subject, Gervase said,

'That's highly irregular. Even as his fiancée, you weren't his next of kin. The things should have been sent back to his parents.'

'Well he didn't have any, did he? He was brought up by his grandparents, so... Anyway, it was only right that my grief and my loss should be acknowledged. But, if you don't like it you will have to take it up with your father. He was a chief inspector at that time, wasn't he? And working on this very case?'

Gervase nodded. 'Yes, he was,' he said, and he didn't look at all pleased.

Michaels came to the door and announced that dinner was ready.

But the meal was never to be eaten. Whilst they were still taking their seats in the dining room, Michaels rushed back in. He was in a terrible flap and all trace of his usual calm manner had vanished. He said, 'Mr Gervase! Mrs Reggie is on the phone. She's in such a state. She says Mr Reggie has locked himself in his study and she can't get any answer from him! She wants you to come at once.'

Gervase stared at the man uncomprehendingly. He began to shake his head and say, slightly irritably, 'Well why doesn't she just...' He shrugged and pulled out his chair ready to take his seat.

But Michaels pulled him by the coat sleeve into the hall saying, 'No sir. Mrs Reggie is afraid something terrible has happened. She needs you to go to over there immediately. Please sir!'

Again Gervase tried to calm the man, but Michaels's agitation was contagious. The three women exchanged looks and Dottie went to

Gervase's side. She felt a sense of foreboding. 'Gervase, let's just go and set our minds at rest. I'm sure Deirdre wouldn't ring unless she was very worried. Perhaps your brother has been taken ill.'

Gervase still seemed reluctant to leave, and actually went to the telephone. But Dottie took the receiver out of his hand and set it back in its rest, as Michaels brought Gervase and Dottie their coats due to the heavy rain that was falling.

Without even thinking of the other ladies, Dottie and Gervase went out and got into his car and set off, Gervase still insisting quite angrily that it was all ridiculous, and that it was bound to be a mare's nest, and variations along those lines. Dottie began to feel horribly afraid.

In spite of his assertion that it was all a waste of time, he drove much too fast all the way there, and almost hit the gatepost as he swung the car off the road and onto the driveway that led up to the house. He slammed on the brakes and leapt out of the car, without turning off the engine, forgetting Dottie, forgetting everything, as he ran up the steps to the house. He turned the handle of the front door and the door opened. They went inside.

Chapter Fifteen

The hall was empty and echoed the sound of their footsteps and hurried breaths. Outside it was still daylight so no lights had been put on inside the house, and it was quite dark.

'Deirdre! I got here as soon as I could, what's going on?' Gervase threw open the drawing room door, and Dottie followed behind him, curious at the silence of the house.

'Oh Gervase, thank God!' Deirdre was sitting on the extreme edge of a chair, her hands twining and twining a handkerchief, her eyes red with weeping, her face otherwise pale. She jumped up on seeing them and launched herself into Gervase's arms, breaking into fresh sobs. She poured out her tale, between sobs and hiccups, and as she did so, Gervase was handing her into Dottie's care, and turning to leave the room.

The gist was, Reggie had gone into his study after their visitors had left that afternoon—if not slightly before, Dottie mentally added—and he had not come out since. She had knocked a number of times, and gained no answer, so she had tried the door, and found it locked. There was no other key that she was aware of. She had even gone around the outside of the house to the garden door, she told them, but although one of the panes of glass was broken, the door was locked, and the curtains had been pulled across, preventing her from seeing inside.

'I knocked on the garden door, but he didn't open it, I don't know if he heard me. Or—or... Oh Gervase, what if...?'

'Nonsense,' Gervase said briskly, though the set of his jaw told Dottie he was as anxious as they were. 'He's just fallen asleep, I expect. I'll go and see.'

He went to the next door along the hall. He thumped on the door and at the same time tried the handle. The door was locked, just as Deirdre had said. Frowning, Gervase pounded again. There was no response. Bending to look through the keyhole, Gervase recoiled with an oath and set himself to kicking at the door.

'My God, Reggie! He's in there, he's lying across his desk. There's—there's blood—lots of it.'

The door wouldn't budge. For a brief mad second he thought about using a chair to try to batter it down, but the door would be too strong for that. Instead, he turned and ran out of the house into the garden, round to the door, Dottie and Deirdre in his wake. Deirdre was clutching at Dottie and sobbing under her breath and saying some garbled form of a half-remembered prayer from Sunday school. Dottie felt like doing the same; all the way she was thinking, please let it all be a mistake, but she knew in her heart it was real.

None of it had been any use. Eventually Gervase had managed to break the lock and get the garden door open, but it was all too clear from the way Reggie leaned forward with his head on his desk, the blood pooled on his blotting pad in front of him, that there was nothing anyone could do.

Glass crunched under foot as Dottie and Deirdre stepped into the room. Gervase tried to prevent them from coming up to the desk, but the women wanted to see, wanted to be sure that there was nothing left to do other than mourn for Reggie Parfitt. Dottie tried to prevent Deirdre from clutching at him, though she did just stroke his hair back from his face, wiping his blood on her dress.

He was still sitting at the desk, his hands neatly folded in front of him on the desk-top. There was a wound on the side of his head, and the impact of whatever blow he had received had knocked him sideways so that his hands were in front of his mouth. The blood had run down his forehead and onto the blotter, spilling over the edge and onto the shining wood. His eyes were open and staring ahead, fixed on some spot no one else could see.

Deirdre became calm at this point, and it was she who unlocked the door to the hall, put an arm around Gervase, who was overcome with emotion, and with Dottie's help led him back to the drawing room. It was Deirdre who quietly and calmly summoned the police in spite of Gervase's harsh cry of, 'No! What are you doing that for?' It was Deirdre who explained gently to Gervase that Reggie's death could not have been natural and that the police must be informed.

Dottie went to make tea. It had transpired that it was the maid's afternoon off, and that they had no other full-time staff. As she had found before in times like this, focussing on practical matters helped her to cope with an upsetting situation. Whilst she waited for the kettle to boil, she wondered if she should try to find something stronger for Gervase. He was so upset, and that was hardly surprising. He had now lost all three of his brothers: the eldest during the war, then Artie just two months ago, and now Reggie. It was terribly sad. If a man was born into a family with three brothers, he surely had every right to expect some of them to grow old with himself.

But who could have done such a terrible thing? She wondered briefly if there was anything odd about Deirdre's calm manner. The kettle came to the boil and she poured a little water into the teapot to warm it. As she did so she reflected on Deirdre's behaviour, eventually concluding that, in the face of her worst fears being proved true, Deirdre had nothing left to fear, and was able to calm herself. Or perhaps it was simply delayed shock.

Dottie finished making the tea and took it through to the drawing room. Gervase was red-eyed but calm, not quite able to smile at her as she came in, though he got up to take the tray from her and set it on the table, and thanked her for making the tea. Deirdre was wiping her eyes, so she had been weeping again, Dottie thought. Nevertheless, she was touched by Deirdre's quiet composure.

As she began to pour the tea, they heard the sound of cars arriving.

'The police are here,' Deirdre said. Gervase stood up, straightening his shoulders and scrubbing his face on his sleeve.

'Right then, let's sort out this bloody mess.'

As soon as he'd let the police into the house, he took the senior fellow into the study. Dottie hoped Gervase wasn't trying to pull rank and take over the investigation. Somehow though, she had a feeling he would be doing exactly that. She thought from things she'd heard from himself and from Penny that he was rather inclined to use his position, and no doubt this would put the policeman's back up.

Dottie and Deirdre stayed in the drawing room, waiting. The young police constable was on the telephone summoning all the people needed in such cases. Dottie took Deirdre's hand

and said, 'There will be rather of lot of people arriving, I'm afraid. They will ask a lot of questions and will be backwards and forwards to the study taking photographs. Then at some point an ambulance will come and take poor Reggie away.'

Deirdre nodded. She didn't say anything for a full minute, but then she said, 'What on earth shall I do about all his lupins?' She burst into tears on Dottie's shoulder, fortunately making enough noise that Dottie's suddenly smothered laugh was drowned out. It seemed terrible to laugh at such a time, but when Deirdre had said that, Dottie had immediately wondered to whom Reggie had bequeathed his precious plants. Poor Reggie. Dottie's eyes stung with tears. With Dottie's arm about Deirdre's shoulders, they sat and waited.

The young policeman finished telephoning eventually and knocked on the study door and went in. Dottie wished she knew what was going on in there, and what they were all saying. But then practically straight away Gervase came out. He had on his inscrutable expression, Dottie saw: his feelings and thoughts were hidden behind an impassive face. She thought this was what Penny had referred to when she had talked about his 'policeman's head'. It was a useful expression for a policeman or a card player, but not for a boyfriend.

He stood in the doorway and said, 'How are you both holding up?' but in such a toneless voice, Dottie didn't know if he was really interested in the answer, or if it was just something to say.

Nevertheless, Dottie said that she was all right, and Deirdre simply nodded.

'Good, good,' he said. He half-turned away, saying in a distracted manner, 'I'll telephone to Michaels and let him know what's happened. I'll ask him to send a car for you both to take you back to Penny's. Dottie, help Deirdre to pack a few things, will you?'

'Of course,' Dottie said, with a glance at Deirdre. Would she want to leave her home and go to Penny's?

But Deirdre simply nodded meekly once again and said, 'Yes, Gervase.'

'As soon as I've phoned Michaels, I've got to go to my parents and break the news to them before some idiot of a delivery boy tells the cook. I can't have Mother finding out like that.'

Dottie called to him as he was about to walk away. 'Gervase, are—are you quite all right?' She knew it was a ridiculous thing to ask but his calm detached manner worried her more than his earlier grief.

He gave her a fleeting smile that seemed entirely automatic. 'Quite all right, dear, thank you.'

'Do we need to wait until the inspector had spoken to us?' she asked.

'Certainly not. I've told him he may come and see you in the morning.'

'Oh.' Dottie watched him walk away to make his phone call, then moments later she heard his voice speaking softly.

She turned to Deirdre. 'Shall we go and pack a few things?'

Deirdre looked as if she had come to the end of what she could take. She managed a brief nod. Dottie helped her upstairs, persuading her to lie down for a rest, and Dottie went about the room, putting Deirdre's things into a suitcase. This reminded Dottie she was supposed to be going home in the morning: her own suitcase was almost packed and ready to go. Well, she thought, that's all off. I shall have to let Mother know I'm likely to be staying on a bit longer.

When they were ready to leave, Dottie went in search of Gervase. She found him outside the study garden door with the inspector and the constable, huddled under a huge fishing umbrella. The men looked up as she approached.

She smiled and nodded at the policemen, then to Gervase she said, 'We're going now.'

'Of course,' he said, and kissed her on the cheek. The constable was dusting the door with the grey powder they use for checking for fingerprints. Dottie looked at the ground by the door. There was a single stone step that led onto paving stones that went right around the house to the front door in one direction and the patio across the back of the house in the opposite direction. She pointed at the broken glass on the stone step.

'That's rather odd, isn't it? But I expect you've already noticed it.'

The three men looked at her as if she were raving.

'What do you mean, dear?' Gervase asked. His tone was rather chilly. He wasn't happy with her for speaking. But she felt she had to explain now that she had said something.

'I'm sure you've already discussed it. It's just, well, when we were trying to get in, we stepped on the glass.'

'Yes, Miss, the broken glass comes from the broken pane in the door,' the constable explained to her in an excessively patient voice, which infuriated her, as he waved a hand at the door to demonstrate the obvious. He and the inspector exchanged a look of amusement. Gervase merely looked annoyed.

'Of course,' Dottie said. 'But when one breaks a window from the outside, the broken glass should be mainly on the inside. If you are inside and smash a window, the glass will fall outside. As can be seen by the glass that fell on the carpet when Gervase—I'm sorry, Mr Parfitt, I mean—broke the little bit of glass by the lock, when he was attempting to open the door.'

Now they were all frowning at her. They were annoyed that she had seen something they had overlooked.

'Real life is not like the pictures, Miss,' said the inspector coldly.

'Science is science, inspector,' she snapped, 'whether in the pictures or in real life. That pane was broken from the inside. Which means the killer did it deliberately to make it appear someone broke into the house, when in fact they obviously were let in by Mr Reggie Parfitt himself. It's quite clear that he was killed by someone he neither feared nor distrusted, someone who was known to him.' With that she turned and stormed off.

Chapter Sixteen

It was a long and difficult weekend.

On arriving back at Penny's house a little after ten o'clock on Friday evening, they found the doctor there, administering a sedative to Penny, who had succumbed to an attack of hysterics on hearing the news about Reggie. So much so that Michaels had called an ambulance. Miranda had accompanied Penny to hospital where Penny had been seen by a matron, who told her to pull herself together, and sent her home again less than half an hour later.

Dottie was relieved that Penny was confined to bed, and hoped she would sleep and not make a nuisance of herself. Deirdre had enough to cope with as it was. Miranda looked as if she was enjoying the whole event, for which Dottie could have cheerfully slapped her. Margaret bustled in and out with cups of tea and cocoa, looking ghostly pale and shocked.

When Deirdre had gone up to bed, to Dottie's room, as they were sharing, Dottie went in search of Margaret. She found her in the scullery, putting some cloths to soak overnight in bleach.

'Are you all right?' she asked Margaret.

Margaret shook her head and continued to get on with what she was doing. 'I just can't believe it,' she said eventually. 'Poor Reggie. He was rather boring, but a sweet man. To think that such a terrible thing could—could happen. It's beyond bearing.' She wept softly.

Dottie still wasn't completely certain what Reggie—or indeed any of the Parfitt men—meant to Margaret, but she felt sorry for her, seeing her so upset.

Margaret wiped her eyes on her apron and finished what she was doing at the sink. Then she came over to put out the light. They returned to the kitchen. 'Well, if there's nothing else you need?' Margaret asked. Dottie felt as if Margaret had once again donned her professional persona and retreated across the distance that placed between them.

'No nothing, thank you. Goodnight,' Dottie said. She went back upstairs.

Seeing that Deirdre was asleep when she reached her room. Dottie pulled out the envelope Gervase had given her what felt like aeons ago at his home.

Caron Allan

She took out the wallet first of all. It was made of rubbed and worn brown leather, with no distinguishing marks or monogram. It was simply very plain, very well-used. Inside there was a cinema ticket stub, a pound note and a ten shilling note, and a tiny, creased photo of a girl smiling at the camera. She wore a flower in her hair, and a long, formal evening gown, with another matching flower on her shoulder. On the back of the photo it said, 'Forever in my heart, Lois'. There followed three Xs—kisses—and the date, which was February 14th 1914.

In addition to the wallet there were the cigarettes and book of matches, but they seemed ordinary, there was nothing personal about them. Lastly there was the small reference book, which was about animal anatomy. It had the name 'Clifford J Bell' written neatly in ink on the flyleaf.

Saturday was long and tedious. Penny and Miranda continued to make the most of the shocking news, with little regard for Deirdre's feelings. They were excited by the arrival of the police inspector, who took first Deirdre, then Dottie into the dining room to ask them questions.

Dottie was only surprised Gervase didn't accompany the inspector. She hadn't heard from him since the night before. It was only to be expected, she thought. After all, he would be busy with his parents. What a terrible shock it had been for all three of them. She would have liked to phone, but felt reluctant to intrude on their grief, especially after Gervase had been so annoyed with her over her comments about the glass.

As she took the seat at the dining table opposite the inspector, Dottie wondered if he would say anything about what she'd said the day before. She felt rather like a schoolchild summoned to the headmistress's office for a reprimand. She could feel herself blushing before he even asked her anything.

In fact, it was all quite easy. She told him her name and address and explained briefly how she came to know the assistant chief constable, which was how the inspector referred to Gervase. Then he asked her what had happened to make them go to Reggie Parfitt's home. At last he told her she was free to go, thanking her for her time. As she was about to leave, he said, 'By the way, what you said about the glass on the ground.'

She sighed. She had almost got away with it, she thought. She knew she had gone red again, but said with as much gravitas as she could muster, 'Yes, inspector, what about it?'

'What you said. That was the first thing our forensic specialist told us.' He gave her a grin. She left the room smiling.

On Sunday, Miranda and Penny insisted on going to church, though Dottie knew that they were far from regular attendees. She wondered if this was simply another way of enjoying the latest tragedy to its fullest. They asked her to go with them, and she intended to decline, but then she thought it might be a relief for Deirdre to have some time alone, so she accepted.

She saw Margaret sitting at the back of church with her little boy. He looked bored, his legs swinging and occasionally kicking the pew in front of him and earning him an annoyed glance from the stout lady who occupied the pew. Margaret seemed distracted and unaware of what her son was doing. Dottie saw with concern that Margaret looked terribly pale. Her eyes had deep dark circles under them. She wasn't sleeping. It could be anything that was on her mind, but to Dottie it seemed logical that it was sorrow about Reggie's death. Dottie made up her mind to ask Margaret again later if she was all right, and if there was anything she could do. Perhaps this latest event would push Margaret into leaving sooner rather than later.

Dottie was surprised to see Gervase and his parents arrive and take their seats in a pew enclosed by waist-high wooden railing. They spoke little to one another, and kept their eyes on their prayer-books or the floor throughout the service.

When it was over, Miranda and Penny rushed to speak with the Parfitts, and Dottie followed them over. After the others had turned from Gervase to talk to his parents and the vicar, Dottie took her chance.

'Are you still angry with me?' she asked.

He smiled and leaned to kiss her cheek. 'No dear, of course not.' He looked pale and tired, but his smile was warm. 'Is it all right if I come over later?' He took her hand and put it through his arm. They turned and began to follow the parishioners from the church.

She was surprised. 'Yes of course. You should know you don't need to ask.'

'Just wanted to check. I'm afraid I had completely forgotten about your plans to go home yesterday. I'm so glad you're still here. Do you know when you're leaving?'

She shook her head. 'I haven't thought about it yet. But Deirdre is going home tomorrow. I think it will be a lot more restful for her to be in her own home. Miranda and Penny are being mawkish to a ludicrous degree. It's fraying my nerves, so I hate to think what it's doing to poor Deirdre.'

'Ah yes,' he said. 'My parents are going to stay with Deirdre for a while, and help her sort things out. It will be good for all of them.'

'Do you know if she plans to stay in the house, or will she sell it and move into something smaller?'

He shrugged. 'I don't know. It's probably still a bit soon to ask her about that.'

'True.' Dottie and he walked out into the bright sunshine. Her mood seemed to lift as soon as she felt the sun's warmth on her. The church had been so cold and dark. She felt as though she was coming to life after a long sleep. 'And how are you, Gervase?'

'I'm a mess,' he said frankly. 'But I'm going to get to the bottom of this, if it's the last thing I do. I owe him that at least, my little brother.'

Dottie shook her head, frustrated. She knew it. 'You must leave it to the inspector. You're too close. You can't get involved in this.'

He glared at her, but undaunted she continued. 'Surely you realise that if Reggie was killed by someone he knows, why, then it's someone you are likely to know too! You must leave it to the inspector to investigate.'

'He's taking too long. I need to know—I need...' His voice broke and he turned away for a minute. When he turned back, he kissed her cheek again and said simply, 'See you later, dear.' He turned back a second time, and called, his voice anxious, 'You won't go home to London without telling me?'

She smiled. 'Of course not.' He nodded, content with that, and strode off.

When he arrived later, though, it was with his parents. Penny and Miranda dominated the conversation as if it were an ordinary social occasion and not a time of great sadness for them. They stayed a bare hour. Dottie went out to the car with Gervase to see them off, in the hope of some moments alone with him. But his mother called to him. Although she spared a smile for Dottie, it didn't reach her eyes. Dottie felt Gervase's mother didn't like her, but told herself it might just be that she was in mourning. But there was no time for talking together, no time for a kiss. He didn't even wave as he drove them away.

On Monday morning, Deirdre returned to her own home, and Dottie went with her just so that she wouldn't be going into the house alone. The plan was that Edwin and Evangeline Parfitt would join her around mid-morning; as soon as she saw that Deirdre was unpacked and settled, Dottie would return to Penny's.

Deirdre's maid was there, pale and sorrowful. She kept following Deirdre around, wringing her hands and saying repeatedly, 'Oh my dear ma'am!'

It was very trying, Dottie thought. Finally, feeling that she couldn't cope with any more of it, Dottie said to the maid, 'Please take Mrs Parfitt's suitcase upstairs and unpack it, and then we'd like some coffee in the morning room.'

The maid seemed glad to be reminded that she had things to do. She hurried off.

Dottie turned to see Deirdre opening the door of the study, about to go in. With trepidation, Dottie followed.

The desk was still there, of course. The blotter had gone—taken away by the police as part of their evidence-gathering, Dottie assumed. The room reeked of death. Deirdre went to open the garden door but it was nailed shut following Gervase's forced entrance, and several planks had been put across the outside until it was repaired.

Deirdre looked around helplessly and sat down on the arm of a deep leather chair in a corner. She began to cry. Dottie let her weep. There was nothing she could say or do that would lessen the impact. She stood beside Deirdre with her arm about Deirdre's shoulders and waited. As the crying subsided, Dottie went over to the doors and looked out between the planks.

The maid came in and said, 'Please Miss, I've put the coffee in the morning room, and now I'm taking up the suitcase and I'll put Mrs Parfitt's things away. Is there anything else you need before I do that?'

Dottie shook her head, then said, 'Could you arrange for someone to come out and mend the door tomorrow? And make sure that Mr Parfitt's study is thoroughly cleaned and aired once Mrs Parfitt goes upstairs to lie down. Mr Parfitt's parents are coming to stay for a few days, and Mr Parfitt senior may wish to use this room.'

'Very good, Miss.'

Dottie took Deirdre into the morning room and they sat drinking their coffee. Soon Edwin and Evangeline would be here. Dottie hadn't had a chance to observe them together, so she didn't know whether or not Deirdre got on well with her in-laws. Surely, they would be united in grief and support one another? That said, Dottie wasn't sure how much comfort she might derive from them, if she were in Deirdre's place.

They arrived a little sooner than expected. Again, Dottie felt that they showed no pleasure in seeing her, and although she tried to make allowances for the circumstances, she felt they had taken against her. She stayed only long enough for the impatient, irritable Edwin to carry all their luggage upstairs, and for the quiet, competent Evangeline to coax Deirdre to go up to her room to rest. Then the Parfitt's driver took Dottie back to Penny's.

On the way there, Dottie leaned back against the seat and tried to block everything out. She dreaded getting back and finding Penny still indulging in hysterics. It was all too much.

Fortune smiled on Dottie. Miranda was playing soft little piano pieces in the morning room, and Penny was in her room lying down: the house was, for the first time since her visit began, an oasis of peace. Dottie decided to have a bath. It was rather an odd time of day, but she wanted to be able to go in, lock the door, and be alone.

She ran the water, adding just a little cold so that the temperature was slightly too hot: just the way she liked it. She threw in a good handful of scented crystals and gave them a swish round in the water. She got in, and within a minute, she was asleep.

She awoke to find the water cold and that she had a crick in her neck. Getting out and scrubbing herself briskly with the towel, she wondered how Gervase was getting on and whether he was back in his office today. She hoped he would visit that evening—it felt like forever since she had been in his arms. She was worried about him. In addition she wanted to know how the police were getting on with finding his brother's killer.

Dottie was dressed and towelling her hair dry in her room when she heard the phone ring. After several rings Dottie thought she had better go down and answer it. As she ran down the stairs, she wondered what Margaret was up to. She was beginning to feel that she was the only one who ever answered the wretched machine.

Somewhat breathlessly, Dottie snatched up the receiver, afraid the caller would grow impatient and ring off.

'Hello?' was all she had time to say.

'Well I have to say, Miss Scott, it really is too bad of you!' began the woman at the other end. Dottie had no idea what she was talking about.

'I'm sorry, this is not Miss Scott speaking. My name is Miss Manderson,' she interrupted, 'I'm a guest of Mrs Parfitt. Can I help you at all?'

The caller caught her breath and apologised with embarrassed haste. 'Miss Benson here. Simon's teacher, you know. At the school in the village. I know he is perfectly capable of coming home on his own, but Miss Scott did promise to come and see me today, so naturally the child stayed here to be collected. But she's half an hour late! Really, I can't hang on any longer. I shall send Simon home. He has a note for his mother; please remind him to give it to her.'

'Oh! Yes, of course. I'm sorry...'

The teacher said goodbye and hung up. Dottie, frowning in puzzlement, went into the kitchen.

There was no one there. The stove was cold, the lights were off, the room was empty. Where was Margaret?

Dottie went upstairs and knocked on Penny's door. Nothing happened. She knocked again. Now there was a sleepy murmur which Dottie chose to take as permission to enter. She went in to find the room gloomy in spite of the bright sunny day. Penny had the covers pulled up to her chin. Surely, in this heat, she was sweltering under all those layers, Dottie thought.

'Sorry to disturb you, Penny. There was just a phone call for Margaret from the school teacher. She was expecting Margaret to come and see her, but Margaret hasn't turned up. Do you know where she is at all? I can't seem to find her.'

'Margaret is receiving calls on my telephone? How dare she!' Penny said crossly. 'I'll soon put a stop to that. What a cheek!'

Dottie repressed a sigh. As usual the focus of Penny's thoughts was Penny herself. 'Yes, it is rather. Er, but about what the teacher said... would Margaret have gone somewhere, do you think?' She felt rather helpless. Was it odd that Margaret wasn't there? Perhaps it wasn't.

'How should I know? She could be in her room, I suppose.'

'Ah yes, I'll check,' Dottie said, feeling foolish for not having thought of that sooner. Perhaps Margaret had been taken ill, or—or she could even be doing some work up there. Dottie hurried across the upstairs hall, through the door and onto the back stairs that took her up to the next floor, and the attics.

She found a little dark bathroom, and a sitting room not much bigger, and twice as gloomy. Dottie shuddered. She had never seen a house so full of dreary dark rooms as this. The next room appeared to belong to Simon—there were some toy cars and a model ship on a shelf beside the bed, with a bear and a book of adventure stories on the counterpane waiting for the boy to come home. There was an adjoining door, and when Dottie tapped on the panel and looked round the door, she saw it was another bedroom, clearly that of Margaret herself. There was no one there.

Chapter Seventeen

Dottie set the plate of mashed potatoes, diced carrots, and fishcakes in front of Simon, relieved she'd only had to reheat the fishcakes and not make them from scratch.

Simon said a clear, polite, 'Thank you,' and began to eat, neatly and with precision. His actions reminded Dottie forcibly of Reggie's dancing. Was it possible...? Or was she seeing a ghost of the overall Parfitt pattern, a collection of general attributes rather than Reggie's own specific qualities?

'It's all in my head,' she murmured. Simon gave her a questioning look. She smiled at him. 'Don't you worry,' she said. But the fact that she'd said these words out loud made her feel even more uncomfortable about Margaret's absence. Simon had been home for almost two hours now, and still there was no word from Margaret. The kitchen was silent with the lack of her. Her cigarettes and a box of matches sat on the dresser beside the table, alongside a pair of Simon's socks she'd been darning, the needle still attached and sticking up from the top of one. Her slippers were pushed tidily under the chair where she sat when she was taking a break from cooking or cleaning.

The little boy stoically ate all his food, put his knife and fork together, slid out of his seat and carried the plate across to place it in the sink. He came back and sat down again. His 'Very nice thank you,' brought smarting tears to Dottie's eyes and she had to turn away. She concentrated on dessert.

'Tinned fruit and cream, or apple pie and custard?'

'Apple pie please, and please may I have lots and lots and lots of custard?'

She couldn't help laughing at his cheeky face. 'You may!' She prepared this for him and accompanied it with a glass of milk. That should hold him for a bit. As Simon ate, Dottie went in search of Penny.

She found her sitting at her dressing table, fussing over her nails. Miranda was sprawled across the bed, reading a magazine.

'Penny,' Dottie began, and in the mirror she saw Penny's frown hastily hidden. A bright false smile took its place, and she made a show of setting down her nail-file and buffer and turning to face Dottie.

'Yes, Dottie dear?' Her voice held just the right amount of mild vexation, as if she were constantly interrupted by trivialities and was endeavouring to remain understanding and patient. Dottie felt the role of demanding house-guest had fallen on her. But Dottie had more important things to worry about.

'I'm worried about Margaret. Where is she, and what am I to tell Simon?'

Penny's forehead furrowed delicately. Dottie knew exactly what Penny was going to say. It was as though she was in a three-act play. Every line had been studied and absorbed, every spontaneous gesture carefully practised in advance of need.

'Who is Simon, dear?' Her tone was patronising, as if he was some imaginary friend Dottie had invented. In the mirror, Penny exchanged a sly glance with her sister, who hid a snigger.

Through gritted teeth, Dottie said, 'Simon is Margaret's little boy. He's been living here for three years. Surely you've noticed?'

Penny didn't like that at all. She snapped back to her mirror and began banging about with brushes and potions. She applied lipstick to her top lip before she replied, 'Don't forget to whom you're talking, young lady. I believe you are still a guest in my home.'

Dottie took a deep breath. There was no point in arguing. She softened her tone. 'You're quite right, Penny, I forgot myself. I'm very sorry. I— I'm just so worried about Margaret.'

'She'll come back when she's ready. It's not the first time. I should think the child's used to it by now.'

'Really? But she seems such a devoted...'

'Oh! Well, you've only just met her, haven't you? I've known her since childhood. She's not terribly reliable, I'm afraid. Never has been.'

'Are you sure we can't call someone—or—perhaps—it might just be worth ringing the hospital, or the police, or—er...'

'Certainly not! I'm not running up a large telephone bill because of her! Absolutely not. Tell the child to go to bed. I'm sure she'll be back in the morning. Now I'd like to finish getting ready for dinner, if you don't mind. Just because we have no guests tonight doesn't mean we lower our standards.'

Dottie almost dropped a curtsey as she left.

Returning to the kitchen, Dottie glanced at the clock. Half past six. It was a little early to send Simon to bed. But he had finished his pudding and his milk. The bowl, spoon and glass were now in the sink with his plate, knife and fork.

'Perhaps Mummy will be back late?' he suggested.

'Yes,' Dottie said, 'I think she may well have been delayed.'

'Shall I do my homework?'

Dottie's heart melted a little bit more. 'Yes, Simon, dear, I think that's an excellent idea. Do you need any help? Because if it's arithmetic, I'm not sure I'll be much use to you.'

'It's Latin and history,' he told her. They both wrinkled their noses.

'I detested Latin when I was at school,' Dottie said. He grinned at her.

'Everyone does. Mummy says it's important for when I go to my new prep school. But I'd much rather learn a bit more about dinosaurs.'

'Me too!' Dottie said. She pulled out a chair, and with a theatrical sigh, reached for his Latin primer.

An hour later and she'd left him in bed reading a book about dinosaurs. There was still no sign of Margaret, nor any message from her, and Dottie was worried sick. In the morning, if Margaret was still absent, Dottie promised herself she would call the police, regardless of Penny's objections.

They ate a light dinner prepared by Dottie and received with little gratitude by Penny and Miranda. As Dottie took her seat at the table, she couldn't help feeling that Penny seemed slightly affronted by her presence. Have I simply become the new Margaret, Dottie wondered. Certainly, neither Penny nor her sister had done anything to help with the meal, nor even seemed capable of thinking about practical matters. They just seemed to think it entirely their due to sit at leisure whilst Penny's guest cooked, cleaned and tidied. And like an idiot, Dottie reminded herself, I did it all. And to think Penny spoke of letting Margaret go. What on earth does she think she will do without her?

Thinking of Margaret gave Dottie a horrid lurching sensation in her stomach. Clearly Penny's plan to dismiss Margaret would not now happen. Even though it had only been a few hours since Margaret had gone, Dottie was as certain as she could be that Margaret would not be returning. Whether by accident or design, Dottie was convinced Margaret was gone forever.

Abruptly, Dottie said, 'I hope you don't mind but I'd like to telephone Gervase. I shall, of course, pay for the call.' She got to her feet.

Penny, caught with a mouthful of meat and gravy, could only shrug her shoulders. Miranda just stared at her.

Dottie took that for permission and hurried to the phone in the hall, but then of course, it struck her she didn't know his number. There was a slim notebook on the shelf above the telephone table, and it was open at the page of surnames beginning with P. Dottie found Gervase's number straight away. She rang, and listened to the clicks before the ringing of the bell at the other end. Thank goodness this locale was more up-to-date than most, with direct dialling there was no need to go through the operator and thus incur delays.

Michaels answered. Dottie gave her name and asked to speak with Gervase urgently. But you couldn't hurry a butler and it took easily three minutes before she heard footsteps echoing across the polished wooden floor of Gervase's lovely hall, then a second later, his voice, warm but concerned, spoke in her ear.

'Dottie? Is that you, dear?'

'Oh Gervase!' Suddenly she felt overwhelmed, and she burst into tears.

When she failed to compose herself after a few moments, Gervase made a decision. 'Right,' he said, 'I'll be there in ten minutes. Hang on, Dearest.'

And he slammed down the phone.

The line went dead. Dottie was left fishing in her sleeve for a handkerchief, still holding the silent receiver in her hand. Hiccupping, she returned to the dining room.

'What on earth is the matter, child?' Penny demanded sharply. Her plate, like Miranda's was empty. Obviously they were not so concerned about Margaret that it spoiled their appetites.

Dottie resumed her seat at the table. She wiped her eyes for the second time and blew her nose.

'It's nothing really, I-I just got upset when I spoke to Gervase. He's on his way over.'

'He's got enough to deal with, what with Reggie!' Miranda said with a laugh of disbelief.

'Oh, for goodness' sake, Dottie, really!' Penny added, 'This is simply ridiculous. You can't expect an important man like Gervase to run all over the place after a silly little girl. Have some control, do!'

Dottie thought that was a bit rich after the fuss Penny seemed to make about the least little thing, and the way she seemed to think Gervase lived only to do her bidding. But then, Dottie thought, Penny was not the kind of person to see someone else's point of view, and her own feelings were always the most important to her. But Dottie said nothing, mainly because she was horribly afraid that there was more than a grain of truth in what they had just said. If only she had had more control, she could have just asked him what she should do, and Gervase wouldn't have had to hurry away from his dinner, and she wouldn't have added to the burden of worry he already had. Dottie cleared the table and went to wash the dishes.

Gervase was as good as his word, arriving a bare ten minutes later. Dottie was by then dreading his reaction when he knew why she had been so upset.

He came in to find her in the kitchen, still drying the dishes and putting them away. Penny and Miranda were sitting at the kitchen table, which Dottie thought was odd, as they didn't offer any help and seemed to find the position uncomfortable. As soon as she saw Gervase, Penny threw herself at him.

'Thank goodness you're here! We're in such a state. It's Margaret. She's disappeared without a trace. We're beside ourselves with worry.'

He disengaged Penny's fingers from his jacket, saying calmly, 'That explains why no one answered the door just now. I had to use your spare key.' He couldn't help seeing Dottie's look of utter disbelief. He turned to Dottie, tweaked the towel out of her hand, and throwing it aside, he put his arms around her.

'Are you all right, darling?' He spoke softly, for her ears alone.

She nodded, not trusting herself to speak. He guided her to the table, seated her, and took the seat opposite Penny and Miranda, who glared at Dottie.

'Tell me everything.' He spoke to Dottie but Penny was the one who began to speak.

'Gervase, darling, now you mustn't be cross, but we're just a little concerned. We haven't seen Margaret since breakfast-time, and there's been no word from her. We don't know what to think. And there's poor little Stephen to think about. He'll have to go into an orphanage.'

'Simon,' both Dottie and Gervase said. Gervase frowned, and Dottie said:

'An orphanage? But—no, Penny, he can't possibly...'

Gervase shot Penny a furious look. 'What on earth are you talking about?'

'I realise it must sound dreadfully harsh, but really, I can't possibly keep him here.' Penny's tone was petulant. Miranda was nodding vigorously.

'Oh absolutely,' she said.

Gervase shook his head. 'I can't believe what I'm hearing. What are you talking about? Surely you can't think Margaret is not coming back?'

Penny said, 'We don't know what to think, Gervase. But I'm adamant I'm not keeping that little brat here.'

Gervase turned back to Dottie. 'Tell me everything.'

The police arrived less than an hour later. Penny, outraged at what she saw as an unnecessary fuss, retired to bed, much to Dottie's relief. Miranda went to sit in the drawing room and listen to the radio. The sergeant listened to Dottie as she explained when she last saw Margaret and gave a little background information about Margaret and the household. He wrote down her description of Margaret and promised a search would commence immediately. Dottie left him in discussion with Gervase in the dining room and went to the kitchen to make the men coffee.

Waiting for the kettle to boil, she stood looking out the window. The intermittent rain had stopped again, and the garden was still sunlit at half past ten. The long summer days were wonderful, she thought, but this one had seemed neverending. The sun streaked the lawn and plants with warm golds and oranges, but Dottie was shivering.

'Where are you, Margaret?' she whispered. In her heart she felt an overwhelming conviction: Margaret was dead. She would not return for her son.

Chapter Eighteen

Gervase came back in the morning. He declined a cup of coffee and stood hovering in the doorway as if ready for action. 'Perhaps we might take a look in Margaret's room?' he suggested.

Dottie said, 'Surely the police have searched her room? They went up there last night.'

'I want to check it for myself.'

'Of course,' she said. They went into the hall. 'I took a quick look in there myself yesterday. But it was only to see if she was in bed, or something. I thought she might be ill. She hasn't looked too well since Reggie... I didn't really have a good look around.'

To Dottie, it felt like a testing moment. She began to feel afraid of what she might discover. When he held back at the foot of the stairs to allow her to precede him, she went on past him gladly, telling herself she would need to show him the way. Her chest felt tight with the tension. She couldn't bear it. Because if he knew the way to Margaret's room...

She went on ahead, talking non-stop. She had no idea what she was saying; it didn't matter in any case. All that mattered was that she should fill the silence, and she mustn't look into his eyes in case she should read the truth there.

'It's this way,' she told him, and turned through the staff door to go up the next flight of stairs. 'Margaret's room is along here, next to Simon's, of course.'

'Is he in his room?'

It was the first thing he'd said for two minutes—the first thing he'd had the chance of saying, with all her talk.

'No, he's downstairs in the kitchen. Mrs Bains is making cakes and he's helping.'

Gervase laughed. 'Excellent. That's one of the favourite occupations of small boys, as I can personally attest.'

She smiled but didn't meet his eyes.

'I know you're anxious about Margaret, Dottie darling, but have I done something to upset you?' He halted on reaching the landing and pulled her to him. With gentle hands he cupped her face and tilted it up to look into his eyes. 'Dottie?' He said her name softly, lovingly, and all her doubts fell away. He kissed her, and she knew she would forgive him anything and everything in that moment. There was a pause, and he kissed her again, lightly this time, on the tip of her nose, and he gave her a sad smile. 'Come on, dear. It might all turn out all right, it's too soon to give up hope yet.'

But he stepped over and opened the third door, Margaret's door, and at that moment her heart knew what her head had always believed: he was Simon's father.

She took a steadying breath as she stared at his shoulders. He went into the room, standing there in the middle of the floor and looking around him. She took another breath. He had lied all along, but only to keep her from being upset, she told herself now. And now, of all times, it was not the moment to argue over the events of the past. She took another breath and willed it all to fall away: her sense of betrayal, the childish urge to be his one and only love, the need to keep him up there on that pedestal.

She went to open the drawers of the bedside cabinet. It gave her a moment or two to hide her tears and pull herself together. With Gervase crossing to the window, it was easy to quickly brush the tears away and put a smile on her face as she turned to reply to his comment, 'Not much here, is there?'

'No, there isn't.' She made herself focus on the moment. She looked inside the narrow wardrobe.

'Her clothes are gone,' he observed, peering over her shoulder.

'Yes.'

He was frowning and she could hear it in his voice. 'So she's simply run away.'

But was he angry because he thought she'd left him without a word, or because the police were looking for her as a missing person, thinking she might have suffered harm?

Dottie sighed. She felt cold and depressed. 'She hasn't run away.' She indicated the empty wardrobe, with its half-dozen bare wire hangers. 'This is all just a smokescreen.'

He stared at her. This time, he was prepared to listen to what she had to say. 'What makes you say that?'

Dottie counted the points on her fingers. 'Firstly, she would never leave her son.' And in her head she said, your son. 'And secondly, no woman goes away without her under-things or her powder compact.' She indicated the drawers by the bed.

He took a look. 'Hmm. Interesting.'

She couldn't help noticing that some of Margaret's undergarments were new and expensive-looking. Well beyond the wages of a domestic servant. A gift then. From her lover. Dottie forced herself to look away, but then she had to look back. She watched him searching through everything and couldn't keep from picturing him buying the garments, running his hands over the fine delicate fabrics. She wondered if he recognised any of the items. He slammed the drawer shut, making her jump.

And then she saw it. A slip of paper that had fallen down between the bed and the bedside cabinet, just poking out from under the bed. She pointed to it, and Gervase bent and pulled it out. He flattened it out and read out loud:

'I'm so very sorry. I've been so wicked. I've done such a terrible thing.

I can't forgive myself. Please look after Simon. I'm so sorry.

Margaret.'

When they returned the following morning, naturally the police insisted on speaking to Simon about his mother. The boy sat, rigid and pale, at the kitchen table, an untouched glass of milk and a slice of cherry cake beside him. Dottie took the seat next to him, and a kindly sergeant sat opposite.

He smiled at Simon and said, 'Now then, young sir, perhaps you'd be kind enough to tell me when you last saw your mother? It will help us to get her back to you as soon as possible.'

Simon sent him a sceptical look, and Dottie covered her mouth with her hand. Simon spoke up clearly and concisely, expressing himself as well as a child of eleven or twelve.

As the sergeant made a note of everything Simon told him, he quirked an eyebrow at Dottie, impressed with the lad's intelligence and composure. Simon's account was still the same as the one he'd given Dottie the afternoon before. At the end, he looked at her a little uncertainly, and she patted his arm.

'Well done, Simon,' she said, and the sergeant nodded vigorously.

'Yes indeed, very clear, thank you, young fellow.' The sergeant sipped the tea Dottie had made for him. By now she had lost count of how many pots of tea she'd made for the police. 'Now then, I'd just like to have a word with Miss Manderson alone, so if you don't mind taking yourself off somewhere for a few minutes.'

'You could take your milk and cake into the garden,' Dottie suggested. 'It's lovely and sunny.'

'I'm not allowed to take glasses into the garden.'

'Oh—er—well, just the cake then. You can have the milk when you come back.'

He slid down from the table, and very carefully, using both hands, he carried the plate of cake to the door. He turned back. 'My mummy's a nice lady,' he said. 'I don't want anyone to think bad things about her.'

Dottie and the sergeant exchanged a look. 'No, of course not, dear. I know your mummy—she's a very nice and kind lady, and she loves you very much,' Dottie told him. She felt as though her heart was breaking.

Simon said, 'Is she dead?'

Completely taken aback, the sergeant said, far too heartily, 'Now why would you think a thing like that? Of course she's not...'

But Simon set down the cake and ran outside with a sob, slamming the door behind him. Dottie's eyes filled with tears.

'Now don't you take on, young lady, we've got to hope for the best.'

'But the note...' She shook her head and dabbed at her face with her handkerchief. 'I've got a terrible feeling he's right. I don't know Margaret very well, no matter what I said to Simon, but I do know this: she loves him, and she always puts him first. She would never go anywhere without him unless she had no choice about the matter.'

'Mrs Parfitt says she's done this before,' the sergeant commented. Dottie wasn't sure quite how much to say about her hostess.

'I'm not sure Mrs Parfitt likes Margaret very much.'

'So you don't think she's the kind of woman to go off like this on a jaunt for a day or two?'

'As I said, I don't know her very well. I only met Mrs Parfitt recently and she invited me to stay with her. But from what I've seen of Margaret, she seems to be a devoted mother. She confided to me just two days ago that she is hoping to leave here and buy her own home with the legacy she received from Mrs Parfitt's late husband. She said she was going to choose a house near to a good school so that her son could get a decent education. And then there's the note,' she reminded him.

He sent a look over his shoulder and leaned closer to Dottie. 'Ah the note. Yes, well let's leave that on one side for the moment. Now I understand Mrs Parfitt's husband left the maid money in his will?'

'Yes. Though I don't know any details. Only that Margaret was so looking forward to getting away from here and giving up domestic work.'

The sergeant made a note. Then he asked Dottie the question she'd been expecting all along. 'Do you know where the boy's father is?'

A face came into her mind, but she said simply, 'I don't have any actual knowledge about that.'

'Just a few ideas, hmm? Well, well, it wouldn't be the first time a man moved his mistress into the marital home.' He secured the notebook with a rubber band then put it into his jacket pocket. He got up. 'Right then, Miss, I'll be in touch.'

'Thank you.'

'And obviously if you hear anything at all, you'll let me know.'

'Oh, of course.' Dottie was wringing her hands. She walked him to the back door. Desperate for hope she said, 'Do you really think she might? Turn up, I mean?'

He shook his head. 'No, me duck, I'm sorry, I don't think she will. The note seems to point that way.'

She nodded and turned away. So much for hope for the best, she thought.

It was a long and anxious afternoon. Dottie and the daily woman between them managed to keep Simon occupied, and got on with the cleaning, and saw to everyone's meals. Over a cup of tea, Dottie said to the woman, whose name was Winnie Bains, 'If Mrs Parfitt agrees, could you possibly come and live in for a while, just until things are a bit less... you know?'

Mrs Bains said she would be delighted. She was a widow with three adult sons all married and living in their own homes so had no one depending on her. Dottie was hugely relieved. Now all she had to do was catch Penny in a good mood and put it to her. Which may well prove to be the tricky bit.

Once Simon was in bed that night, and the dinner things had been washed and put away, Dottie went to sit in the drawing room with Penny and Miranda. The first thing she noticed was that Penny seemed almost surprised that Dottie should emerge from the kitchen and take a seat in the same room as them. She no longer thought of Dottie as a house guest, apparently. There was a restraint between them. Dottie felt certain that, in Penny's mind, Dottie was now the new domestic servant—and no longer a guest or social equal.

'What a mess,' Dottie said, then all too late realised she had spoken out loud.

'Well, when she comes back, she shall have her dismissal,' Penny said, looking up from a magazine. 'I'm simply furious with Margaret.'

'Quite right too,' chipped in Miranda, 'She's got no right to do it. She's put you in a perfectly awful position as regards the child, the housework, everything.'

Dottie thought that was a bit much, seeing that neither of them had lifted a finger to help for the last two days. She murmured a vague response.

It seemed as good a time as any, so very quickly, and approaching the topic with the suggestion of how much easier and more convenient it would make Penny's life, Dottie explained about Mrs Bains, but it quickly became clear that Penny was reluctant to spend the extra money. She even seemed rather surprised Mrs Bains wouldn't do longer hours just for the love of it. Dottie decided to let the matter drop. There was nothing to be gained from pushing Penny, she could be stubborn when she liked.

Just then there was a knock at the front door. Penny looked at Dottie, who bit back irritation and the urge to stamp and scream. 'Shall I go and see who that is?' she suggested mildly.

'Please, dear.' Penny sighed wearily and passed a hand over her eyes.

Chapter Nineteen

It was Gervase. He took in her weary harried look. Leaning forward to kiss her on the cheek, he said, 'Want to get out for a bit?'

'Oh yes please!'

'Right then.' He turned as if to head back to his car, but Dottie pulled him inside.

'Oh no you don't. You can explain to Penny and Miranda while I go and change my dress and put on some lipstick.'

'What? Must I?' But he laughed. 'Very well, go and get ready and I shall generously go and get your leave authorised.'

Running upstairs and flinging wide the wardrobe doors, frantically trying to think what she should wear for an impromptu undisclosed outing, she was half-laughing at the ridiculous situation she'd got herself into, and half furious.

When she came down five minutes later, Penny was petulant and annoyed, and Miranda was just plain jealous. All the more reason to get out of the house, Dottie thought. Gervase was saying to Penny, 'Now look, you've got to stay in because of the child. You can't leave him in the house all on his own. And if you'd got any sense at all, you'd get that daily woman of yours to do more hours to help out. I'm sure she'd like the extra money, and it's not as though you can't afford it.'

His patience, never much in evidence at the best of times, sounded as though it was wearing very thin. Doubtless he'd already said this speech several times in one form or another.

'He's not my responsibility. I don't see why I should have to stay at home. You always take Dottie out, and you leave me behind. It's not fair!' If she had stamped her foot or thrown herself on the floor in a tantrum, Dottie would not have been at all surprised.

'We're going out, and that's that!' Gervase said. 'And kindly remember, you invited Dottie here as your guest. She's not your skivvy.'

Penny muttered something low and unintelligible to Dottie, though Gervase must have caught her words as he looked furious. He stormed out to his car, and Dottie, caught in the doorway as Penny came after him, simply turned and ran after him, annoyed at the guilt she felt.

Penny slammed the door behind him, and Dottie dreaded to think how she would behave when Dottie returned. Hopefully she'd have taken to her bed again. Dottie got into the car, Gervase leaned across to kiss her on the mouth, and they set off.

He halted the car beside a lake, and they sat and watched the sun setting behind the trees, spilling oranges and pinks across the rippling water.

Gervase seemed inclined to be amorous, but Dottie wanted to talk about Margaret. She pushed him away.

'Behave yourself,' and laughed at the way he rolled his eyes in mock irritation. But he settled beside her, an arm about her shoulders, his fingers playing with her hair as she vented her anxiety.

'I'm so worried about Margaret. What if she doesn't come back? What will happen to Simon? We didn't have a chance to really get to know each other,' Dottie said, 'Although she did say that she had been left money by Artie in his will and was going to use it to move away and buy a house, and put Simon into a good school.'

'Ah. Interesting,' he said.

She was frustrated that he didn't say more. 'I know it's none of my business but why did Artie leave money away from his wife to Margaret? I mean, it's not as though he was Simon's father, even though Penny seems to believe he was. Which is why she resented their presence in the house so much.'

'Hmm,' was all he said. She felt like thumping him. Or getting hold of him and shaking him until he said something useful. Or honest.

This prompted her to take a deep breath and making a decision on the spur of the moment, she said, 'I feel it's time for me to go home. I've already been here for a week longer than I intended, and to be frank, Penny and I do not really see eye to eye, and Miranda seems to egg Penny on all the time. Together they are unbearable. Especially since Margaret...'

'I know they've been taking advantage of your good nature, dear, you really should put your foot down. I've told Penny to get the daily woman in for more hours.'

'Winnie Bains? Yes, I've already asked her if she could help out a bit more, and she's perfectly willing, but Penny wasn't at all happy about that, she said I had acted out of turn. And in any case, it's just easier to get on with things. Miranda just sits there laughing at everyone like we're only there to entertain her. And Penny makes such a song and dance about the simplest things, and— sorry, of course I'm completely forgetting they are dear friends of yours...'

'Not so dear that I'm blind to their faults. Neither of them have ever been the sort to set to in a crisis, I'm afraid.'

'Well, Penny talked last week about getting rid of Margaret.' It was a relief for Dottie to vent her feelings. 'Yet she seems incapable of doing the least little thing for herself. I don't know how she thinks she'll manage. And as for poor little

Simon—how can she pretend she doesn't even know his name! What is to become of him, I'd like to know. No one seems to give him a moment's thought. I'm the one who's been getting his meals, getting him to bed, helping him with his schoolwork. When is someone going to give him a home, or—or the care he needs, or...' And suddenly she was weeping. It wasn't about Penny, or the housework. It was all about a small boy seemingly without a home or loved ones.

Gervase took the opportunity to sweep her into his arms and kiss her, assuring her in the most vigorous language that he would make certain Simon was looked after, and soon. It was at least a partial consolation.

There was a banging on the car windscreen. They shot apart. A torch shone in at them through the glass. Dottie was astonished to find it had grown dark as they had talked and kissed; the sunset had faded completely into night. Gervase wound down the window.

'What is it?' he demanded in his rather superior tone.

'Come on, hop it! We don't want no courting couples round here. I'll do the two of you for indecent behaviour!'

Dottie now caught sight of the silver buttons on his tunic, and the tall helmet that bent into view as he spoke to Gervase. She would have laughed, but Gervase seemed quite angry.

'Do you know who I am?'

Dottie felt a dropping sensation inside. She detested men who said that kind of thing. She was surprised at him but felt she had known all along he was inclined to a certain vanity about his position.

The policeman admitted he didn't know Gervase at all, adding, 'And I don't care if you're the bleedin' chief constable, there's no hanky panky round here! Decent folks don't behave this way.'

'I'm Gervase Parfitt. If not exactly the chief constable, I am at least the assistant chief constable,' said Gervase, in the haughtiest voice Dottie had ever heard. 'And, not that it's any of your concern, there's no 'hanky panky' as you put it going on here. My fiancée was upset and I was comforting her during a private discussion. Any more of your insubordination, my man, and you'll be out on your ear. I hope I've made myself clear?'

'Oh—er—yes indeed. Terribly sorry, sir. I meant no offense, it was just a misunderstanding. We 'as problems round 'ere wiv youngsters neckin' in cars.' The man's dismay was unmistakable. He lowered his beam and backed away.

'Very well, then,' Gervase said, and snapped his window shut again.

'You were a bit harsh,' Dottie pointed out.

'Nonsense. Damned cheek.' He set the car in motion. 'I'll get you back to Penny's. I'll pop in for a little while, cheer her up by having a nightcap.'

'I can't believe you told that chap we were engaged, too!'

He shot her an amused look. 'Pure wishful thinking, Dottie dear.' He squeezed her hand briefly before turning the car out onto the road again. She couldn't help smiling at that.

It took Gervase a while to get round Penny and lure her into a smile and a conversation. Dottie was still annoyed with Gervase, and she was certain Penny picked up on this and took it to mean that the romance wasn't going as well as it should. She alluded once or twice to their supposed 'tiff', but neither Dottie nor Gervase felt inclined to satisfy her curiosity about it.

Gervase drank a small brandy, and he and Penny chatted about some show they had seen in the Spring. Miranda listened and joined in the conversation, now laughing and animated with a man in the room to show off to. Dottie went to check on Simon, then made herself a cup of tea. When she came back into the room, Penny said,

'Oh, by the way, Dottie, dear, I thought you'd be glad to know, I've arranged for my daily woman, Mrs—er—?'

'Mrs Bains?' Dottie supplied, not taken in for a moment by Penny's inability to recall the name of the woman who had worked in her house five days a week for almost ten years. Although, strictly speaking, it was of no account to Dottie, as she hoped to be leaving shortly.

'That's it, yes! How do you do it, dear? You're so good at the little details, aren't you? Anyway, yes Mrs Bains. She's going to come and stay for a few weeks until things get sorted. I thought that would be the best thing all round.'

'Oh definitely,' Dottie said. She was too tired to say more.

Dottie had finally fallen into a deep sleep, after lying awake well into the early hours, unable to shake off her concerns about Margaret, and Simon too. She woke and with a sense of dread for the coming day, she made herself get out of bed and go and have a bath. She was dressed and on her way downstairs when the phone rang. The bell echoed around the hall with its strident demand for attention. Dottie was annoyed that her first reaction was one of fear that the sound would disturb Penny or Miranda. She hurried to the back of the hall, and as she reached for the receiver, suddenly the thought hit her: Margaret.

'Yes?'

At once a policeman began to talk in her ear, and as she heard what he said, she turned to see Simon, staring round the newel-post at her from the bottom step. She had the brief thought, why isn't Penny here to help, and could have laughed. Of course, Penny would be in bed, waiting for someone to bring in her morning cup of tea. Once more, Dottie was alone in the situation.

'Thank you, yes, we'll be here,' she said and put the phone down. She looked at Simon again. What on earth did one say? But he knew. He ran across the hall, his feet bare on the tiles.

'Was that about my mother?' he asked. He was composed, too composed for a young child. He was so grown-up, Dottie thought. His eyes were deep and troubled and didn't look away. He would know if she was lying. She had to tell him. She took his hand and led him into the kitchen where it was very slightly warmer. She sat at the table and drew him to her.

'Yes Simon, I'm afraid it's very bad news. You've got to be very brave, dear.'

His eyes filled with tears. He flung himself into her arms, and said gruffly, 'Don't want to be brave.'

'I know, dear.' She stroked his hair. What else could she say? She wasn't sure if she should tell him what the police sergeant had said. Instead she just said, 'Someone is coming to talk to us shortly, so I'm going to go and get dressed. And I need to let Mrs Parfitt know, oh and Mr Gervase Parfitt should probably be told too. Oh dear.'

She looked at Simon who was standing in front of her now, hunched with his arms folded, tears running down his face. He was only wearing his pyjamas and was shivering. 'Why's it so chilly in here?' she asked. It was easier to focus on practical matters.

'My mother usually lights the stove early. That makes it warmer.'

'Of course. Oh Simon!' She hugged him.

She wanted to send him to put on a dressing gown and slippers, at the very least, but she didn't want to send him off on his own, not even just upstairs. She quickly lit the stove, and set a kettle on to boil, then taking his hand she guided him upstairs, helped him to get dressed and then left him in the bathroom whilst she ran to pull on a skirt and blouse, struggling with her stockings in her hurry, then she shoved her feet into slippers and scraped her hair into some kind of order. Simon was waiting outside in the hall. She took his hand and they went back to the kitchen that already felt cosier. She made tea, then left Simon at the table whilst she quickly rang Gervase. He was shocked but he said he would be over right away. She spared a thought for him—was this his second bereavement in a few days?

She went to make tea for Penny and Miranda, placed one tray on top of the other, and two pots and two cups and saucers, milk jugs and sugar bowls on the topmost tray. It made quite a load to carry upstairs, but she wanted to get them up and ready to see the police if necessary.

She heard the police arrive in the hall below, which meant Mrs Bains must have arrived. That was a relief as it meant Dottie could ask Mrs Bains to sit with Simon whilst she explained to Penny and Miranda what had happened without actually knowing many of the details herself, and then came down to speak with the police officers.

When she returned, the policemen were sitting around the kitchen table with cups of tea, chatting comfortably with Simon alone as if it were a purely social visit. There was no sign of Mrs Bains.

'We let ourselves in,' the sergeant clarified. 'And we helped ourselves to a cuppa. Hope you don't mind.'

It was Sergeant Menzies again, whom Dottie had seen the previous day, along with the inspector she had first met at Reggie's house. They reminded her a little of Inspector Hardy and Sergeant Maple, in that they seemed to form the perfect double-act and knew each other's methods and character.

'Is anyone else in the house?' the inspector asked, but before Dottie could reply, the sergeant said to him, 'There's a Mrs Parfitt. I assume she's still in bed?' This last was addressed to Dottie who hastily agreed that Mrs Parfitt hadn't yet come down, though she was awake and aware of the situation. Dottie added that Mrs Parfitt's sister, Mrs Parkes, was also staying in the house.

'While you attend to everything, I see,' the sergeant said. Dottie felt herself blushing.

'Well, Mrs Bains, the daily woman doesn't come in until nine o'clock, and so I am happy to do a few things. But she is coming to stay in the house for a while, to help out.'

They asked her a few more questions about the staff situation and enquired whether Mrs Parfitt was in delicate health.

'Erm,' Dottie began, torn between conventional tact and the desire to be truthful without making Penny sound bad. 'Mrs Parfitt was recently widowed, so she is still recovering from her grief. Mr Parfitt was quite a young man and died suddenly.' That sounded all right, she thought, and fairly tactful. Hopefully it would cover a fair amount. She didn't like that the sergeant was writing it all down in his notebook, but that might be purely procedural.

As soon as Winnie Bains arrived, Dottie left her to give Simon his breakfast, and she took the policemen into the dining room where they could sit at the big table in there to make their notes.

'So you've found Margaret Scott, then?' Dottie said. She already knew this was the case, but she struggled to find a way to start the conversation. She was clasping her hands tight.

The inspector nodded. 'Yes, I'm afraid Miss Scott's body was found by a gentleman out walking his dog very early this morning. She was floating in a pond half a mile from here. In the light of the note you found the day before yesterday, we are certain she killed herself in a fit of remorse following the murder of Reginald Parfitt.'

Dottie stared. She began to shake her head. 'No, no! That can't be right. I'm sure she would never...'

'Well it seems clear enough to me,' said the inspector, and with a slight edge to his voice, added, 'Although if your own investigation has turned up any evidence, I'm sure I'd love to have it.'

'My own...?' Too late she realised he was being sarcastic. She shook her head again. 'I just don't think it was in her nature to do something like that.'

He snorted. 'So you're a student of human nature too, are you, Miss? Well I'm sorry to say that humans don't always react the way you expect. And anyone can lash out in a fit of anger.'

She was about to respond but there was a knock at the door. She hoped to God it was Gervase.

It was, and if he was grief-stricken, he hid it behind his authority which he proceeded to wield. He overbore the inspector's arguments about Margaret having killed herself, using the arguments Dottie had presented to him.

The inspector was disinclined to accept them at first, but Gervase's very rank meant he was at least obliged to listen. The sergeant wrote everything down and looked as if he was enjoying the tense exchange. There was no need for Dottie to say anything, she just watched and listened to the two men.

'Well sir, I'm sure you don't need me to tell you that people, especially women, don't always act in a predictable manner as you might say. And from what I hear, she wasn't no better than she should be, so that's probably why she didn't take no undergarments.'

Gervase expressed his disgust at the inspector's comments. The inspector, somewhat ruffled but determined to stick to his guns, said, 'The other thing is, the woman's bedroom was a crime scene, so there's no call to be allowing civilians,' and here he nodded at Dottie, 'to walk all over the place.'

'A crime scene?' Gervase's voice was clipped and cold.

'Yes sir.'

'Then why wasn't the room sealed or placed under police guard?'

The inspector floundered slightly. 'Well, I wasn't able to get the men. But I gave orders no one was to go in there, and you would have known that, sir, begging your pardon. For all I know there could have been fingerprints that are now smudged and unusable.'

'Were you intending to fingerprint the room?'

'Well, I—I hadn't made up my mind about that. I was waiting to speak to my chief super.'

'I think you'd already made up your mind that Miss Scott had run off without her child and you didn't care about the crime scene.'

'No indeed, sir, I was keeping an open mind.'

'Until her body turned up. Then you had her pegged as a depressive, a murderer, and a suicide case that warranted no further police time.'

'It was only four hours ago,' the inspector protested. He held up a hand. 'Very well. I will look into it.'

'I want a post mortem carried out. I want to know if she was alive when she went into the water,' Gervase insisted.

'Well that whack on the side of her head probably knocked her out first,' commented the sergeant without looking up from his notebook.

That night, Dottie went back through the case-file of Richard Dawlish and reread everything. She had some ideas. They seemed too far-fetched. Yet they were insistent. Little details crowded her brain. She couldn't seem to push them away. It was as if something clamoured to be let out.

Chapter Twenty

The following morning, quite early, there was a phone call for Dottie. She had slept so deeply after all that had happened that she didn't even hear the telephone ring. The first thing she knew was Winnie Bains shaking her awake, saying, 'Beg pardon Miss Dottie, but there's someone on the machine for you. I didn't know whether I was to take a message or what.'

It took Dottie a full minute to understand what Winnie was telling her. Older people still feared the telephone as a device from the devil himself. Still dopey with sleep Dottie stumbled out of bed, followed Winnie downstairs, putting on her wrap as she went. She felt a horrid sense of déjà vu as she picked up the receiver.

'Hello Dottie, it's Catherine. I heard from Flora that you wanted to speak to me?'

After over five years living in London, the full lilt of Catherine's Jamaican accent had softened, but she still had a strong contralto that sounded like she was smiling all the time.

'Oh Catherine! I'm so grateful you called me!' Dottie made herself comfortable leaning back against the coats. Then she remembered getting wet leaning against one of them several days earlier and she put out her hand to check if it was now dry. It was. She went back to leaning and turned her attention to the conversation. She asked Catherine how she was and what she was doing with her life. But she was all too aware of the cost of the telephone bill, and that Catherine, as the wife of a minister, would have little money available for such luxuries. She came to the reason for wanting to speak to Catherine.

'I was wondering about what it was like for someone to come from Jamaica to live in England. I was trying to picture it. I mean—I've never been to Jamaica, but I've heard about exotic plants and fruits, and of course the sea, and the hot summers. So I was thinking how hard it would be for someone to come from all that to live in, for example, London. Was it hard?'

Catherine laughed. 'Oh Dottie, you have no idea! It was like moving to the north pole. It was such a long way, geographically, and culturally—well... Try to imagine going somewhere where everyone who you met or went past in the street would turn and stare at you. Or spit at you. Or tell you to go away—often in the most detestable language. You didn't even need to do anything or say anything, just your very face was enough to set you apart from every single person you met. Because of where we lived when we got to London, you know, with my father's position, it was easily three or four months before I saw another black face. I wanted to hug the woman and say, 'Thank you Lord!' because honestly, I thought we were the only people of colour in the whole of England.'

Dottie said nothing. What could she say? She felt appalled. She felt ashamed of her own ignorance.

'At school they made me scrub my body until I bled, telling me I was black because of the weight of my sin, that I was unclean. And you know what? I believed them too, until I told my father about it. My mother cried for a week after we arrived. She didn't speak to my father for two weeks. They—who had never spoken an unkind word to one another in almost twenty years of marriage. My father was horrified. He had tried to prepare us—and himself—for what life would be like, but I think it was far, far worse than he had ever imagined. He said a hundred times, 'I wish we had never come here.' In the end it was my mother who said, 'The Lord brought us here, we must trust Him.' It got a little better after that. Oh, but it was so dark here, and so cold, and so crowded. I suppose I got used to it eventually. But even now, almost every day, I am insulted and embarrassed by the things complete strangers say to me. I can't go home to Jamaica, because my parents, and my two brothers are here, as well as my husband, and now my baby. We are here and here we shall stay.'

'I'm so sorry, Catherine.' Dottie's voice was barely above a whisper.

'Oh Dottie! It's all right my dear, you were a good friend to me at school. We had fun, didn't we, giggling at the back of Miss Russell's class? But look, I need to go soon, the cost...'

'Of course, please let me help with that. Um, there was something else I wanted to ask.'

'If I can help...'

'I wondered if your father still knows anyone in Jamaica? I know it's a big place, and you haven't been there for quite a few years. But I need to find someone.'

'Well I can ask. He knows a number of ministers and pastors both here and back in Jamaica who might be able to help you.'

Very quickly, and without overwhelming her with too much information, Dottie told Catherine about Richard Dawlish. Catherine promised to speak with her father, and then they said goodbye, vowing to meet up once Dottie got back to London.

That evening, Penny and Miranda had gone to dine at the Maynards' home. Dottie hoped it was a sign of thawing in Norman Maynard's cold displeasure with his daughter. Perhaps Miranda might even move back to the family home. While they were out, Gervase had come over.

She wasn't quite sure how to bring up the subject. How could she make a start on something like that? She looked at him. He smiled, showing her by his very attentiveness that he was listening. She took a breath, and just... blurted it all out in a panicked muddle:

'Gervase, I'm so sorry, but I'm absolutely certain. I can't see any other explanation, I just...' She took a deep breath and started again. 'It's about Richard—he was murdered, I just know it. Richard Dawlish, I mean, obviously.'

He was still staring at her but his expression had taken on a scornful quality. 'That's absurd, Dottie.'

'Not only that, but I believe he was murdered by someone from your group of friends.' She watched him, guessing how he would react.

Now that he realised she wasn't simply teasing him, he looked plain annoyed. He clenched his jaw, the line of his chin and cheek rigid. She reached for his hand to try and take it. To her dismay he shook her off.

He said again, 'That's completely and utterly absurd. What possible reason could you have for thinking such a thing?'

She hesitated. In her head the reasons that had seemed so conclusive and overwhelming in the early hours of the morning now shrank and seemed too small, too chancy, just not enough. But she had a stubborn streak and she met his cold eye with her own gimlet expression.

'Well there's his character to begin with...'

He gave a sarcastic laugh. 'Oh well!' He shook his head, and was hardly able to look her in the eye. 'You didn't even know him, Dottie!' He had half-turned away, she believed he was about to leave, and she again tried to take his hand or grab at his arm. He didn't pull away this time, but his anger was unabated. 'Really Dottie, this is too bad of you. I should never have given you that case-file if I'd known it would lead to this.'

She resented his tone; he was talking to her as if she was a silly child. She wasn't having that. She came out of her corner ready to fight. 'Ah yes. The case-file. Just why did you give it to me, Gervase? I agree, it was a dreadful breach of police procedure on your part. Even though it's been extremely interesting, to say the least.'

'Yes well...'

She had him wrong-footed now, and decided it was a good idea to press her advantage, or she felt instinctively that in their relationship, her soul would never again be hers to call her own.

'How many other girlfriends have you shown files to? Is it something you always do once you get to know a girl? Or do you only do it to impress potential girlfriends?'

'No, of course...'

'So you obviously had a reason? Perhaps on some deeper level you've always felt that there was something unsatisfactory about the investigation?'

She was giving him the chance to save face and lie his way out of the situation. They both knew it was a test. Would he be honest, and admit his foolishness, or would he lie to make himself look better?

'This is ridiculous!' he hedged. Then, more forcefully, 'There was no investigation, because Richard Dawlish killed himself!'

'Exactly.' She leaned forward, eager to impress upon him the truth of his own words. 'Exactly. From the very start, they took all the evidence, the crime scene, everything at face value. The police—your father—had made up their minds from the outset that he had killed himself.' She began to count the points off on her fingers. 'And even the knowledge that there was no suicide note, that he had been decorated for bravery, that he was a deeply religious man with strong moral values, or even that he had a wound on his head—even those things did not make them change their preconceptions about how he had died. They saw him as a valueless inferior with no moral code or personal integrity. They didn't bother to investigate. It suited your father and his best friend, Norman Maynard, to assume Richard had killed himself. And his murderer has been walking around free for the last fifteen years.'

He glowered at her. His chest was heaving with the quick shallow breaths he was taking. He was furious, she thought ruefully. Surely this meant the end of their burgeoning romance? After a pause she added, 'Even your own statement said that he hadn't appeared depressed, and that even as a joke he had never talked of hanging himself.'

That threw him. If anything it made him angrier that she'd used his own words against him. He was silent a moment, thinking of something to hurl back at her. He found it.

'And now I suppose you'll tell me this same person killed my brother Reggie, and even Margaret too! Really, Dottie, it's too ridiculous for words!'

It was her turn to feel angry and off-balance. 'Now you're the one who's being ridiculous!' she snapped back. 'Of course I'm not saying that...'

But things shifted in her mind, a piece here, a piece there, and she stared at him, appalled by her own dawning thoughts.

'Gervase!' It came out as barely a whisper.

'Dottie, you can't—you can't possibly...!' His voice too was softer now, and he leaned towards her until he could kiss her cheek. He took her hand. 'Dottie? Darling?'

'I hadn't... It hadn't even occurred to me that...' She shook her head. 'No, it's too horrible. Surely that can't be true?'

He leaned back again looking thoughtful. 'I need to read those case notes.'

The telephone rang. Dottie knew Mrs Bains was busy in the kitchen, so she went herself to answer it. It was a good thing she did. The caller was an elderly Jamaican gentleman, who began to explain to Dottie that he was a friend of Catherine's father, and had heard of Dottie's enquiries about Richard Dawlish. His slow, gentle voice came to her over the line, and she felt calmed by its soft tone. He might not, as a cleric, be much in the 'fire and brimstone' line, Dottie thought, but as a counsellor, or a comforter of the sorrowful or suffering, he would be absolutely perfect.

'I used to know Richard Dawlish's whole family when I was a young man back in Jamaica,' he told her. He began to reminisce, but after a few moments she felt obliged, through concern for his telephone bill, to bring him back to the point. She asked him if Richard had had a sweetheart. Immediately he confirmed this, and told her a little about Lois, and her father, the noted veterinarian Clifford J Bell, still working in his practise though now nearly seventy-five years of age. Lois, his youngest child, kept house for her widowed father.

'If there is one thing I remember very clearly, it's that she always wore Richard's ring on a chain about her neck, with her cross. When he passed, well, she had to stop wearing it on her finger. Too many people asked her when was the happy day and so on, and it upset her so much. But she couldn't bear to part with it, so she put it on the chain to wear it next to her heart. To this day, she's never looked at another man. I'm sure if she had, my sister would have told me the news. I keep in touch, you see, what with so many friends left behind.'

'It must be so sad to leave your home,' Dottie said.

'Yes, true,' the old man said, 'but if I hadn't, well, I wouldn't get to play chess every week with Catherine's father, now would I?' He laughed heartily at that. In her mind's eye Dottie could picture the two men, laughing together and talking about old times over their chess pieces. It brought a lump to her throat. She hoped she would meet this dear fellow too, when she saw Catherine.

She had one further question, and then she thanked him and said goodbye.

'I suppose Richard was very in love with Lois? Do you think he would have left her for another woman?'

'Never!' There was no hesitation whatsoever. 'I knew that boy. He had loved her since he was fifteen, and she was thirteen and came with her father when he took over from the old vet who retired. The first moment they saw one another, that was it. they were inseparable. No, I asked my sister last night, and she said he wrote his last letter only shortly before we heard about his death, saying how he was about to leave to come home, and that she should start making plans for the wedding because he was tired of being apart. 'Never again,' he told her. 'Never again will we be parted.''

When Dottie returned to the drawing room, Gervase was still reading. But she could see from the little pile of pages leaning against his chest that he was nearing the end. She sat down to wait.

He set the papers aside with a frown. He said nothing for a few minutes, but just stared into space. Dottie could almost see him gathering his thoughts. What if he told her he still believed she was being absurd? She needed him to tell her what he was thinking. But she couldn't push him, so she had to wait. At last he turned to her and said,

'My first thought is 'how'? How exactly did he kill himself?'

It wasn't what she'd been expecting. She didn't know quite what to say.

He got to his feet and began pacing the floor as he spoke, one of those men who can think and talk better when he is active, she thought. It was clear immediately that he was now on her side.

'Think about it, Dottie, darling. Say you want to kill yourself, and you settle on hanging as the way you want to achieve this. Let's ignore for a moment that there are far easier methods to make away with oneself, especially for someone used to handling weapons as Richard most certainly was.'

She thought for a moment, then said, 'Well, I suppose I'd need a rope.'

'Yes! And luckily, there is a rope already there. All you need to do is to knot it.'

'I wouldn't know how to do that,' she pointed out, and he laughed.

'Girls never do know how to tie a decent knot. Let's say you're a chap, and you can do all kinds of useful knots. Now you've got this rope that someone has already most obligingly cut a swing seat off, leaving you with a good bit of rope, already attached to your chosen tree, and you tie a nice noose in the end of it. What do you do next?'

She shook her head. 'I don't know. I suppose I put my head through the noose?'

'How?'

She looked at him. 'What do you mean?'

'How do you get your head in the noose?'

'Well, you hold the noose open and slip it over your head so that it sits around your neck.'

'Hmm. And then?'

She shook her head. 'I don't know.'

'Suppose I told you that the noose, when examined by the medial officer, was found to be precisely eight feet above the ground.'

'Oh!' She frowned in thought. 'You mean he had to have something to stand on? How tall was he?'

'Well he was tall, but nowhere near eight feet! He was about five feet eleven. I'm six foot and he was very slightly shorter than me. When you hang someone, you have to allow for a drop. You can't have people standing on their tiptoes, cheating the hangman. So the noose is quite a bit higher above the ground than the height of the man to be hanged, either that or a trap door is employed.'

'Then he would have needed a box or—a chair—or—something. Would it have needed to be exactly two feet tall?'

'No, just anything that would be able to get his head through the noose eight feet above the ground.'

'But nothing was found?' She saw now what he was driving at. He smiled.

'Nothing.' He pulled a packet out of the inner pocket of his jacket. It contained the photographs from the file. He riffled through them until he found the one he was looking for. 'I know I said I didn't want you to see these, but well, this one isn't too horrid, if you think you can bear it?'

'I can.'

He handed one to her. A little nervously she took it and saw a black and white grainy picture of a man hanging from a tree. It gave her a jolt to see him—this person known to her only as a name, a sad story. Here he was, dead, but present, and all too real. Richard Dawlish.

Two men in business suits stood to one side of Richard's body. One of them, the one closest to the body, was smiling, for all the world like a proud fisherman standing beside his catch. It reminded her forcefully of the photographs hanging in the hall at the Maynards' home. The two men and their trophies. It made Dottie's stomach churn with disgust.

'That's my father,' Gervase said, though she already knew this. His shame was clear in his tone.

'And the other is Norman Maynard,' she said.

He nodded. He sounded as though he was still thinking about this. Slowly he said, 'Yes. He was a rising star of politics in those days, just got his knighthood a year or two earlier. He was destined for great things, and even recently he was tipped for Prime Minster.'

She looked back at the photo. Made an effort to concentrate on the details. 'Yes, there's nothing in the photo to show there was something for Richard to stand on. Unless they moved it out of the way to give the Honourable Gentleman a bit of space.'

'I don't think so. There's no box or anything in this one either.'

'Let me see.'

Gervase hesitated. 'Dottie, dearest, you can't, it's not very...'

'I loathe being protected,' she said and whipped it out from between his fingers. Sure enough it was a close-up picture of Richard's face, but taken at a downwards angle, it also showed much of the grassy area around the swing. To one side, there was the slat of wood that made the swing seat, and nothing else, apart from the doctor's bag.

'No box,' she murmured. She looked at Richard's face.

'He looks quite peaceful, as if he's asleep.'

'Yes, dear, so perhaps he had wanted...'

'Oh rot, Gervase! I'm sure you know as well as I do that if he had hanged himself, his eyes would be bulging, not peacefully closed, and his tongue would be lolling out! He looks very handsome and relaxed, as if he were simply sleeping. He had to be already dead when he was hanged.'

If Gervase was disconcerted by her knowledge of the graphic details of hanging, he didn't show it, instead leaning over her arm and saying, 'Good God, Dottie! I believe you're right!'

He sat back, holding up his hand to count off the points as she had done. 'So there was no box; the rope was already there, as was the tree, obviously; he had a contusion on his temple; and died before he was hanged, yet death was by asphyxiation.'

'Or bleeding into the brain,' she reminded him. 'According to the report in the file. The bleeding could have been caused by a blow to the head. The medic dismissed that as of significance initially due to the presence of tiny bits of wood in the wound. But what if, rather than bumping his head on the tree trunk or branch as he tried to hang himself, he was hit with something. Something made of wood. Something close to hand?' She handed him the photo again. His eyes widened as he saw what she was getting at.

'Right there the whole time for the whole world to see!' He leaned back and passed a hand over his eyes. She saw now how tired he looked. He'd had a terrible time lately, she thought. But he smiled at her. 'After all my original bluster, for which I apologise unreservedly, I'm now convinced that you're right, you clever, clever girl. I believe there was some kind of official cover-up, concocted between my father and

Norman Maynard to avoid any scandal attaching itself to him and blighting his career. Richard Dawlish was murdered.'

Chapter Twenty-one

They talked long into the night. By three o'clock Dottie felt she knew exactly what had happened. She had it all worked out in her head, and as she discussed it with Gervase, she became more and more certain she was right. If she had expected him to be hard to convince, she was wrong. He agreed with her on all the main points, and trusted that she was correct on the fine details too.

She wished she had the courage to confront him about Simon, but she wasn't ready. She timidly ventured to suggest yet again that something urgently needed to be done for the little boy, but Gervase simply said, 'I've been in touch with Margaret's parents. We've had a long chat. They are arriving tomorrow to take him back to live with them. They are good people and will care for the young fellow.'

Dottie decided to leave it at that. She would hear news about Simon through Gervase's connections with them in the future. She didn't need to do everything right now.

With all that out of the way, he began to tell her about the arrangements being made for Reggie's funeral. It would not be for at least another week, as the family had to wait for some relatives to arrive home from overseas.

Dottie began to try to explain that she wanted to go home. She wasn't quite sure how to tell him she wouldn't be there for his brother's funeral, but he stopped her with a kiss, saying a moment later, 'It's all right, dearest, I realise you can't stay here until then. It would have been vastly easier to have you there by my side, if I'm honest, but I know you've already stayed longer than you intended to, and you must go home. May I drive you home tomorrow afternoon?'

She leaned her head against his shoulder. She was overwhelmed with relief. 'Thank you. If you truly don't mind, I'd like that. It'll be such a help not to have to worry about catching trains and so on. And I would so like to introduce you to my parents.'

'And so you shall. But there is one more thing I want you to do for me,' he said. He placed a kiss on her hair.

'What?'

'Don't you mean, 'anything for you, my love'?' He laughed, and Dottie snorted.

'Oh yes, that's exactly what I meant. So sorry, your lordship!' She thumped him gently on the arm. 'Well, go on, then. What is this onerous task I must fulfil for you?'

'I want you to do the thing they do in detective stories, where all the suspects are invited, and the detective unmasks the perpetrator.'

She sat up to look at him. 'I'm not doing that! And just think what the inspector would say!'

He left a short while later. She was glad he had gone by the time Miranda and Penny returned from the Maynard's at half-past three. It seemed all was forgiven, and Miranda would be moving back to her parents' home the following afternoon.

'After all,' she crowed, 'It's awfully late. I doubt I shall be out of bed before lunch-time.'

'Did you have a terribly dreary evening, Dottie dear?' Penny asked, with a slight sneer. 'I must say I'm surprised to find you still up.'

'I was about to turn in,' Dottie said now, getting to her feet. 'I'm so glad you had an enjoyable evening. Goodnight.'

They were all gathered in the drawing room at Gervase's house that evening. Dottie looked around her and felt a stab of fear. She took a deep breath, then nodded to Gervase. He cleared his throat loudly to quieten everyone. Into the silence, Dottie spoke.

'For a long time, I believed that Miranda was responsible for these three terrible crimes,' Dottie began. The room felt oppressively silent.

The proverbial pin, dropping now would have given everyone a dreadful fright, she thought. They were all there: Gervase, Miranda and Penny, Algy with Deirdre beside him. Mike Maynard. Norman and Augustine Maynard sat beside their dear friends the Parfitts. And the inspector and sergeant sat on upright chairs by the door, whilst out in the hall, two constables waited.

All eyes were fixed on Dottie, and her voice quavered slightly, showing her nerves. The thought sprang into her mind, what if you're wrong? You'll never hold your head up again. And Gervase will despise you. But she wasn't wrong. She knew it as soon as those treacherous thoughts struck her conscious mind.

Miranda, blowing out cigarette smoke, sat forward in her seat. She shrugged off Mike's arm and stared at Dottie with undisguised hatred, her eyes daring Dottie to say any more.

Dottie rose to the challenge. She cleared her throat and continued, happy that her voice was strong now. 'As I say, for a long time I thought it was Miranda who was behind the murders. Let's call them what they are. We're not talking about something minor such as a few shillings missing from someone's piggy-bank. We're talking about the cold act of snuffing out a human life, as if they were of no more importance than an annoying fly at a picnic. Not once, but three times.'

Gervase was watching her with frank admiration. She spared a moment to be thankful that he was not the guilty party. She couldn't have borne that.

'As soon as I met Miranda, or, I may say, even before I met her, I was aware that she was the sort of person who always had to be the centre of attention. No matter whom that attention came from, she wanted it to be focused and dancing upon her. It was almost entirely male attention she craved, and as I quickly saw, she basked in it. Men fell over themselves to talk to her, to do things for her, they competed for her smiles and her gratitude.'

There was a snort of derision from Penny, in the corner of the sofa beside Gervase. Dottie turned to her. 'It's true. Anyone who spends more than a few minutes with all of you in your group will see it immediately. Miranda has always been very much the flame around which the moths flutter, at their peril.'

'This is completely ridiculous,' Miranda said. She stubbed out her cigarette in three or four sharp angry movements, and getting to her feet, she grabbed her little evening bag. Turning back to face the rest of them, with a wave of her hand at Dottie, she said, 'She doesn't have any right to do this! She's just making up all these ludicrous accusations, there's no basis, no truth to any of them. Why are the police letting her do it? I'm going to contact my lawyer immediately, she can't do this, it's libel.'

'Slander,' Gervase corrected automatically.

'Shut up! Mike, take me home! I'm going back to Mummy's.'

Mike, also looking furious, leapt up, all too willing to comply. Gervase stepped in front of him, and placing a hand on Mike's chest, he said, 'I'm sorry, old chap, but I'd very much like you to stay and listen to what Dottie has to say.'

Miranda shoved Gervase's hand aside and grabbed Mike by the arm. 'I've had enough of your silly little tart, Gerry, I'm leaving. You can't stop me.'

'You're staying put and that's that,' Gervase said firmly but quietly. 'Mike, sit down. We all need to hear this.' They locked eyes, then after a few seconds, Mike shrugged and resumed his seat.

Miranda was not so easily persuaded. She gave an angry laugh, tried to step around Gervase who was there ahead of her at every turn. She lost her temper then, and made to slap him, but he was again too quick, catching her hand before it touched his face, and none too gently he pushed her back into her seat. The police officers watched with interest, but didn't need to stir themselves. With a nod at Dottie, Gervase said mildly, 'Do go on, darling.'

There was a definite frisson through the room. All eyes turned once more on Dottie.

She said, 'All along I've asked myself the question, why did Richard Dawlish kill himself? I know I wasn't there, and I know I'm very young, but I do understand people.' Her voice faltered over the sudden intrusion of William Hardy's face into her thoughts. Mentally she pushed it away, adding, with slightly less confidence, 'Well, some people.' She took a deep sigh and brought herself back to her point once more. 'The thing is, everyone talked about his good moral character and his strong religious faith. Penny and Margaret both told me he was gentlemanly and not given to crude jokes or taking liberties with the ladies. And he had been decorated twice for valour.'

'That doesn't mean a thing,' Mike pointed out, 'You're too young to remember, but I was there and I know how terrible it was. Plenty of chaps came back from the war and found they couldn't hack it. Normal life was just too much for them.'

'It's true, I wasn't there,' Dottie admitted. 'And I never met Richard or got to know him as all of you did. But I've learned a lot about him from talking to all of you. Mainly I've learned that actually no one much liked him, purely on account of the colour of his skin; that he was despised, and his truly outstanding war record was largely dismissed even though it was as good if not better than most white-skinned soldiers, men who were—quite rightly—lauded and treated as the heroes they were. And even though everyone said that they knew nothing about an engagement between Miranda and Richard, even though everyone agreed Richard and Miranda were little more than casual friends, when he was found dead, Miranda stated that they were engaged to be married, and no one ever questioned that.'

Miranda screamed vile words at Dottie, and Mike had to forcibly hold her down in her chair when she would have launched herself at Dottie. The two constables looked as if they might come into the room.

Dottie looked her full in the eye and said, 'There was no engagement, there never was. You made it up on the spur of the moment. Even in death you couldn't bear the thought that he might take the attention away from you. And you couldn't allow him to overshadow you there at the front of the stage, could you? You invented the story of the engagement so that all of the sympathy and concern was not for Richard as it should have been, but was directed at you, the suffering lover.'

'You bitch! You nasty little bitch!' With almost superhuman strength Miranda threw off Mike's arms and rushed at Dottie, who fell backwards and bumped her head on the edge of the coffee table. She was shocked but unhurt. Gervase and Algy both helped her to her feet. Penny was in front of Miranda and there was the sound of a slap, and Penny's hand was swinging back to her side. Across Miranda's cheek was the livid outline of a hand. Miranda fell back onto the sofa whimpering, all the fight gone out of her.

Penny, tucking her skirt neatly about her as she sat, smiled gently at Dottie and said, 'Sorry about that, Dottie dear. Do go on.'

Dottie, somewhat shaken, took a seat on the other side of Gervase, who pressed her hand gently then released it. Dottie looked around the room. The police inspector was looking extremely interested, and by comparison,

Gervase's father looked as though he'd like to be anywhere than here. His wife was cold and impassive.

'As I was saying, there was no engagement. Richard had no desire to stay in England. He longed to go home to Jamaica, to his family and, more importantly, to his fiancée there. Her name is Lois, in case anyone is interested. She still has the engagement ring he gave her. She's never married, and she keeps house for her father who is a much-respected veterinary surgeon. Richard was planning on training as a vet too, and the idea had been that he would go into partnership with Lois's father once he qualified.'

She paused, then said, with scorn in her voice and her nose wrinkled in disgust, 'He didn't want to work as an office boy in Norman Maynard's business. He was going to have a profession. I know it's hard for all of you to understand. You never wanted him here in this country, he was only here because he was useful in a time of crisis. Once the crisis was over, well, he'd served his purpose, and he and all the other thousands of men of colour, could be, should be, sent back to 'where they came from'. Never once did it occur to any of you that he might not want to stay here in this cold, unfriendly place. No. Richard's life was there in Jamaica all along: his love, his family, his career. He wasn't depressed. He just wanted to go home. He didn't kill himself, he was murdered.'

There was a soft gasp from someone, though Dottie didn't know who. It had sounded like a woman, but she couldn't discern who it was between Augustine and Deirdre. They both were staring at her, pale, shocked. They all were. Only Miranda smiled.

'But you said it wasn't Miranda,' Penny said. 'You did say that, didn't you? That at first you thought it was her but now you realised it wasn't. So if it wasn't Miranda, then who on earth was it?'

Dottie sighed. 'Oh Penny, it could only have been one person. It was you.'

Chapter Twenty-two

It was as if the earth had stopped turning. Then into the silence came Penny's grating little laugh.

'Oh Dottie! My dear child! What a perfectly idiotic thing to say!'

Everyone looked from Penny to Dottie and back again. They all looked incredulous. Mike was shaking his head. Only Miranda looked down at her hands, no longer interested in what was, for her, old news. The spotlight had moved off her now and it was cold in the shadows.

'It was you, Penny,' Dottie repeated. 'Your love of attention is, if anything, even greater than your sister's, though you lack her daring, her audacity. You were always overshadowed by her, I imagine: the big sister, so confident, so popular. You tagged along behind everyone like a little puppy, eager to be included but always dismissed as Miranda's sweet little kid sister. You told me that yourself. And I'd even heard you talking to Gervase about how you had a crush on him when you were a teenager but how he didn't even notice you.

'But you didn't have your sister's flair for creating drama, did you? You'd never have thought of claiming a dead man as your lover and fainting, or running away from home to India. No, you stayed meekly at home and married the brother of the man you really loved but who saw you only as a friend. Men just never looked at you the way they looked at Miranda, did they? Even the black man you threw yourself at when he walked you back to the house that night. Surely his standards were lower than that of the others? But no, even he rejected you.

'But it wasn't just Richard Dawlish who failed to please you. It was you who killed both Margaret Scott and Reggie Parfitt.'

Around the room there were gasps and protests. Mike once again had to be persuaded to resume his seat, and Norman Maynard began to harangue the inspector. The constables came in and 'helped' Maynard to find his seat. Eventually order was restored, and this time it was the inspector who told Dottie she may continue.

'Margaret knew you went out that afternoon just before Reggie was found dead. We came back from the lunch with Reggie and Deirdre, and immediately you and Miranda went up to lie down. You could easily have gone out again. No one would have known. I was in my room packing. Margaret would have been in the kitchen, I should think. Gervase has discovered that a phone call was made from your house to the Parfitts' in the afternoon. I imagine it was picked up in the study by Reggie himself. You arranged to go and see him.

'It would have been simple to go out of the house, drive over to Reggie's, to go around to the study door and get him to let you in. He was expecting you. You probably said you needed to talk to him about Miranda. He wouldn't have paused for a second. And then... it took no time at all. All you had to do then was to lock the study door to stop anyone getting in that way before you were ready. Close the study curtains. Break the pane of glass to make it look as though someone had broken in from outside. Then get home and lie down in your room. Easy.

'But your coat was wet from going out in the rain. I noticed it when I went to use the phone, although the significance just didn't dawn on me at the time. Somehow Margaret knew what you had done. Perhaps it was Reggie dying so soon after his scene with Miranda. Margaret wouldn't have heard his comment about, 'After all I've done', which at the time I didn't understand, but now it makes perfect sense. At first, she couldn't believe it was true, but she thought about it and realised what had happened.'

'This is all so entertaining, Dottie dear, really you ought to go in for writing adventure stories for Girls' Own!' Penny smiled, still poised and secure. 'How exactly did Margaret find me out, pray do tell!'

'I'm not sure. She saw you leave, perhaps,' Dottie said, 'Or she might have looked into your room, bringing you a cup of tea, or something like that, and found you gone. Or perhaps she saw your wet coat later and that gave her the idea. It could even have been that she heard the car start up. The garage is quite close to the kitchen, and if she was in there, working quietly, darning Simon's socks for example, she would have heard you start up the car and drive away.'

'Oh, this is fascinating!' Penny clapped her hands softly as if applauding a play. Gervase, Mike, and the others frowned at her. She didn't seem to notice that they were no longer on her side, but drinking in every word of Dottie's, they were becoming convinced by her argument. 'And I suppose I killed Margaret because she threatened to rat on me, I think that's the word.'

'Yes. She was horrified by what you'd done. And you knew she would tell Gervase everything, and he, as assistant chief constable couldn't possibly ignore or overlook her information.'

'Perhaps it was Reggie, not Artie, who was the father of her brat? Perhaps she thought I'd killed her lover?' Penny's voice was heavy with malice, and out of the corner of her eye, Dottie saw Deirdre start. Dottie couldn't have Deirdre's memory of her husband so tainted.

'Neither Artie, nor Reggie was Simon's father,' she said softly. 'I think we all know that much.' There was an awkward silence around the room.

She couldn't bring herself to look at Gervase. But there was no point, that didn't matter right now. 'But yes, I think she told you what she knew, I think she told you she was going to the police. Perhaps she asked you for more money. She had her child to think of, after all, and wanted to get away to make a new life for herself and Simon. So yes, you lured her out to the garage on some pretext and hit her over the head. You bundled her body into the car, and then, at night when everyone was in bed, you disposed of her in the pond.'

Penny was leaning back now, calmly shaking her head and tutting every now and then. Her hands, though, wrung each other, the knuckles white and strained. Everyone in the room was focused on Dottie and collectively holding their breath.

She went on, 'You took her clothes from the wardrobe and made a clumsy attempt at a suicide letter, making it sound as if she had a guilty conscience that she couldn't live with any more. Unfortunately, you forgot Simon's name once again, and a close examination of the letter shows that where there should be an S followed by an I in his name, it is in fact an S followed by a carefully adapted T. In any case, it's nothing like her writing of his name on the picture in the kitchen. And because you've never done your own packing, you forgot to pack her underclothes and make-up. She wouldn't have packed her outer clothes but no underwear or face powder, no woman would. But let's not forget Simon. Margaret would never, ever have left behind her son.'

'Well, she's left him behind now!' Penny's voice was practically an insane cackle. There were horrified gasps all around the room.

'But surely—I mean—how on earth could a kid of Penny's age hang a full-grown, healthy man? No, Dottie, this all has to be absolute rot, and I'm not at all happy that Gerry has allowed you...'

She had a sudden brief attack of nerves, but she held up her hand to halt him. 'I know this is not at all easy to hear, Mike. And yes, obviously Penny couldn't have hanged Richard all on her own. No, Penny did what she always did in those days. She got her sister to help her out of a hole.'

'No!' Mike's exclamation was more of shock than denial. Looking at him, Dottie could see that he was—in spite of his words—ready to believe it all. Convention and good breeding, even family loyalty might demand that he defend his sisters' honour, but he wasn't genuinely surprised.

'I believe that Penny lashed out at Richard. The medical report mentions a blow to the side of the head. I think Penny threw herself at him as he walked her back to the house that evening. She was desperate to be seen and treated as a desirable woman and not as a child. She was so enraged by his kindness, and doubtless his scruples, that she hit him with something, I've got an idea it was...'

'It was the wooden seat of the swing,' Deirdre's voice was so soft, it barely reached Dottie's ears. Nevertheless she did hear it, and she looked from Deirdre to Gervase. Gervase was looking alert, sitting forward in his seat. This was further proof of what they suspected.

'The wooden seat?'

'Yes,' Deirdre said. She looked up, her face was ashen, her hands trembled. Algy put an arm about her shoulders. She said, 'Do you remember? The seat of the swing was made from a bit of the copper beech tree itself, a piece cut from a fallen branch. It was only about as wide as a cricket bat, and perhaps eighteen inches long. Anyway, it kept breaking off, it wasn't really strong enough, and it broke again that evening. Penny said something about taking it to show the butler; she said he would send one of the gardeners out to fix it. I remember she was carrying it when she and Richard left to go back to the house, but when I saw her later, she didn't have it.'

'You saw her later?' Gervase said. His tone showed everyone that this was significant. 'That wasn't in your statement. I thought you went home a few minutes later.'

'I—I did, but I c-came back. Algy walked me home, he wanted to come in, but I said he couldn't. I knew he was—well, you know—drunk and a bit amorous. I was frightened we'd get caught by my parents, so I said no. So he said goodnight at the gate, and I went in, but my parents weren't back, so I ran to get a jacket—I thought I might get cold later—and I went back to the party. On the way, I heard Penny sobbing, and muttering, and then I heard Miranda saying, 'It'll be all right, you go in and go to bed, don't say anything to anyone. I'll get Reggie to help me, he's practically eating out of my hand at the moment. Men are all out for what they can get, aren't they? Well I'll make him pay for it first.' I didn't really know what it meant at the time, then later, I couldn't quite work out... I mean it's only as you get older you understand about things. Anyway, I just turned and went back to the pavilion. Algy walked me home again two hours later, I got in just as the clock struck two. I put on my nightgown then went downstairs for a glass of water, and my parents came in just then. They thought I'd been back for hours.'

Dottie continued her narrative. 'What we don't know, is whether Richard was already dead at that point, or whether he was simply unconscious. We might never know. But Penny did what she always did when she was in a fix. As I said, she got Miranda to help her. And Miranda did what she always did, she turned to whichever man was enamoured of her at that particular moment. In this case it was Reggie who had been openly and noticeably following her about; 'like an orphaned puppy', one person said. If anyone other than her had asked him for help, I doubt he'd have been quite so forthcoming, but I'm sure she managed to put on a jolly good display of hysterics and no doubt she clutched at him and begged him, and he, only too willing to do anything for Miranda, would have gladly stepped into the breach.

'Not that I believe for a minute he knew what had really happened. I'm sure she spun him a story about Richard taking liberties, her being forced to defend herself, or perhaps she simply said he'd tripped and fallen, I don't know. But I doubt Reggie was sober and thinking straight, and somehow, she completely overcame all his scruples, and he helped her. They concealed the body, probably in the shrubbery—it's quite dense there, thick with huge rhododendrons and things like that. No search appeared to have been made of other areas of the grounds apart from the bit by the beech tree. Then, when everyone else had gone, they carried his body to the swing, threw the seat aside, which Miranda had got from Penny, in the hope no one would connect that with the injury on the side of his head, or rather, no one would connect Penny or Miranda with it, then they hanged him with the rope of the swing, leaving him to be discovered a few hours later when the staff came to clear up after the party.'

Silence enveloped the room, deep and thoughtful. Dottie knew they were all with her, believing her, picturing the scene in their minds. No one denied or refuted. No one looked at Miranda or Penny. Deirdre wept softly into her hands, and Algy gave her his handkerchief. She took it and wiped her face.

'And what about Reggie?' she asked. 'Did he kill Richard, then?'

Dottie said, 'We don't know. But he must have felt great guilt and regret over what happened all those years ago. Then to suddenly be faced again with Miranda's betrayal: well, in fact she betrayed him twice. The first time when she left to go to India. I'm sure she had promised to marry him—or—or something, he was so in love with her, I feel sure that is what she would have said. The second time she betrayed him was when she came back a week ago and pretended not to recognise him. Miranda, that was a ridiculously stupid thing to do. I mean, yes it was heartless and cruel, but from your own point of view, it was stupid. If you'd only shown him a small sign of affection, if you'd simply hugged him and said, oh I don't know, something like, 'Oh Reggie, how lovely to see you again', he'd have been easier to deal with. But you had to humiliate him, didn't you, and that made him angry. After all these years I believe he was sick of keeping quiet about his part in your little drama that night. I'm sure he threatened to give away your long-held secret, purely because of that childish need you had to hurt him. And so Penny had to silence him.'

Miranda gave a sigh. But all she said was, 'I don't know what you're talking about. And I certainly never asked him to hang Richard for me! That's a completely ludicrous idea! If he did such an insane thing, he did it all on his own, obviously. Though I must now admit that he told me at the time what he'd done, and naturally I was horrified and appalled. That's why I had to run away as soon as possible, I was afraid of his violent temper.'

Gervase was on his feet, shaking with rage. Dottie grabbed his arm, as did Algy, and held him back.

'My brother did not have a temper, he was not a violent...' He choked on the last word and sank down into the seat. 'My brother,' he said through his fingers, 'My poor... if only he'd told me what had happened that night, I might have been able to do something.'

'But you said nothing at the time,' Dottie said to Miranda. 'An innocent person would have spoken out.'

'Oh, I was too young to understand!' Miranda said airily. She gave a delicate little yawn. 'Mike, dear, I'm rather bored with all this. Take me home now.'

Mike made no move, though. Miranda kept her seat, and Dottie thought she appeared tense.

'Left to himself, Reggie would never have done such a terrible thing,' Gervase said, and next to him, Deirdre nodded. 'He's always been a follower, never a leader.' Gervase's voice wobbled slightly, but he added, 'And back then, he worshipped you, Miranda, he'd have done anything, absolutely anything you asked of him. I'm sure he did do exactly that. Poor old Reggie. He was never a go-getter, but he was a good man.'

'Nonsense!' Miranda snapped. She nudged her brother, 'Give me a cigarette, Mike, I'm gasping.'

Mike lit her cigarette, and she made a show of leaning back in her chair, taking a long drag on it then slowly exhaling. Smoke wreathed the air, and slowly she smiled.

Watching this, Dottie thought with surprise, she's going to confess, she's enjoying this whole thing, and she's going to confess!

'Oh fine, I give in, you're right of course,' Miranda said. 'Poor dear Reggie was putty in my hands. Another couple of drinks, a few minutes fumbling round the back of the pavilion and he was ready to do anything for me. I got him all riled up over what Richard had supposedly tried to do to me, told him I'd pushed him away, and he'd fallen and hit his head, and that he was dead. It was so easy to make Reggie think this was the best way out of a tricky situation. He didn't see why my life should be damaged by Richard's ungentlemanly behaviour. It was, after all, just an accident. Dear Reggie! I didn't tell him I saw Richard's chest moving—that he was still alive. Though not for long, of course.' She gave a little laugh that chilled Dottie to the bone and made gooseflesh stand out on her arms. Out of the corner of her eye, she saw Deirdre's hand go to her mouth in horror.

Time to shift the spotlight, Dottie thought and said, 'Of course this was all just to get Penny out of trouble. I imagine Penny expected to be the centre of attention somehow: the youngest one there, the sweet little schoolgirl Richard had been so kind to, her innocence horribly blighted by such a terrible occurrence. And then Miranda came forward with her big announcement and a theatrical swoon, and ruined that as well. It's a good thing Miranda did go to India—who knows what Penny might have done to her in a fit of rage?'

Penny was now smiling again. In spite of the terrible indictment levelled against her, Penny preened as all eyes fixed on her once more. 'I thought it was very clever of me,' she said, and Gervase drew a sharp inward breath. Dottie thought, he's thinking what I'm thinking, that this is another admission of guilt. 'But yes actually, you're right, Dottie dear. I was incensed by what Richard said. 'Why would I want to stay here,' he said, 'it's cold and it rains all the time. Back home I've got my darling girl and my whole future. Why anyone would want to stay here is beyond me.' He was so—so ungrateful. He was just a—a common darkie, throwing all that back in our faces—the hospitality, the honour, the offer of a job in my father's office, of a better life...'

'Not for him,' Dottie said. 'It wasn't a better life for him.'

'I decided that I didn't really like him after all. In fact I hated him. Hated the stupid way he touched my arm and said, 'Don't worry, Penny, you'll meet someone. You've got your whole life ahead of you.' How dared he patronise me like that? He—oh, he deserved to die! I hated him for that!' She was practically snarling. Saliva threaded down her chin, and her eyes were mashed tight. She was like a wild thing. Dottie was frightened. Gervase, still on his feet, drew close to her, sitting on the arm of the chair, his hand on her shoulder. The sudden turn of Penny's temper had everyone taken aback; even Miranda was white-faced with shock. They've known her all her life, Dottie realised, and this is the first time any of them have seen her as she truly is.

'What about Margaret?' Algy asked abruptly, from the other end of Miranda's sofa. His voice was calm though his fist clenched and unclenched on his knee. Dottie had a theory about that, but remained silent. Penny leaned forward in her seat to look across at Algy.

'I'm so glad you asked, Algy, dear,' she said in her usual voice, smiling at him sweetly, all trace of rage wiped away. 'Dottie is right. I'm afraid Margaret confronted me about Reggie. She'd overheard my telephone call, and heard me go out. She wanted to have it out, she followed me outside. She was angry and upset—I know that, though I'm afraid I was too—and so I didn't make allowances. Perhaps she might have calmed down given a little more time, but I couldn't take the risk.' She paused then continued in a lighter tone, 'And you know, I'd been thinking of getting rid of her for some time, I really just don't need her now that dear Artie is no longer with me, so I was planning on letting her go anyway.'

Dottie felt the nausea rising in her. How could someone sound so normal, so perfectly reasonable and yet be speaking words of madness? Penny actually gave a little chuckle, as if they were discussing something—ordinary. She seemed oblivious of the horror her words had instilled in all those present.

'But Penny...' Even Miranda's voice shook. Her jaw was slack, her mouth slightly open, as if she were in shock.

'Oh, I knew you'd all take her side.' Penny said, waving Margaret aside with a flap of the hand. 'Wonderful Margaret. Beautiful Margaret. How the men all flocked around her like flies on...'

'But she had a little boy,' Gervase said.

'Oh yes, her little bastard. Well she'd have sucked my bank account dry. It would have been an impossible task to silence her. Even then, I'm sure at some point after the money ran out, her scruples wouldn't have allowed her to keep what she knew to herself. She heard what I said to Reggie. There is just time to tell you about it before I go.'

'Go? Go where, Penny?' Gervase asked her gently.

'Well I'm not staying here, am I? I don't want to hang. I'd have thought that was obvious.'

Gervase nodded as if this made perfect sense. He said, 'Sorry, I interrupted you. What had you been about to say?'

'Well nothing much, that was it really, just that Margaret had to go, the stupid cow, she wasn't sensible enough to keep her mouth shut. I knew I couldn't trust her, so it just seemed easier to get rid of her and have an end of the matter.'

Penny stopped and looked around the room with a little frown. Several people were not even looking at her any more. Deirdre had her hands over her face, and Augustine was leaning against Mike, her eyes shut, her face a ghastly pallor. Gervase stared at Dottie. He was biting his lip as if wondering what to do next. The inspector nodded to the sergeant who got to his feet.

Suddenly bored with the whole thing, Penny slapped her hands on her knees and said, 'Right then, I'll be off,' and got to her feet.

The inspector grabbed her right arm as the sergeant took her left. 'Not so fast,' the inspector said, 'Penelope Parfitt, I am arresting you for the attempted murder of Richard Dawlish, and for the murder of Reginald Parfitt and Margaret Scott.'

He took two steps, pulling an amused Penny after him, when with a screech, Miranda launched herself across the room at him, pounding him and scratching at his face.

'Let go of my sister! How dare you! Leave her alone!'

It took several minutes for the two constables and the sergeant to subdue Miranda, whilst the inspector took charge of Penny who began to wail and plead with them to let her go. Dottie sat and watched the whole scene as if it were some strange and unbelievable avant-garde stage show.

Chapter Twenty-three

'Let me look at you,' Dottie said, and took a step back. She was holding back the tears, but only just. She smoothed his hair. 'This bit at the front always seems to stick up,' she said, shaking her head. It was foolish of her, she knew that. But she just couldn't seem to help it. To focus on the physical, practical, that helped. Otherwise she didn't think she could cope. She didn't want him to go. Just one minute more, just...

There was a sound behind her, and Dottie turned, her arm automatically going about Simon's thin shoulders to protect him. An older couple came in and they hovered uncertainly in the hall, Gervase just beyond them. Dottie put their ages as early to mid-fifties. There was something of Margaret in the brows and straight nose of the man. The woman put a hand to her trembling lips, and Dottie knew that look. It helped to see that Margaret's mother was just as overwhelmed as Dottie was, if not more so.

Their grandson regarded them with steady eyes, but his body seemed to have stiffened.

'It's all right, Simon,' Dottie told him. 'These people are your...'

'I know who they are,' he said clearly and firmly, 'Mother had a photograph of them. They are my grandparents. How do you do?' he said gravely, going forward and holding out his right hand to Margaret's father.

Taken aback, the gentleman, with a half-smile, shook Simon's hand and said, 'I do very well, thank you, Simon. And how are you?'

'Not too bad, thank you,' said Simon.

There was a sob from his grandmother, and rather to everyone's surprise, she flung herself at Simon, pulling him into a tight hug, saying as she wept, 'Oh my darling, my dear boy!'

Her husband came forward to put an arm about both of them, tears flowing unchecked down his face.

Dottie backed away to the door, stepped outside, and softly closed the door upon them, leaving them to be private. She turned to Gervase and went into his arms.

He stoked her hair. 'They'll take care of him,' he said softly. 'They feel terrible about abandoning Margaret; they won't do it to Simon.'

Dottie nodded, but she had no voice. She was happy, but her emotions had suffered so many knocks of late that she couldn't seem to hold herself in check any longer. Gervase held her, and when eventually the storm passed, he provided Dottie with a clean handkerchief to blow her nose and wipe her eyes.

She almost had a relapse when Simon hugged her goodbye and went out to get into his grandfather's car.

There would be big changes for him, and it would take a huge adjustment, but at least he would not be alone, and there was no doubt in Dottie's mind that he would be loved.

In London, William Hardy had finally found the time... no, it wasn't time he had been short of, he was forced to admit to himself. He had been reluctant to come back to this house for several reasons. He took out the envelope Mr Bray the solicitor had given him almost two weeks earlier, and from it he extracted the bunch that held the front door key. With a sense of foreboding he went up the steps to the front door, took a breath, then slipped the key into the lock and turned it.

The hall was quiet, and empty. Of course it was. But his memory furnished the details of a night not so long back. Of coming into the hall to see the dead body of Mrs Carmichael lying at the foot of the stairs, of the little hall table, the broken vase.

It took him a moment to push that aside and look about him. He had been here twice now, the last time to attend to her death, and once before that to interview Mrs Carmichael about a case he had been working on. He smiled sadly to himself. She had been a real character, a formidable, impressive woman. If only he could have spoken to her again.

'I knew your father,' she had told him. 'For almost a year...'. Little had he realised at the time that there would never be another opportunity to ask her about that. She was the mother of his half-brother, whose existence he had never even suspected, until recently. William shook his head.

The hall was still draughty and damp. He would have to get that seen to. The place was his now, and with it a little bit of money that he could use to make the repairs Mrs Carmichael had failed to carry out. He began to look about him now with the eye of a proprietor, not a policeman.

On his first visit, Pamphlett, Mrs Carmichael's maid had shown them into the sitting room. He crossed the hall now to open that door, and cautiously looked inside. He had only the haziest memory of the room itself, though its occupant, in her lurid lounging pyjamas was imprinted on his memory for eternity. Thinking of this, he smiled again.

It was a relief to arrive home at last. Dottie viewed the house of her parents as she ran up the steps to the front door, and found it slightly strange-looking, as a familiar place is when you have been away for a long time.

But it was home. She had no need to ring the bell or knock, because Janet the maid was watching for her and the door opened before Dottie even reached it. Half out of her little tweed coat already, Dottie hugged Janet.

'Stand still, Miss, or I won't be able to get it off you!' Janet said, trying to grab the trailing coat sleeve. She was beaming from ear to ear. 'It's so good to have you back!'

Before Dottie could answer, Gervase came up the steps behind her, and Janet sent her a questioning look. At the same time, Dottie's parents came from the drawing room, smiling and arms outstretched.

There was a moment of stiff embarrassment before Janet went off with the outer wear and Gervase and Dottie were chivvied into the drawing room and introductions were made.

Gervase stayed for an hour, then made his way to his club. Mrs Manderson, happy with his rank and good looks, if not his age, extended an invitation to dinner the following day.

As soon as Dottie came back from seeing Gervase off, Mr Manderson said, 'He's just asked me for your hand in marriage! Quick work, I call that. How do you feel about it?'

'Oh!' Dottie stared, unable for the moment to think of anything intelligent to say.

'Surely he isn't really the assistant chief constable of Derbyshire?' her mother broke in.

'Um, well, yes, he is.'

'Policemen certainly seem to hold a mysterious appeal for you,' her mother added.

Dottie had to laugh at that. She couldn't deny it. 'Yes, they do!'

'Has he already asked you to marry him?'

'Not yet. But he has hinted that's what's on his mind.'

'Do you really love him that much? You're ready to marry him after just a mere fortnight's acquaintance?' her father asked.

Dottie huffed. Her fringe flew up in the air and settled neatly back on her forehead again. 'I like him, he's a jolly nice chap.'

'But you don't love him?'

'I don't know, Mother! Father, as you say, it's all happened so quickly. I just want to get to know him a bit more.'

'Hmm,' said her mother in that disapproving way mothers have. 'Well don't let him rush you. Or take advantage. I must say, he's a little older than I would have liked for you, and although he's quite nice looking, he's not so attractive as W...'

But Dottie wasn't about to have yet another discussion about Inspector Hardy. 'Well that is over!' she said with finality, and she got to her feet to make an end of the conversation. 'I'm going up for a wash and to change my skirt.'

George's father for once was speechless. Piers Gascoigne de la Gascoigne was wooden-faced and pale, clutching his wife's hand. But if in the past Dottie had ever thought him cold, she knew now that he was not. As his daughter's coffin was lowered into its place in the ground, he sobbed like a child.

White roses had seemed the most appropriate. Dottie abhorred lilies and nothing else seemed quite so fitting. She dropped her posy down onto the coffin lid, and it lay there on the gleaming wooden surface, beside those of George, his parents, and Mr and Mrs Manderson. William Hardy was not there, of course, though Dottie had half-expected to see him, but in the end, this was a time just for family, a private affair.

Cynthia Gascoigne, reunited with her husband after an absence of two weeks, dabbed her eyes for the dozenth time with her handkerchief and turned a tremulous smile on Dottie, saying for the hundredth time, 'Thank you, dear,' and squeezing her hand. Her gratitude served only to make Dottie feel worse about the fact that she had been with Diana when she died and had not saved her.

Dottie assured her no thanks were necessary, kissed her cheek, and went to stand beside her mother, leaving Diana's family some privacy at her graveside.

'Are you sure you're all right?' Dottie asked Mrs Manderson. Her mother had been subdued for most of the three days since Dottie's return from Nottinghamshire. Dottie was becoming concerned. Was her mother sickening for something? Or was she worried about Flora? Or Dottie and her new relationship with Gervase? It was so unlike her to be silent and lost for words. And she was so pale.

'I'm perfectly all right, dear,' her mother said yet again, but Dottie wasn't convinced. She resolved to get her father to herself and ask him.

They went back into the barrack of a place—practically a castle really—for a light lunch, then at half-past two, they said farewell and set off back to town. George was carrying a small box of things from his sister's old bedroom that he was taking back with him. He said a formal, cool goodbye to his father, shaking his hand, then kissed his mother. Dottie reflected it was the best anyone could hope for in the circumstances. No doubt, given time, he would soften, but at the moment, it was all still too fresh, too raw for forgiveness.

'Flora had wanted to come, of course,' he said, as they stood beside the cars, 'But obviously in her condition...'

'Oh no, certainly not!' Mrs Manderson agreed. 'We'll see you both the day after tomorrow, dear.' She kissed him and allowed her husband to assist her into their vehicle. She was silent practically all the way back to London. Dottie's concern grew.

On arriving home, Dottie went straight up to her room to change out of her black dress. A few moments later there was a tap on her door. Mrs Manderson was there. She looked upset. Dottie looked at her.

'What's the matter, Mother? What on earth has been wrong with you today?'

Mrs Manderson took a seat on Dottie's bed—almost unprecedented—and inhaled deeply. Her breath was unsteady. Dottie felt alarmed. 'What on earth is it? Flora...?'

Mrs Manderson drew Dottie to her side immediately, taking her hands. 'No, dear, Flora's perfectly all right. It's not that. There's something else.' She sighed. Dottie could only remember anything like this happening a handful of times during her life. The last time had been when Dottie's cat died. The time before that had been when her grandmother had passed away.

'You're not ill?' she asked, in a sudden panic. Her mother shook her head. 'Nor-Nor Father?'

'No, dear, nothing like that. Um...'

Dottie could tell her mother was feeling for the right words. The very knowledge of this made Dottie feel cold and afraid.

'With all that's happened lately, happened to you, or happened to others but involved you, well, my dear, you've seen rather a lot of life just lately. I'm very proud of the way you have dealt with difficult situations and how you've shown yourself to be loyal and caring, and not afraid to help others. But I've seen how you've been hurt by some of the things you've discovered, and I know you've come to see that people aren't always what you think, and don't always behave as one would expect.'

'What is it you're trying to tell me? You're scaring me, Mother.' Dottie felt she could hardly move her lips. Her whole body felt frozen and fixed, like nothing could move or bend.

Mrs Manderson was looking down at her folded hands. Her voice was low and unsteady. 'You've seen that men and women don't always behave as they should,' she said, 'and Dottie, dearest, I'm sorry to have to tell you that I—I've kept something from you all these years.'

Before Dottie could make sense of the words, her mother rushed on, as if afraid to stop.

'You see, you're not my daughter. Not our daughter, I should say. I only wish you were. You're my sister's daughter. Your aunt Cecilia's. She was very young, and foolish. She had an affair. She got caught, and she was afraid that her husband would find out, so she went away. Like—like Diana. And when you were born, she gave you to us to adopt. I hadn't been able to have another child after some difficulties when Florence—when Flora was born, and of course, your fa—Herbert—and I were delighted to be able to take you.'

There was an abrupt silence as Mrs Manderson broke off and sat looking at Dottie, who was shaking her head.

'Wh—I...' Dottie fell silent. Words ran out. She had no idea what to say. There was nothing she could say. She couldn't seem to understand. She fixed her eyes on a pigeon on a branch outside. 'So you and...' She couldn't say Father, because he wasn't. They. Weren't. She turned to face Mrs Manderson, and the tears ran down her face. She had no words. She just looked at her.

Mrs Manderson leaned forward, her hand outstretched. 'Oh Dottie, darling! I'm so...'

There was a sudden sound across the room, and Mr Manderson stood in the doorway looking agitated. His wife looked at him, dashing tears away, saying a little sharply, 'What is it, Herbert?'

'Sorry to interrupt, my love. That was George on the telephone. Flora's gone into labour. The doctor is with her now. George has been told it won't be long, things are already quite advanced. He asked that we go over.'

Mrs Manderson was already halfway along the hall to her room, calling over her shoulder to him. 'Of course, we shall, dear, we'll go immediately. Go and get the car, Herbert, and I'll just change my outfit. And don't forget the cigars and the champagne! Two minutes, that's all I need. Oh, my goodness!' She sounded breathless with the surprise of it all. The baby was arriving a good couple of weeks early. Dottie could only pray that wasn't a bad sign. She struggled with so many thoughts at once. Thoughts of Diana and her baby, thoughts of what her mother had just told her. Mother? Dottie froze for a second. Mrs Manderson wasn't her mother. Flora—oh, Flora wasn't her sister. After all these years of sisterhood and intimacy. Not her sister. Where did that leave them now? Flora was her cousin. Not her sister.

Dottie stood in front of the mirror fighting back a fresh outbreak of tears. She should get ready, she had to be quick, they would be leaving shortly, but she couldn't seem to...

'Dorothy!' Mrs Manderson was in the room again. 'Could you help me with my gown, dear?'

'Of course, M...' The name died in her throat. Their eyes met in the mirror. Mrs Manderson's eyes filled with tears, and Dottie's overflowed. She was enclosed by arms hugging her tightly.

'I'm so so sorry about the shock, my dear. To tell the truth, I had hoped you'd never need to know. It's always been so easy to pretend to myself, to ourselves, that you really are our own little girl. But then, after all that's happened lately, I thought I had no right to keep it to myself. And now... oh my darling girl, if only you were my own child, I could not love you more dearly than I do now, than I always have. I beg you, Dorothy—Dottie—dear, please, don't let it change anything.'

Hebert Manderson's shout from the hall downstairs made them draw hastily apart and repair their complexions. The two women hurried downstairs, grabbing a few necessary things on the way. A minute later the car was pulling out of their road, and they were heading across London to the Gascoignes' home. Her thoughts were by turns stumbling then racing. She couldn't seem to take a hold of them. The only thing that mattered was that Flora would be strong, the baby healthy and delivered safely. Nothing else... She shook her head. Everything else would just have to wait.

It took them fifteen minutes to reach George and Flora's home, and the first thing they saw was the shiny black car belonging to the doctor. Greeley, the butler, must have been watching for them because the door was already opening before they got out of the car. They hurried up the steps and into the house, and immediately they heard the sound of a baby's cries.

Greeley took their things and, beaming all over his face, said, 'Such happy news, the baby's here! I can't tell you how glad we all are!'

Mrs Manderson clutched Dottie's arms, tears already forming in her eyes. But unlike half an hour earlier, these were tears of joy. There was no sign of George. The daily woman and Mrs Greeley the cook hovered at the end of the hall, waiting to hear the news, and Greeley went to his wife's side. It warmed Dottie's heart to see how happy and excited the staff were.

Just then there came the sound of footfalls on the stairs, and they turned to see the doctor coming downstairs, with George following behind him, laughing.

'Come upstairs, come up all of you! He's here! My son. Sorry, I mean of course, our son!'

There was a happy confusion for a moment whilst George tried to give instructions to Greeley regarding champagne and cigars, and to say a heartfelt thank you to the doctor, who was leaving, and to urge the family, and the rest of the staff to follow him up to see Flora and meet the new arrival.

There was a scurry of rushing feet and excited chatter, and they were all crowding into Flora's bedroom, to see her sitting up in bed, looking exhausted but happy, and cradling the bawling bundle in her arms. Cissie, Flora's maid, was straightening the fresh bedlinen, which was a struggle as she could barely see past the happy tears in her eyes.

'Aww Miss!' she said to Dottie. 'I'm ever so happy. It's the first time I've been in a house where there was a baby. It's ever so exciting!'

Dottie and Mrs Manderson went to Flora, kissed her and gazed at the baby. George took up a manly protective position beside the head of the bed, looking down proudly at his wife and son, his hand on Flora's shoulder

'This is Freddie,' Flora said, smiling down at the finally-quiet infant. 'Frederick George Gascoigne de la Gascoigne. Isn't he just perfect?'

They all agreed he was.

*

THE END

Caron Allan

ABOUT THE AUTHOR

Caron Allan writes cosy murder mysteries, both contemporary and also set in the 1920s and 1930s. Caron lives in Derby, England with her husband and two grown-up children and an endlessly varying quantity of cats and sparrows.

Caron Allan can be found on these social media channels and would love to hear from you:

Facebook:
https://www.facebook.com/pages/Caron-Allan/476029805792096?fref=ts

Twitter:
https://twitter.com/caron_allan

Also, if you're interested in news, snippets, Caron's weird quirky take on life or just want some sneak previews, please sign up to Caron's blog! The web address is shown below:

Blog: http://caronallanfiction.com/

Also by Caron Allan

Criss Cross: book 1: Friends can be Murder trilogy
Cross Check: book 2: Friends can be Murder trilogy
Check Mate: book 3: Friends can be Murder trilogy

Night and Day Dottie Manderson mysteries book 1

The Mantle of God Dottie Manderson mysteries book 2

Scotch Mist: Dottie Manderson mysteries book 3: a novella

The Last Perfect Summer of Richard Dawlish Dottie Manderson mysteries book 4

Coming 2019

The Thief of St Martins Dottie Manderson mysteries book 5
The Spy Within Dottie Manderson mysteries book 6

Easy Living: a story about life after death, after death, after death.

CARON ALLAN

The Thief of
St Martins

Dottie Manderson mysteries: Book 5

Coming Summer 2019

Made in the USA
Columbia, SC
27 November 2020

25621974R00221